I0629817

Promise of Salvation

Book 2

by

Clifford M. Scovell

www.scovellbooks.com

A RED MOONS PRESS PUBLICATION

First Printing

A RED MOONS PRESS PUBLICATION

ISBN-13: 978-0-9908536-0-2
ISBN-10: 10:0990853608

Printed in the United States of America

Cover artwork by Kari Angle

Chapter 1

Salem, Oregon, Spring of 2011

"I know this is going to sound a bit strange, Gerry," Jasmina confided as she nudged me away from a small clutch of people and toward her newest purchase: a Chinese instrument called a *guzheng*, which she pronounced *goo jung*, "but I had a really powerful vision and…it was about you."

The petite, red head's statement sent my heart racing, and I was suddenly overwhelmed with a strange mix of curiosity and revulsion. She had invited me and my parents to her party with the promise that we would hear Oriental music played by a master of the *guzheng*. Now I was wondering if she didn't have something else in mind.

In addition to her success as a writer and lecturer, Jasmina Maxell is an accomplished psychic and healer. She is also the favorite aunt of my totally-cute girlfriend, Remmy Reed.

My name is Gerry Patterson. I'm nineteen, a thin six-foot-two with wavy blond hair that Dad says is too long and Remmy thinks is too short. I'm also a sort of involuntary time traveler. At least, I had one past-life experience about six months ago that connected me to an abused woman in 1890's England. If not for Jasmina's help, that experience would have been the death of me. So you can understand why my heart races when she has a vision involving me.

"What did you see?" I asked, my eyes jerking to Remmy, who looks so much like her aunt, it's hard to believe they aren't mother and daughter.

Ignoring my question, Jasmina motioned for me to sit on the stool in front of the glossy-black instrument with a dozen or so strings spanning its top, but I hesitated.

"This is a reproduction of an ancient version of this instrument," she explained as she fixed her green eyes on me and smiled knowingly. "Unlike those made today, this one has only thirteen strings, but according to what I saw in my vision, you already know this."

"Why would I?"

She sighed. "Because you were playing it."

Feeling really tense, I looked again at the instrument I'd never even heard of before this evening, and was surprised by how familiar it did look. As I examined it more closely, I started to relax until Jasmina said,

"Play something for us."

Panic, dread, fear, angst, horror: a torturous soup of emotions filled my head as I looked up to see a crowd of people staring at me.

"No way!" I squeaked. "I don't know what you saw, but I wouldn't even know where to start."

Jasmina's hand pressed down on my shoulder as she whispered in my ear, "Trust me. You'll do fine."

"This is going to be so totally embarrassing," I moaned while slowly lowering my butt to the stool, my heart on its way to a thumping bongo-drum cardiac meltdown.

To my surprise, when I looked at Jasmina again, her face seemed transformed: her rosy cheeks were more rounded and pale, her curly red hair now straight and black. Seeing the change should have increased my stress, but it actually brought on a sense of calm as the word *teacher* formed in my mind.

"Give it try," said a voice that was higher-pitched than Jasmina's and strongly accented.

I looked at the approximately four-foot wide, rather flat, boxlike instrument with all those strings stretched across its arched top, and a different bridge roughly in the middle of each one.

"I think it's kind of like playing a guitar," Remmy was saying as I tried to make sense of the strange apparatus.

I don't know why, but I knew it was not that simple. Even so, I was surprised to feel myself relax again as my eyes scanned the exotic instrument, taking in its inlaid ivory symbols and figures.

"Show what you can do," the teacher was saying as she took a step back.

The suggestion was absurd, but even as I prepared to protest again, something outside myself took over my body. Without wanting it to, my right hand moved close to the *guzheng's* surface, fingertips tingling, and I thought,

What the hell.

The tip of my right index finger hooked a string, and when I plucked it the sound was melodic and pleasing. I repeated the move with another string, then another, starting slowly to create a haunting, oriental sound. The movements became automatic, like I'd done this a million times, and I was no longer thinking about what to do as my other hand pressed strings on the left side of the bridges to add a depth and variation I would never have expected. The effect was dreamlike, as though I was watching someone else in my skin, but what struck me most was the overwhelming feeling of longing for a homecoming that could never be.

This was taken from me by a betrayal.

There was so much anger in that statement it made my heart ache, but I knew it had not come from me.

Crap! It's happening again.

That last thought came from me, but as I prepared to pull away from the instrument, sounds of surprise and pleasure filtered in from the people around me. I couldn't make out words, but was struck by the sense that not everyone was speaking English. I tried to turn and see who was talking in that strange tongue, but another force kept my fingers on the strings, producing a melody that gradually increased in tempo, climbing to a frenetic pace, like a wild stream filled with spring snowmelt. The volume rose along with the pace then softened as it briefly slowed before exploding into a furious roar that excited a part of my soul much older than my nineteen years.

I wanted to stop when the strings blurred, their grayness blending into the instrument's dark surface, but my fingers continued to move as though in their own universe, pouring out something eerie, then exciting, and finally so soothing it made me feel at one with the...

"Ow!" I cried, my hand jerking up to cover a sharp pain in my right cheek.

The room darkened as I gawked at my blood-smeared hand.

Shit!

The room seemed to spin and a sudden flash of sunlight made me blink, and stumble.

I'm on my feet?

Regaining my balance, I realized there were thousands of men around me marching in perfect rows, their knee-length, red wool shirts and bright blue caps nearly glowing in the glaring sunlight. Blinking again, I looked down at the dull-brown overcoat of metal-plated armor covering my chest and belly.

Soldiers? What the…

Lifting my hands, I realized that like the others, I held a small shield in one and a long spear in the other. Something slapping my left thigh pulled my attention back down to see a sword hanging from my waistband.

Some kind of military parade?

I looked again at the guys on each side of me, and realized they looked like the ancient Chinese soldiers we talked about in history class.

I'm one of them? Damn!

Aching lungs made it clear I had not been breathing, so I sucked in a breath, but the putrid, sickly sweet air I inhaled nearly gagged me. Though I didn't know how or why, I knew this smell came from violent death.

This isn't a parade.

Feeling panicked, I wanted to run away, but could do nothing more than march along with this mass of people, spear in one hand, shield in the other, chanting loudly in sync with those around me.

Across the dust-fogged field, sunlight glowed off the yellow and green uniforms of a different row of men marching towards us in a line that stretched as far as I could see in either direction. As row after row of them moved down a short rise, I saw archers preparing to fire their crossbows.

One of that group stood out from the rest, and though he was some distance away, he was in full sun, and I could clearly see his scowling face: cold, calculating, almond-shaped eyes; black eyebrows; lean cheeks; a slight smile, accentuated by a thick mustache and an arrowhead-shaped clump of hair under his lower lip. His hair was pulled back severely into a topknot held in place by a bright-red ribbon. While the soldiers around him looked nervous, or angry, he seemed to be staring directly at me with the confidence of one who has been here many times.

Tearing my attention from his face, I could see this particular soldier held a brightly painted composite bow, while the others had dull-brown crossbows. His shiny, black armor was made up of large metal plates, rounded at the bottom, and looking much like overlapping fish scales compared to the dull, rectangular plates covering the other archers' chests. I gasped at the realization that this was the only soldier whose face was painted green.

Ju ji bing, flashed in my head, and I immediately knew it was Chinese for sniper!

The skills of such a person are wasted in a battle where brute force and mass killing are the objective.

The thought was clearly not mine, but was as powerful as if it had been.

"Forward on the double!" our sergeant cried, and we surged ahead as one.

I couldn't stop watching as the enemy archer jerked a hand back over his shoulder, and in one smooth motion pulled out a bright-red arrow with white fletching. Nocking it so quickly I didn't have time to cry out, he yanked the bow string back, aimed, and let it fly.

Certain that arrow was for me, I wanted to duck, dive to the ground, hide somewhere, but I was shoulder-to-shoulder with a line of screaming, panting, sweating men, and from the roar of voices behind me, I would certainly be trampled into the dirt if I did anything other than run full tilt toward the oncoming soldiers.

As we stupidly tried to cross the expanse of field between us before being killed, I looked up to see a sky darkened by thousands of arrows.

"Shields high!" someone shouted, and in one swift move we all held up our only defense against the deadly cloud.

When the black rain descended upon us, I heard agonizing screams when those arrows struck home, and tried not to think about the fallen, or the fate that might soon be mine. Terror can either reduce you to a helpless lump of shivering bones, or numb you with an overdose of adrenalin as you charge into an unknown future. I am not sure this was a choice, but I sucked in a desperate breath, bellowed to vent my fear, held up my only defense against the pounding arrows, and kept pace with those around me.

I was in mid-stride when the red arrow slipped under my shield, slammed into the center of my chest, and knocked me back. The stool toppled over, and made those behind me cry in surprise as I crashed to the floor. Something slammed my head and the roar of voices was instantly replaced by concerned shouts of alarm. My head throbbing, I opened my eyes to see a dozen startled Caucasian faces gawking down at me.

"Son of a bitch!" I cried, my hands trying to grab an arrow that was no longer there.

"Watch your tongue, young man!" my mother protested.

Jasmina was on her knees and bending over me, her hair now red, green eyes wide.

"Gerry! My God! What happened?"

So in shock I could barely breathe, I looked again at my chest, the arrow now gone but not the pain.

"You're bleeding," she cried while magically producing a napkin. I jerked when pain exploded in my cheek as she added, "It looks like someone cut you with a knife."

"That's not possible," my father protested, his broad shoulders suddenly blocking the ceiling light and bringing welcome comfort. "There was no one within arm's length of him."

"What did you see?" Jasmina asked.

"S...some k...kind of b...battle," I stammered.

"A battle? But that's not what I saw."

"What you saw?"

She gave her head a sharp shake. "In my vision, you were in a home, surrounded by friends and family, and playing the *guzheng*. You were definitely not fighting in a war."

I looked at my chest to see a red blotch expanding into the fabric of my shirt.

"Gerald," Mother cried as I pulled down my collar to see blood oozing from a small hole where the arrow had hit me.

"Christ Almighty," I gasped before looking at Jasmina.

Now also kneeling beside me, my hyper-religious mother protested my sacrilege, but I was totally focused on the solemn Jasmina, and her attention was on her wide-eyed niece.

"I think we found Gerry's next adventure."

Chapter 2

Jingzhou Province, China, Spring of 197 AD

"You should be dead," the physician protested loudly, his eyes narrow slits, hands fisted in front of his chest as he glared at the remains of the arrow embedded in his patient's skin. "Why you not dead? Why you not dead?"

Jerking awake when the man wiggled the broken scrap of wood protruding from his chest, An-Chi sucked in a sharp breath, and looked up at the physician's profile as the curious doctor leaned over to squint at the arrow stub.

"Something not right here."

Grabbing it with his fingertips, the physician yanked out the largest remaining piece of the arrow and stared at its bloody wooden end.

"Ha!" he barked, his tired eyes contradicting the broad grin on his round face. "No tip." He held up what remained of the arrow, as though displaying it to his patient. "You do more damage to it than it do to you."

Still disoriented, An-Chi squinted at the artifact drenched in blood made dull by the room's gray light.

After a brief hesitation, the surgeon's smile vanished as he pulled An-Chi's shirt open to peer at his bare chest. Without comment, he twisted around to grab a pair of long, slender copper tweezers. Turning back, he stopped with the tweezers hovering over the hole in his patient's chest but did not look at An-Chi.

"This gonna hurt," he warned at almost the same instant he stabbed the instrument into the hole.

An-Chi gritted his teeth against the pain when the tweezers' tips thumped against his breast bone.

Grunting, the physician squinted at the pieces he had extracted before straightening and tossing the instrument back onto the table. Facing An-Chi again, he waved a hand at two stretcher bearers.

"Get this fool out of here and bring soldier with real wound."

An-Chi felt his stretcher rising while the surgeon tossed a rag onto his chest. He wanted to protest, but before he could think of what to say, the surgeon waggled a finger at the cloth.

"Stuff in hole until bleeding stop. You be OK in no time."

The surgeon stepped back and was soon lost in a noisy forest of moving bodies, bandaged faces, blood-stained clothes, and slashed arms. An-Chi's ears filled with the shouting, moaning, screaming, and even singing from those around him while his nose scrunched up in reaction to the acrid mixture of sweat, excrement, urine, and blood.

His bearers stopped, and a cry ahead pulled An-Chi's attention forward to see another stretcher bearer on his knees, struggling to regain his footing on the slick floor while his patient lay on the ground. The confusion produced much screaming and swearing and An-Chi looked down to see the patient lying on his side, facing him. The bloody bandage on his head was askew, exposing a gash that ran from above his right eyebrow down through his cheek. Half his eye hung out of the gap, stuck to his flesh by drying blood as flies crawled in and out of the wound. His good eye appeared to be looking at An-Chi, but he knew the soldier wasn't seeing him.

Bile rising in his throat, An-Chi pulled back and closed his eyes. Though he had seen plenty of blood and gore on the battlefield, it was a struggle to keep his churning stomach in check.

Your are weak! he thought angrily when they started moving again.

He opened his eyes when the light grew suddenly brighter, and found they had just left the surgeon's tent. He was preparing to rise when his bearers tilted the stretcher and dumped him onto the ground, the leader anxiously motioning for him to get up.

"You be OK," he said in the crude dialect of the uneducated. "Go back to unit. This place for dead and dismembered only. You OK. You fight again."

Still on the ground, An-Chi picked up the cloth, and watched the two men hurry back into the tent, followed immediately by other bearers carrying a steady stream of injured and dying. Slowly rising to his feet, he tried to gently touch the cloth to his exposed chest while he got his bearings, but was roughly bumped and pushed by others scrambling to make their way in or out of the hospital tent.

His chest throbbing, he weaved through the fast-moving crowd, stumbling over muddy ground made worse by a drizzling rain that chilled his shocked body. Slogging through the cold mud, he looked down, not surprised to see the bits of sinew, chunks of flesh, a finger, and an eye mixed into the muck.

A reminder, he thought while grimacing against the pain in his chest. *There are always others far worse off than you.*

Chapter 3

Still stunned by what had just happened, I sat on a chair in Jasmina's 20th-century kitchen, and felt relief as I stared at the mirror Remmy held. Instead of the angry glare of a green-faced soldier, I was relieved to see my own features illuminated by light from the nearby doorway: blue eyes, unruly blond hair, and pale skin emblazoned with a few too many zits. Of course, I wasn't thankful for my aching head or the butterfly bandage Jasmina used to close the painful cut on my cheek, but it could have been worse.

I had just turned my attention to the throbbing red hole in my chest when Remmy cried, "No way," in response to my description of what I saw.

I looked up, feeling conflicted. Remmy and I had argued earlier this evening because she believes I should tell my mother that I'm not as adamant about religion as she is. But it wasn't just that. About six months ago, I had somehow connected with a woman in 1890s England and Remmy was her abusive husband. I had never had a past-life experience before and it left me seriously confused about both who I was and what my feelings were for this feisty woman.

"How else do you explain it?" I asked, angry frustration making me almost spit out the words as I stabbed a finger in the direction of my aching cheek. "No one was close enough to do this, and I surely didn't."

Running fingers through her auburn hair, Remmy continued to shake her head. "But the last time you connected with a past-life no one was able to reach across time to cut you."

This conversation, my thudding headache, the painful injuries to my cheek and chest were all too much. I wanted to lash out at someone, but didn't want that someone to be her.

Sucking in a breath, I pushed down my anger, and tried to keep it out of my voice.

"The last time I was more an observer. I didn't really interact with the people in the past. This time, I was totally there, doing what this guy was doing, feeling, smelling, and hearing it just like he did." I pointed at my chest. "How else can you explain this?"

Pressing fingers over her mouth, Remmy jerked her body around, her short, black skirt bouncing above black tights as she danced in her new glossy red shoes with three-inch heels. She was cute, sexy, and I longed for her, but that was tempered by memories of our former life, where her persona had beaten and nearly killed me by throwing me off the roof of our home.

How much of him is still in her?

The question stopped me from saying more, and after a moment, Remmy bobbed her head once and turned back.

"But if the first arrow cut your cheek, why didn't the second one k...?"

When a sob cut off her sentence, I looked up to see a tear trickle down her rouged cheeks, her hand flying up to cover her lips. Her reaction made my heart ache. It was as though that tender moment made me want to forget the ancient past, jump out of my chair, and give her a big bear hug.

Bad idea, Bro.

I'd learned from past experience that when Remmy was upset, she didn't like having her movements restricted, and hugging was the ultimate no-no. Stifling the urge, I looked again at the throbbing injury to my chest, thankful that Jasmina's initial ministering had stopped the bleeding, but it also brought me back to Remmy's unfinished question.

Why am I not dead?

"No idea. Maybe they just..."

"That was TOTALLY AWESOME!"

I nearly fell off my chair as I twisted around to see a fellow classmate, Barbara Foltzman standing in the doorway, her eyes wide with excitement, hands fluttering beside her face, mouth wide.

"That music was soooo incredible, but your finale -- throwing yourself onto the floor like that with the blood and everything -- totally made it."

"It wasn't fake blood and it wasn't planned," I protested while pointing again at my wounded cheek.

Her smile faded, but not the excitement in her eyes. "What? But how did you get..."

"Son," my father interrupted as he appeared behind Barbara while jerking a thumb over his shoulder in the direction of the front door. "Your mother is really upset. We need to go."

"Are you serious?" Remmy cried, her heavily made-up eyes wide. "Someone from his past tried to, like, kill him. Jasmina is his only hope of defending himself."

"Tried to kill him?" Barbara cried, her frizzy brown hair bouncing back and forth as she looked from Remmy to me and back. "What do you..."

"Enough of this," my mother announced angrily as she stormed into the room, a virtual tornado of fear, anger, and natural energy. "We can deal with this ourselves."

Her straight, shoulder-length blond hair whipped around her head as she grabbed my arm and tried to yank me to my feet, something she hasn't been able to do since I was ten. "I'm sure Father Raymond has a better explanation for all of this than..." She jerked a nod toward the room into which Jasmina had gone. "...the likes of her."

Standing on my own, I looked into Mom's tense face, knowing this wasn't just about what happened to me today. My mother is a seriously devout Episcopalian, and from her perspective, any ideas that don't follow church doctrine are sacrilegious.

I, on the other hand, have been drifting from the church for years. Though I'm finding it hard to tell my mother, I'm guessing she knows and that's why she's so protective of me. I know I need to take my own path, find my own way to who or whatever is pulling the strings down here, but it's just never the right time to make my mother cry.

"Mom. This isn't a religious issue. The church can't protect me from…"

"Jesus rose from the dead and healed the sick. Surely He can help us deal with those who have died."

"Are you totally serious?" Remmy cried. "What does…."

"We've all had a terrible shock," Jasmina announced loudly as she hurried into the room. "I think it best if we take a deep breath and calm down."

Her angry eyes jerking from Jasmina to me and back, my mother said no more as Jasmina quickly moved to me and pressed a square of gauze over the wound on my chest. I winced as she smoothed out the tape before looking at me, her back to my mother.

"This salve will help with the pain," she said soothingly, her voice not reflecting the tension in her face. Her eyes flicked to my mother and back to me before she grabbed my shirt from a nearby table and handed it to me. "And prevent infection."

Seeing my mother's face screw up in a way that implied she was about to blurt out something nasty, I jerked my arm up to get her attention. When her eyes met mine, her expression softened briefly before her lips tightened, corralling the rebuke, but the determination remained.

"We're leaving," she insisted as I was pulling the shirt on.

The finality of the statement ignited a flash of primal rage fired by injustices that had little to do with the present moment. Yes, I still lived at home, but I was also nineteen-years old and could make my own decisions. I took a deep breath and prepared to shout a biting rebuttal, but before my lips parted, Jasmina gave my arm a squeeze. The electricity in her grip pulled my attention to her before she released me, stepped back, and held up both hands, palms out.

"No one is trying to stop you." She motioned toward the hallway leading to the front door. "I'll see you out."

The contradiction between my mother's unyielding demand and Jasmina's conciliatory gesture left me confused and uncertain as to what to do next. On the one hand I wanted to vent my frustration at being treated like a child, but on the other, how could I involve Jasmina in that ugliness?

My mind in total turmoil, I looked from Remmy to Barbara to Jasmina, and finally to my mother's determined face. As soon as we made eye contact, Mom moved in, grabbed my arm and led me straight to the front door which my red-faced father pulled open. Though I wanted to yank my arm free, I knew that doing so would only make things worse, so I let her pull me outside.

"Mom. I don't see how praying is going to…"

I stumbled and nearly fell when she stopped abruptly and faced me.

"You put too much faith in her mystical mumbo-jumbo, and not enough in what can really help."

"Jasmina didn't start this. The nightmares I had last time came long before I met her."

"She twisted your dreams into something far beyond reason. No one believes in that past lives stuff. It's all trickery and devil worship designed to make you stray from the Right Path."

"Jasmina doesn't worship the devil. She's only trying to help me cope with what's happening."

"Father Raymond will surely know what needs to be done about this."

"A priest?"

"He'll get this sorted out."

Frustrated beyond belief, I looked back to see Remmy standing on Jasmina's porch, biting her thumbnail. Behind her, Barbara was waving, her expression a mixture of concern and expectation.

Expectation of what?

Now thoroughly confused, I turned my attention to Jasmina who was standing behind the girls. She looked briefly at Dad, nodding as he said something to her, his demeanor apologetic before he turned and followed with our coats over his arm. I seriously wanted to hurry back to her, but Mom's angry expression made it clear that would only make things worse.

Worse? I wondered while folding myself into our pale-blue Prius. *What's worse than some crazy Chinese dude trying to kill me?*

As we drove down the street, I looked back to see Jasmina's white house vanish from sight, and felt my stomach cramp as the whole street seemed to darken while I mentally flashed back to the soldier with the green face.

Was that guy really an assassin, and was he after me? If so, how can I convince mom that a holy-water-sprinkling priest is no defense against a bloodthirsty killer?

After looking back again, and seeing nothing but an empty street, I settled back in my seat and closed my eyes to visualize the reverend holding up a large cross in an attempt to stop the barrage of arrows descending on us.

I am so totally toast!

Chapter 4

After visiting the auxiliary medical tent where his "minor" wounds were stitched, disinfected, and soothed with a pain-killing salve, An-Chi cleaned and repaired his uniform before bathing. Though he hurried as fast as his aching body would allow, by the time he approached his sergeant's tent, the sun had dipped low in the sky, the long shadows adding an anxious tension to the growing aches in his body as the effects of the pain-killing salves wore off.

In addition to the gash in his cheek and the painful hole in his chest, he had received a nearly concussive blow to the head, and while unconscious, his arms and legs had been stomped on, his body kicked and tread on many times. It was not that his comrades were indifferent to his plight, but they were in a life-and-death situation and were intent on not getting killed or wounded themselves.

Though his many injuries were painful, they were not distraction enough to mask the tightening in his chest as he approached his sergeant's tent.

At the entrance, he hesitated a long moment to regain his composure before standing at attention and calling, "Permission to enter, Sir."

"Come," came the curt reply.

Pushing through the entrance flap, he bowed to his superior officer, and despite the pain, tried to keep his face neutral.

"I am ready to return to duty, My Sergeant."

"You are not seriously wounded? Why did you not stay with your troop?"

"I was knocked out during the charge, and did not regain consciousness until I was on the surgeon's table."

"The surgeon's table for a blow to the head?"

"An arrow hit my chest, sending me back into those behind me. When the surgeon removed the remains of the arrow, he found it had no tip and did not penetrate far enough to reach my heart."

The sergeant was silent for a long moment before he shook his head. "I must punish you just the same."

An-Chi wanted to argue his case, but protocol forbad it. Common soldiers did not talk back to their superiors, under any circumstances. Defiance was death.

"As you say, My Sergeant," he responded.

"Is the wound painful?"

"Most certainly, My Sergeant."

The sergeant eyed him for a moment before asking, "Where did this arrow hit you?"

His eyes down, An-Chi pointed at the injury.

"Stand at attention!"

Straightening, An-Chi grimaced when the movement brought more pain, but was caught completely off guard when his sergeant took two quick steps toward him and slammed the heel of a hand into An-Chi's chest.

Crying out, he dropped to one knee, but almost as quickly jumped up to stand at attention again.

"Was *that* painful, Soldier?"

Though he wanted to shout yes, An-Chi knew the question was a test, one he had experienced many times in training camp. If a soldier could not tolerate pain, he was a liability to his comrades on the battlefield.

"No, Sir," he shouted, his voice cracking in response to the screaming agony in his chest, his knees buckling slightly, head spinning.

"Are you ready to return to the fight, Soldier?"

He sucked in a desperate breath, locked his knees, and fought to keep his body rigid.

"Yes, Sir," he gasped. "Victory for the Emperor. Victory for…"

Spots dotted his vision as he struggled to stay at attention, his head spinning, muscles weakening while his sergeant's stern face faded to black.

*   *   *

He was sitting cross-legged in a vaguely defined, though familiar place. Faceless women moved quickly around him in the subdued light, at times passing so close the air from their wake brushed his cheeks.

A door burst open and a figure -- broad-shouldered, straight-backed, proud in bearing, determined in stride -- entered. Though he did not speak, the women stopped what they were doing and hurried from the room, quietly closing the door behind them.

"What have you done?" the man asked, his attention fixed on a jade vase.

"I have done nothing to dishonor you, Father," he protested.

"What have you *done*?" his father repeated more forcefully as he turned to glare at him.

His father's aide had been murdered, and evidence pointed to An-Chi. He struggled to come up with an answer that might appease this towering figure, but he had no alibi, there were no witnesses, or other suspects. It did not matter that he was innocent, or that his father believed he had not done it. Even the appearance of guilt was dishonorable.

He felt his head bow, tears on his cheeks, the shame of a thousand generations of ancestors watching, weighing, judging, and being disappointed.

"I am nothing, Father."

"Yes," the figure sighed angrily, his voice thick with disgust. "And that is what you will remain."

*   *   *

Gasping in air, An-Chi opened his eyes to see the dingy-gray ceiling of a tent. Surprised by the change in scenery, he started to take a deep breath, but a shot of pain stopped him. Jerking his eyes down, he found his shirt open and a square of cloth lying over the hole. A movement on his left pulled his attention to a beautiful young woman, the small nearby lamp illuminating her almost perfectly round face, eyes wide with surprise, mouth partially open. She uncharacteristically stared at him for a long moment before shying away, turning sideways, and looking down.

"Most sincere apologies, Sir," she said. "I did not intend to be rude."

A red-and-green bow bound her jet-black hair into a single tail at the back of her head. Her straight, simple dress was not tied at the waist and modestly hid whatever figure the woman had. In her profile, he saw smooth, tan cheeks; small lips; a short, flat nose; and black eyes that alternately flicked to him and back to the ground, not typical of the traditionally submissive Han peasant woman.

He tried to sit up, but the pain in his chest cancelled the effort, and forced out a groan. It was then he realized she was not speaking like an ignorant peasant girl.

Who is this woman?

"Is it painful?" she asked, her attention now fully on him.

Relaxing back onto the cot, An-Chi sighed, "Yes, but it does not matter. I must return to my unit."

Moving quickly to his side, she gently touched his right cheek, making him realize it was numb.

"What have you done to my face?"

"The poultice I applied has numbed it," she responded. "You will heal faster if the pain is less intense."

"But I have already been treated for these wounds."

She nodded. "When you fainted, the wound on your chest tore open and started bleeding again. It was necessary to remove the original stitches and sew it up again."

Putting her long, slender fingers on the bandage on his chest, she briefly made eye contact with him before concentrating on her task.

"Even so, none of your wounds are serious, but the injury to your breastbone must be quite painful," she said confidently before putting her other hand on his shoulder. "Sit up now. I must secure the bandage."

Grunting as he complied, he looked around the small, sparsely furnished space. "Where is the physician?"

She tugged at his shirt with one hand as the other held the bandage in place.

"He is busy with more serious cases," she answered indignantly. "Take off your shirt."

Looking into her eyes, he saw an uncommon intelligence and determination that surprised him. Just the same, he was not accustomed to taking orders from someone of the opposite sex.

"When will the physician be in?"

"He will not be," she answered sharply. "I am caring for you."

"You? Where is his assistant?"

"I am his assistant."

"How can that be? Women cannot attend medical school."

"A medical education is not needed to treat such minor injuries."

An-Chi hesitated for a long moment before slipping out of his shirt, and watching as she deftly wound the cloth around his chest to hold the bandage in place. The action brought her face close to his, and the smell of her filled his nostrils. Despite the pain, he found her closeness arousing.

"Are you a midwife?" he asked as she was tying the cloth.

"I have delivered babies."

"Where are you from?"

Tugging the knot tight, she took a step back and glared openly at him.

"You ask too many questions." She waved a hand at the exit. "Go now and return to your unit."

An-Chi's laugh was stopped by the sharp pain in his chest. When he looked at her again, she had backed away to the tent's entrance, both hands holding the roll of bandaging cloth at her waist, her eyes appropriately demure.

"May long life and prosperity be yours," she said while freeing a hand to push back the tent flap.

The ancient greeting struck him as absurd. He was returning to the front lines. Even if he managed to live a long life, a man did not become a soldier to get rich.

"Long life and prosperity to you as well," he heard himself saying as he rose from the cot, surprised to feel the pain easing.

Stopping at the entrance, he finished attaching his sword to his waist before turning back to her. "I do not know your name."

"It is not important. You will most likely be dead by the time this engagement is over."

Surprised by her apparent indifference, he scowled. "And if I am not, how will I find you?"

She shrugged. "An intelligent man will figure it out."

His intended protest died on his lips when she looked up, her eyes smiling even though her mouth was curved down. It was then he noticed the small T-shaped scar on her chin: an unexpected blemish in otherwise perfect skin.

"Go now," she said abruptly. "Others need my attention. Die bravely and be forgotten."

She gave his shoulder a shove, and though he could have resisted, he let her push him out the entrance. After carefully pulling on his shirt, he turned to watch her march to another tent, stop at the entrance, and look back, her eyes on him for a long moment.

However, it wasn't just her eyes that captivated him. She was now facing into a breeze and the wind pushed her loose clothing against her slim body. The sight aroused him in a way he had not been for a very long time. Seeming to recognize the lust on his face, she shook her head and moved inside.

He started to follow, but stopped when a deep baritone voice called, "Soldier. Are you ready to fight?"

His libido instantly deflated, he turned to face his superior and bowed his head. "Apologies, My Sergeant. I will rejoin my troop."

Upon hearing a derisive snort, he looked up to see his sergeant's head shaking. "You have no troop. I just learned that they were wiped out to the man."

The news hit him like a bamboo rod across his face. Anguish nearly overwhelmed him as another failure piled on top of the others.

He had not saved his father's aide, had been disgraced in the eyes of his family, and had failed to die honorably with his troop.

Staring wide-eyed at his superior, An-Chi cried, "Every one?"

His sergeant's shoulders slumped only slightly. "We lost two thousand today."

The image of his father's face mouthing the words, "What have you become?" flashed in his mind.

I have failed them all!

An-Chi jerked to attention and yanked out his sword. "I will perform *Zi Wen*, My Sergeant."

He pressed the blade to his neck, hardly feeling the steel edge slicing his skin. Closing his eyes, he tried to yank the sword down to finish the deed, but it would not move. His eyes snapped open to see his sergeant's hand holding his.

"No," his superior protested.

"But I have disgraced myself and my unit. I am of no use to the Emperor or you."

The sergeant pulled the blade away.

"A noble sentiment, but I need a leader who can get more from his men than even they believe they have." After An-Chi relaxed his arm, the sergeant released it and took a step back.

"I am told your troop fought valiantly, even after you went down. It is because so many of the other troops did not that so many died. Even so, protocol demands that I demote you, but I have a situation that might give you the chance to redeem yourself. If you fail, you have lost nothing. If you succeed, your honor will be restored."

Confused and disoriented, An-Chi glanced back at where Mei-Xiu had disappeared. The thought of her anchored him in a way he barely understood, but the feeling was strong. Of course, in his present state of disgrace, he could never hope to see her again. Why that mattered, he could not say, but it suddenly did.

"What can I do for you, My Sergeant?"

After An-Chi sheathed his sword, the sergeant motioned for him to follow.

"Prepare to die, Soldier."

Chapter 5

"Mom," I protested from the back seat of our car. "This isn't about religion."

Though her back was to me, I could see Mom's head shake. "That woman's pagan beliefs are corrupting you."

"She's not a pagan."

"Then what was that silly ritual she performed the last time, when she said you were possessed with a spirit? It was surely nothing a good Christian would do."

"It wasn't silly. There really was another soul in my body. She got it out and sent it home."

Her head continuing to shake, she turned to point a finger at me, her thin lips pinched together, blue eyes locked on mine. "You weren't possessed, because possession is the work of the devil and you are *not* a devil worshiper."

Now my head was shaking. "No, Mom. I'm not a devil worshiper, and neither is Jasmina. She just sees things that you and I can't."

"Poppycock! That's nothing but trickery to make you believe her fantastic stories and give up the church."

I looked away, struggling to resist the urge to tell her I had given up on religion a long time ago, but was long-since tired of arguing about it.

"She's not trying to get me to give up anything, she's just…"

"Oh no? Then why are you arguing with me?"

Her question angered me, but just the same, I should have let it go. The problem was, I am my mother's son.

"But Mom, it's not what you…"

"That's enough, Son," Dad interrupted, and before I could respond, he added, "We'll talk to Father Raymond and see what he has to say."

Dad was looking in the rear-view mirror, his expression more pleading than determined. He knew, as did I, that Mom would never let this go.

Grunting angrily, I settled back into the seat and scowled. It was a wasted effort since he was no longer looking at me, but it didn't matter, and yet it did. I could see a growing rift between my mother's intractable religious beliefs, and mine. It wasn't just that we had different ideas of God, redemption and all that, but she adamantly refused to even consider my opinion. The thought that my ideas didn't matter, that I wasn't capable of understanding how the universe worked, that I was still a child to be told what to do and how to think, seriously pissed me off.

By the time we reached St. Marks on Commercial Street, I was in no mood to speak with anyone. What did I care about some priest's take on what I was going through? He wouldn't believe me anyway.

I don't remember much of my talk with Father Raymond, if you could actually call it a conversation. He asked questions, but I was too angry to answer, so Mom filled him in with her distorted view of things. He was kind and conciliatory, and said lots of things that made my mother nod and toss out a couple of amen's before we ended up in a pew with the priest praying, Mom's head bowed over folded hands, me feeling like a trapped animal and getting angrier by the minute.

It infuriated me even more when Mom insisted I speak with Father Raymond alone. I so wanted out of there. This priest had no solutions for me, and after several painful minutes of him talking and me grunting, I ended the conversation by just walking back to the car.

Dad rolled down the window as I approached, his eyes jerking from me to where Mom was moving toward the reverend.

"How did it go?"

"Didn't!"

"What do you mean?"

"Don't want to talk about it."

Yanking open the back door, I climbed in. I wasn't just pissed over what my mother had done, but there was also a confusing conflict nagging at me. I felt a strong sense of disappointment at letting my ancestors down, and that meant my grandparents, and great-grandparents, and even further back than that. It didn't make sense. My great-grandparents and the people who went before them were long dead. They lived in different times with different rules. What did I care what they might have thought of this situation?

When Mom got back into the car, I stayed on the driver's side and made a point of staring out the window, but out of the corner of my eye, could see her look at me for a long moment before she turned around and fastened her seatbelt.

It was a very quiet drive home.

Chapter 6

Chu Mei-Xiu gawked at the thin, nearly bald man in front of her, his light-blue robe stained with the blood, vomit, and other body fluids of his many patients.

"You cannot be serious, Father," she moaned. "I am not ready to perform your duties."

His face painted with exhaustion, Chu Gao shook his head as his bloodshot eyes scanned the small, sparsely furnished tent he shared with his daughter. "You have been a more enterprising student than any I have ever had. None could be more qualified."

"But a division commander? He will never let a woman treat his wounds. I am sure he will kill me before I can even explain why I am there."

Goa continued to shake his head. "As of our last report, he was unconscious and too badly injured to move. He is a cousin of the Son of Heaven, and I would go myself, but my superiors do not want to risk experienced surgeons at such a critical time. Though the emperor's personal physician will undoubtedly be sent to tend him, we must first get him back into our camp. Before that can happen, his wounds must be bound and he needs to be prepared for transport."

"His guards will not let me into his tent."

Holding up a rolled-up sheet of paper, her father nodded. "This is a pass from our general. None of our soldiers will dare harm you."

"Did you say this was near the front? How do I get there?"

"For that, you will be given your own troop as escort."

"Will I command them?"

Barking a laugh, Chu Goa passed the scroll to her. "That would be more dangerous than sending you into enemy territory alone."

"But a woman on the battle field? Is that allowed?"

His expression serious, her father pulled a hat from the pocket of his loose-fitting surgeon's robe and handed it to her. "Cover your hair, bind your breasts, and wear several layers of clothing. It is doubtful any of the soldiers escorting you have even met you before. Speak only when necessary and they will think you are a young man."

Taking the hat, she twisted her hair into a bun, slipping the cap over it as she moved to a nearby mirror, and scowled at the image.

"I do not look much like a man."

"With the right clothes, you will not look much like a woman either.

Chapter 7

"Stay away from Jasmina?"

Daylight filtered through the shades covering our kitchen windows, throwing soft light on my mother's determined, though no-longer-angry face.

"Your father and I have discussed it and we agree that you've lost perspective on this matter. We think Remmy's aunt is only confusing you."

"So," I grunted while glaring at her, my partially eaten breakfast already forgotten. "You're going to lock me in my room?"

Her laugh sounded condescending, and implied I was too young to grasp what was really going on. The resulting flare of anger made my muscles spasm when I rose from my chair, almost knocking it over as I lurched from the table.

"You think I'm totally stupid."

"No, I don't think…"

"You think I'm too dumb to understand right from wrong, too addlebrained to think for myself, too idiotic to even walk across the street alone. Is that it?"

She looked shocked and hurt, and I felt guilty for the outburst, but that only made me angrier.

"I don't think any such thing."

"But you're telling me who I can and can't associate with."

She looked at her hands. "Just Remmy's aunt."

I felt my head shaking. "I'm nineteen. I can talk to whomever I wish."

"As long as you are living under our roof, you will abide by our rules."

"Can I go to school, or am I, like, too stupid to handle that as well?"

"Don't be disrespectful, young man," she said, her voice on the edge of breaking. "You can go to school, but you are to come straight home afterwards."

"What about basketball practice?"

"Yes," she answered begrudgingly. "You can go to practice, but you are to have no more contact with that woman. If you do, we'll pull you off the team."

"You can't be serious."

"We are," she said with determination as she glanced at her wristwatch. "Your father and I are in complete agreement on this. We are paying your tuition, and have a right to say what you can and cannot do while in college."

I felt my muscles tense, my fist coming partway up with the overpowering urge to hit something. I couldn't do it, but the need was so strong I froze for a long moment before storming out of the kitchen, steam probably shooting from my ears as I marched to my room to snatch my backpack from a chair, and hurry to the front door.

"You haven't finished your breakfast," Mom called, but I couldn't stop, or speak.

Slamming the door, I flew down the steps, my eyes on the ground as I mentally regurgitated every swear word I had ever heard, and even invented a few new ones. The deep thunk of a closing car door made me look up, and the sight of Father Raymond standing by his car made me livid. Mom had obviously tried to arrange another little chat between us, but I was having none of that.

I broke into a trot to get to the sidewalk before he could block my way.

"Hello, Gerry," he called as I took a sharp right and kept going without a response.

Hearing his footsteps on the pavement at the same time as our front door opened, I gave up any expectation of a dignified escape and broke into a run, hoping to put as much distance as I could between them and me before one of them tried to call me back.

I wouldn't have stopped if they had.

Chapter 8

"What are your orders, My Sergeant?" An-Chi asked as he stood outside his superior's tent.

Beckoning for him to follow, the sergeant pointed at a dozen disheveled soldiers standing in a loose cluster.

"You will retain your position as troop leader and are to take charge of this lot."

Though the soldiers stirred when the sergeant drew near, and a few stood straighter, most either pretended to ignore them, or stared blankly as though lost in their own private world.

"With respect, My Sergeant. Them?"

Nodding, the sergeant turned to An-Chi. "Think of this as an opportunity to regain your honor. Survive this mission and you will be returned to the ranks."

"With these misfits?"

An-Chi regretted the words as soon as he spoke them, but as an experienced former leader in his father's army, he knew that not every insubordinate solider was immediately put to death. Family connections were vitally important in both society and the military. Generals could not raise and maintain large armies without the support of rich benefactors. That meant every effort was made to make sure these supporter's relatives did not die dishonorably. An-Chi knew that even if they could not be made into true soldiers, these well-connected fools should at least appear to die in an honorable manner.

Out of the corner of his eye, he could see the look of disgust on his superior's face, and knew for certain that the order had come from the higher ranks.

"You are to escort a doctor to the front and bring back a wounded commander."

"What is this commander's status?"

"He is badly injured, and cannot be moved until he is stabilized by the doctor. Unfortunately, he is in territory now controlled by the enemy."

"How will I find him?"

Pulling out a map of the valley, the sergeant pointed at a section outlined in red. "We are here." He moved his finger to a spot just north of the red section. "And Division Commander Liu is here, hidden in a cave surrounded by a cluster of low hillocks. His division was cut off just before we lost control of this area. Many were killed, but one of his men made it back to report their status and position."

"But shouldn't we be going in with more men?"

"He has about fifty warriors for support once he is ready to be moved, but if you are captured, you will be tortured for information. You can tell them nothing."

"What will my men know?"

"The less they know the less they will reveal under torture. The doctor, on the other hand, cannot be captured."

"Take off his head before I slit my own throat?"

"That is correct."

An-Chi was not being sarcastic when he nodded and said, "Whatever it takes to protect our side."

"Precisely."

Realizing the odds were nearly unsurmountable, he stifled an insubordinate sigh, and asked, "And if we return without the division commander?"

The sergeant pointed at his mouth. "A pound of salt."

An-Chi flinched, knowing what being force-fed salt did to its victims. It was a slow and painful death that made the offender desperately thirsty, while at the same time shutting down their kidneys. It often took many excruciatingly-painful days for them to drown in their own internal fluids.

"And how much time do I have to get this lot in shape?"

"You are to leave at sunset."

"That does not leave me much to work with."

The sergeant smiled. "Remember the words of Sun Tzu, 'Place your army in deadly peril, and it will survive; plunge it into desperate straits, and it will come off in safety.'"

"But I have only twelve undisciplined men."

"You have half a day before the sun sets. Plenty of time to beat sense into them."

"I must do what their former troop leaders could not?"

"It is your job to convince them that the greater their discipline, the greater their chances of surviving."

Trying hard not to react to the irrational thinking, An-Chi jerked a nod. "Then let us get this doctor on his way."

The sergeant waved at the cluster of men. "I will introduce you to your men."

Instead of snapping to attention as they approached the troopers, the men seemed to ignore them.

"Stand at the ready," An-Chi commanded, his bamboo switch slapping his right leg.

For their part, the grumbling troopers slowly shuffled into two unevenly spaced rows, their spears loosely held, shoulders slumped, uniforms unkempt.

His disgust obvious, the sergeant stopped a dozen paces from the first line, making An-Chi painfully aware that this was a test. He moved quickly to the nearest soldier and slammed the butt of his hand into his chest. The surprised soldier fell onto his back, and laughter erupted from his comrades.

"Silence!" An-Chi barked while keeping his attention to the prone soldier. "Rise!"

While looking at his fellow soldiers, the trooper chuckled nervously and clumsily rose. As soon as he was standing, An-Chi knocked him down again.

Scowling at his superior, the soldier sat up, but did not try to rise further.

"On your feet, Soldier," An-Chi demanded.

"I am trying, Troop Leader, but you keep..."

His bamboo switch whistled through the air, striking the soldier's cheek with a smack.

"No talking. On your feet!"

The soldier scrambled up, looking lost and unsure of what to do next.

"Stand at attention," An-Chi demanded before turning toward the others. "All of you! Stand at attention!"

Making a sharp-right turn, he walked briskly to the tallest soldier in the front line. Yanking out his sword, he held it inches from the man's face and made sure his own expression clearly showed he would not hesitate to kill him.

"Discipline is to be maintained at all times," he stated adamantly. "This is your last chance. If I reject you from this troop, you die. Is that clear?"

When the troop mumbled a disorganized response, he shouted, "Is that clear?"

"Yes, Troop Leader!"

"Louder!"

"Yes! Troop Leader!"

"Form up! Straight lines! Even spacing!"

Each man shifted his position to accommodate the command, and even though the formation was not yet perfect in An-Chi's eyes, he at least had their attention. Moving slowly down the line of soldiers, he made eye contact with each man before returning to the center of the line and sheathing his sword.

He waited another long moment before marching back to his sergeant.

"I will get them properly outfitted and make them ready, My Sergeant," he announced. "We will not fail the Emperor."

His own eyes scanning the still poorly organized troop, the sergeant shook his head. "See that you do not, Troop Leader. Many lives depend on you."

"Yes Sir!"

Without further comment, the sergeant marched away. After he was out of hearing range, An-Chi looked at his troop to see shoulders already slumping, feet shuffling, weapons at various angles.

"I am a dead man."

Chapter 9

"I'm so totally grounded," I blurted while approaching Remmy in the school hallway.

"Grounded?" she asked, her eyes wide with curiosity. "They can't do that, can they?"

I felt my head shaking, and at that instant, wanted to cry.

"My parents think Jasmina is, like, corrupting me. If I don't stop seeing her, they'll pull me out of school."

Remmy barked a squeal of protest. "They don't see what's happening?"

"They don't care. Mom's afraid I'll stop going to church."

"No way!"

I nodded. "She took me to see a priest right after we left Jasmina's."

"What happened?"

"Nothing!" I shouted, feeling suddenly self-conscious when people nearby looked my way. After giving my head a quick scratch, I let out a breath and continued, "I wouldn't talk to him. What good would it do?"

"So what's your plan?"

Feeling paranoid, I took another look around before moving closer to Remmy, and lowering my voice. "Could you call Jasmina? I so need to see her today."

"But your Mom said…"

I stopped her with an upheld hand.

"I had another -- what can I call it? -- vision on my way to school."

"What did you see?"

"I was looking at this guy who totally looked like one of those terracotta soldiers we learned about in class last week."

"Seriously? What did he do?"

"He was talking with the soldier I'm connected to. I don't know what they were, like, talking about, but then I suddenly felt really bad. Before I knew what was going on, I pulled out a sword and tried to slit my own throat."

"Your own throat?"

I nodded. "Yeah. That's how it felt, but that's not the worst of it."

It was Remmy's turn to look around. "What's worse than that?"

Sucking in a breath, I let it out but felt no relief.

"I could feel the sword against his neck, and it totally felt like the blade was cutting into *my* skin."

"You're joking."

Opening my coat, I pulled up the bandage covering the thin line on my neck. "And it really was."

"Shit!"

"That's what I was thinking," I said while releasing my coat collar. "But at least I know the guy I'm connected to is still alive, so that arrow didn't kill him."

Looking perplexed, Remmy shook her head, but her eyes were on me. "Sorry. I don't understand."

Frustrated, I held out my arms, palms up.

"Everything that happens to that guy, happens to me, in real time."

Her eyes widened as realization dawned.

"If this guy gets killed while you're still connected with him…"

I felt my head nod. "I'm toast."

Chapter 10

After marching his troop around the camp for most of the afternoon, An-Chi led them to a low ridge to watch the spectacle of thousands of General Sun Ce's troops preparing for the upcoming engagement.

As they watched, tens of thousands of soldiers marched in front of them, the many iron plates on their armor rattling in rhythm with uncountable feet stomping the hard soil to dust. A brown mist billowed up as row upon perfect row of disciplined soldiers marched across the field, their spears pointing skyward, banners flapping, heads rising and descending in perfect unison. Horses by the thousands pranced along with the soldiers as captains, colonels, and generals used hand signals, horns, drums, and bellowing voices to pass orders to their subordinates, who passed them on to others below them to orchestrate the perfectly-ordered movements.

Dust rising on the opposite side of the valley made it clear that General Lü Bu's troops were making similar preparations.

"Why we not wear armor, Troop Leader?" one of An-Chi's troopers asked as he leaned on his spear.

"We are sneaking into enemy territory tonight, an impossible task when rattling armor is giving away your position."

Smiling knowingly, the trooper nodded. "Maybe that why I lowly foot soldier, and you troop leader."

"And if you want to survive this, you had better remember that."

"I will, Troop Leader," the soldier answered. "My name, Chong Dai. I very good soldier. Make excellent number two."

Still watching the troops parading below, An-Chi shook his head.

"Show me," he said without looking at Chong Dai. "Line up the troop for inspection."

Flashing a smile, Chong Dai hesitated only briefly before bowing. "Quickly, quickly, Troop Leader."

An-Chi continued to watch the spectacle below, pretending to ignore Chong Dai's efforts to get the troopers in line while watching them from the corner of his eye. Though most of the tired troopers were now sitting, and resisted his call to rise, An-Chi was impressed with how he prodded them until they formed their usual uneven lines and then continued to work until the troop was properly ordered.

After a moment, Chong Dai announced, "All men ready, Troop Leader."

Keeping his face neutral, An-Chi slipped a bamboo rod from his belt, and turned to face Chong Dai. He was mentally preparing a biting rebuke, but the sight of his rag-tag troop lined up in two almost-perfect rows forced a sigh of relief from him. And then he wanted to laugh. They looked fairly good now, but how would they hold up on the long march that lay ahead? Even if they avoided contact with the enemy, this group might still not make it to their objective.

Struggling to stop his head from shaking, he moved in front of the men and pointed his rod at the marching army.

"Our mission will be difficult, but the upcoming battle will be a great help to us." He turned to point at a cluster of low hills north of their current position. "That is our destination, and though it is in enemy territory, they will be busy preparing for combat, so it is unlikely anyone will be watching for such a small troop.

"Of course, that does not mean the enemy won't be have men patrolling the area we will be passing through." Pointing at the hills again, he added, "I am aware of the last known positions of their encampments. We will do our best to avoid them and move as quickly as possible to our objective."

"In dark?" Chong Dai asked.

An-Chi glared at him for a long moment before continuing. "For most of the way, we will have a sliver of moon to march by, but that also means we will be visible if someone is looking in our direction. We must make no sounds that will alert the enemy to our presence. That is why you are not wearing armor, but it also means there will be no talking, smoking, rattling gear or weapons, and if you injure yourself, no crying out."

He turned his head slowly, eyeing each individual in turn. "If any of you fails to maintain discipline, all will die. Is that clear?"

When the troopers grumbled their assent, An-Chi shouted, "Is that clear?"

"Yes, Sir," they shouted back.

"Good," he said as he waved the troopers back. "Rest here for now. We leave just after sunset."

As his men returned to their resting positions, An-Chi turned his attention to the marching army for a moment and recalled a maxim of the revered military tactician Sun Tzu.

"The clever combatant imposes his will on the enemy, but does not allow the enemy's will to be imposed on him."

Turning to look at his unenthusiastic, disheveled troopers, An-Chi shook his head. "In this case, my first task is to impose my will on my own soldiers."

Chapter 11

"Jasmina!" Remmy shouted into her cell phone as she sat on a bench outside the school's main entrance. "You've so got to help us."

"What is it?"

"We need to see you, like, as soon as possible."

"I have to go to Portland this afternoon, but can meet you tonight after I get home."

"No. It has to be sooner. This is getting too dangerous."

"What's going on?"

Turning toward Gerry, she suddenly realized he was no longer aware of her.

"Gerry's connecting with this Chinese guy more and more frequently."

Reaching up with a free hand, she gave Gerry's shoulder a shake, but he did not respond.

"What else happened?"

"The guy Gerry was in his past life tried to kill himself and Gerry could feel the guy's sword cutting into his own throat."

"Was he seriously injured?"

Remmy shook her head. "Oh, it's, like, not so bad. Someone stopped him before he could do much damage."

"Where is he now?"

After shaking Gerry's shoulder again, Remmy answered, "He's right next to me, but he's totally lost in the past."

"Can't you wake him?"

"I've been trying, but he doesn't respond. I don't know what to…"

"Gaaa!"

"Gerry? Are you OK?"

After looking around for a moment, he locked eyes with his girlfriend.

"This is so totally bad," he gasped, a shudder rippling through his body.

"What is it?"

"The soldier is being sent on a suicide mission with a bunch of rejects from other divisions."

"When do you leave?"

"Just after sunset."

"How soon is that?"

He shrugged. "Its maybe, like, mid-day there right now."

"Jasmina?" Remmy shouted into her phone. "Did you hear that?"

"Yes, Dear. Get over here as soon as you can. We must find a way to connect with this spirit and break the bond between him and Gerry."

"We're on our way."

Chapter 12

"I'm here to collect the physician," An-Chi announced as he stood at the entrance of Chu Gao's tent.

"Ah yes," the doctor responded with a nod before turning to wave at someone inside. "This is Chu Ju."

When Mei-Xiu appeared, An-Chi was struck by how familiar she looked, but it did not occur to him that this "man" might be a woman. Her braided hair was coiled up inside her wool cap. A second leather cap had been pulled over the first, its wide straps hiding her delicate ears as they swooped down to a knot under her chin.

She was pulling a soft-leather coat over her wool shirt as she stepped out of the tent, but her ill-fitting clothes, thin frame, and tentative steps made An-Chi want to protest the inclusion of someone so apparently unsuited for this task.

Knowing it was not his place to question his superiors, he suppressed the anger, and bowed politely. "I am troop leader, Ban. My soldiers will escort you to your patient."

"Thank you, Troop Leader," Goa acknowledged when Mei-Xiu said nothing. "Please bring my doctor back quickly. We are seriously shorthanded, and Chu Ju is one of my most promising assistants."

"I will do my best."

Remaining silent, Mei-Xiu lifted her medicine kit's carrying strap over her head, and settled the bag under her left arm before bowing silently to the soldier.

When she started walking, An-Chi fell in beside her. "I trust you are able to make this journey. We must make good time and have no cart to carry you."

"I do not need a cart," she said, keeping the pitch of her voice low. "You need not worry about me."

Without looking at her, he shook his head. "I have to worry about everyone on this mission. All our lives depend on it."

When he finally looked at her, he was surprised to see her staring up at him, her expression questioning, even disapproving, and that added to his growing irritation.

"You have a great responsibility, Troop Leader," she finally said.

What does this doctor know about my responsibilities? he thought angrily.

He quickened his pace to put himself in front of her, his thoughts filled with the daunting task ahead; his disgrace at not dying with his troop; and, considering the nearly useless soldiers he must work with, the slim hope he had of redeeming himself.

It was nearly two *li* to his troop's encampment, and though An-Chi maintained a brisk pace, he was surprised to find the doctor right behind him and not breathing hard when they arrived.

"Troop leader in camp," he announced loudly, feeling embarrassed when his soldiers slowly rose to greet them.

While they should have jumped up and run to form two lines, they simply stood wherever they were, and if they made any acknowledgement of his arrival, it was a simple nod or wave of a hand.

"Line up," Chong Dai shouted as he rushed in amongst them. "Are you listless dogs?"

Their tired muscle obviously aching, the men started moving, but sluggishly. An-Chi remained silent as his number two hurried to the nearest soldier and slashed a bamboo rod across his shoulder.

"Fall in, you unworthy worm!"

Howling, the soldier ran to the center of the encampment, but Chong Dai was already marching toward the next unresponsive soldier, his rod held high. Before he could reach him, that soldier hurried to join his comrades. When Chong Dai turned to face the rest of the troopers, they were already moving to the middle of the encampment.

"Form two lines, and be sharp about it," he demanded as he moved in front of them. "Who wants to feel my rod next?"

Fighting the urge to shake his head, An-Chi watched in disgust when the irregularly spaced solders looked around nervously, until Chong Dai shouted,

"Straighten your lines! Even spacing! Spears upright! Hurry! Hurry!"

Though it took them a long moment to do so, the troopers finally lined up properly.

An-Chi moved to stand in front of them.

"Remain as you are until I tell you to move," he ordered before turning to face Mei-Xiu.

"It is hot in sun," one soldier complained. "We stand in shade. OK?"

Though shocked by the impudent question, An-Chi kept a straight face as he looked at Chong Dai.

"What you say, Soldier?" his number two demanded as he rushed to the complainer, his bamboo rod at the ready.

"The sun is very hot. Why can't…"

WHAP!

The soldier cried out as he covered his face with a hand.

"Say again?"

Still holding his cheek, the soldier looked up cautiously before responding. "I only ask why we…"

WHAP!

Howling, the soldier dropped to one knee, released his spear and brought his other hand up to cover the new welt.

"Stand up, Soldier," An-Chi bellowed as he moved to him.

When the whining soldier slowly rose, he stopped in front of him and pointed his own rod at his face. The whining immediately stopped.

"Pick up your spear and stand at attention!"

After the soldier did as ordered, An-Chi moved back to the middle of the line.

"Anyone else want to feel my rod?"

He paused a moment before slapping the shaft against his thigh.

"Anyone ELSE want to feel my rod?"

"No, Sir!" the entire troop responded.

Slapping his thigh again, he slowly turned to look at the mixture of faces: some dark, some pale, some round, others narrow. It was obvious his men were drawn from different regions of China, and quite recently, but where they came from, or what their former lives were did not matter.

"I will have discipline in this troop. Is that understood?"

"Yes, Sir!"

"Remain where you are, at attention, until I tell you to move."

"Yes, Sir!"

Without further comment, he marched back to Mei-Xiu, who was looking confused.

"I apologize for this," he announced when he was close. "I only took command a few hours ago."

Mei-Xiu shook her head, but said nothing.

"Yes," An-Chi said sadly while turning to face his troop. "In times like these, we must make do with what our leaders give us, but rest assured, Doctor Chu. They will do what is necessary when the time comes."

"When do we leave?" she asked, carefully keeping the pitch of her voice low.

He looked at the sun floating a hand's width above the horizon. "Just after the sun has set, and we will pass through enemy territory under the cover of darkness. I am told our path will not be heavily patrolled."

"I will be ready."

An-Chi looked back at his troop again, seeing several of the soldiers already slouching.

"But will they?" he muttered.

Chapter 13

"What has been happening?" Jasmina asked excitedly as she ushered us into her home.

"Thankfully, nothing since Remmy called you," I answered.

"I'm glad to see you haven't been injured again, Gerry," she said while leading us into her large office painted with cool, comforting colors, and outfitted with an overstuffed couch and chairs.

Making herself at home, Remmy plopped down in an overstuffed chair, her legs over one arm, back against the other, head wobbling from side-to-side as she looked from one of us to the other, her casual recline not an indication of how anxious she was.

"What can we do?"

Jasmina shrugged. "If I hadn't seen Gerry's injuries for myself, I'd have a difficult time believing it. I've done hundreds of past-life regressions and have never had one like this."

"Maybe that's the difference," I noted while sitting opposite the two women. "In the other cases, you've been the intermediary, telling people about their past lives. It's kinda like you've been a barrier between them and the experience."

Jasmina nodded. "And because you're actually going back there yourself, you are more tightly linked with them?"

"Well that's the real issue, isn't it?" I asked. "I'm not intentionally going back there. This person is coming to me."

"As I see it," Jasmina explained, "metaphysically speaking, this Chinese soldier's body is somehow merging with yours on a physical plane outside our own."

"But how it that possible?" Remmy asked.

My body humming with nervous energy, I ejected myself from the chair to pace the room, feeling much like a wild animal in a cage.

"I don't care *how* it's done. I just want it to stop before this guy gets seriously injured or killed."

Though the room was large, furniture restricted where I could go, forcing me into a C-shaped path that ran from the right side of the couch, around its front to the left side. Upon turning at the wall, I looked over to see Jasmina staring quizzically at her hands.

"Gerry," she said when I was once again in front of her. "Do you think he is aware of you?"

The thought brought me to a stop, primarily because it hadn't occurred to me. "Wouldn't that, you know, freak him out?"

"Maybe not. The Chinese have always been far more involved in the spiritual realm than we are. He might see this as a connection to an ancestor. Have you tried speaking to him?"

I felt my head shaking. "I...I don't think I know how. When I'm connected to him, I'm totally outside myself. It's like a dream I have no control over."

"He can't risk influencing him," Remmy protested. "That will change history."

Jasmina shook her head. "Unless this encounter has already happened."

"What do you mean?"

"We westerners think of time as linear, but there are other cultures, even some American scientists who believe it isn't. In this case, the ancient Chinese thought their ancestors were as much a part of their present as their past. They prayed to them, talked with them, and even asked for advice. In their culture, a person's place in society might have as much, if not more to do with who his ancestors were than his personal accomplishments. But the person was important to the ancestors too. To bring the shame of dishonor onto yourself also shamed them."

She cupped her hands over her face for a moment before lowering them to look first at Remmy then at me.

"What if everything in our existence has already happened -- past, present, and future -- and we're only experiencing one thin slice of it?" Rising from the couch, she pointed at me. "You, on the other hand, have somehow managed to penetrate the barrier that limits most of us to a single slice of time, and are now experiencing two instances at once."

"Are you serious?" I responded, feeling a mixture of anger and fear. "I'm in two places at the same time?"

In my current mental state, Jasmina's shrug really irritated me. I was desperate for something concrete and that wasn't it.

"More precisely," she answered. "Two time periods simultaneously."

I was starting to visualize my body merging with the soldier's, and found the whole thing unsettling. "So tell me this: if I cut myself, will this soldier also feel pain?"

She shrugged. "We know it goes one way. The only way to know if the reverse is true is to injure yourself while you are connected and see."

"You mean cut myself?"

"Nothing that extreme," Jasmina countered. "A simple pin prick would do it."

"Oh great," I complained. "In addition to suffering when others abuse him, I have to hurt myself."

Sighing, Jasmina gave an exaggerated shrug. "It may be the only way of knowing if the connection is two way."

"Why does that matter?"

"If he thought you were one of his ancestors, and that his death would also hurt you, he might have more incentive to survive this mission."

Chapter 14

Light from the setting sun was only a faint glow in the western sky by the time An-Chi led his troop past the last sentry post along the northern edge of General Sun Ce's encampment. Between them and their destination lay ten *li* of rolling hills and grasslands.

After they passed the dimly lit sentry's camp, he turned to his soldiers and pointed to a small cluster of trees one-hundred paces ahead of them.

"From here on, we go in one line. That wood will be our cover for a short time, but from then on we will be crossing grasslands, with little else for cover. The darkness will make us difficult to see, but because most of this area is without trees, noise carries very far. Strap your spear securely to your back so it does not rattle, and keep your shield in front of you." He pointed at the sliver of the waning moon, already halfway across the western sky. "We must make good time while the moon still lights our way. After that, we proceed in the dark."

"Troop leader," Chong Dai called as they started marching. "Maybe it better we go east, get behind hills, far from enemy outposts. If so, we maybe travel in daylight."

An-Chi shook his head. "Our orders are to reach the division commander's cave before sunrise."

"No problem. Sun come up, we make good time. Enemy come, we make holes in ground. Hide very good. You see. We be safe."

Keeping his eyes on the path ahead, An-Chi shook his head. "Being safe is not in my orders. If the division commander dies while we hide in rabbit holes, our punishment will be death."

Chong Dai shook his head. "But if we die before we get…"

"Huh!" An-Chi interrupted while holding up a hand, palm out. "We have our orders. I will lead the way. You cover our rear."

"But…"

"That was not a request, Soldier. No speaking unless it is an emergency. Is that clear?"

Chong Dai hesitated for a long moment before bowing his head. "Yes, Troop Leader. No speaking."

As he was turning to face forward again, An-Chi saw the doctor looking back at Chong Dai. After a moment, she moved up beside him.

"You do not speak like a common peasant. Where did you get your education?"

The question made his heart ache, and though he longed to tell her about his disgrace, he shook his head instead.

"Sorry, Doctor. No more speaking until we arrive at the division commander's cave."

Feeling unwelcome emotions rising in his chest, An-Chi increased his pace and moved ahead of the troop, embarrassed to be fighting back tears as they marched away from the protection of General Sun Ce's camp.

Chapter 15

Sitting on the couch in her office, Jasmina patted the cushion next to her. When I sat in the designated space, she held my hand, and closed her eyes, her body gently rocking from side to side. A nervous, twitching Remmy sat upright in a chair opposite us, her attention shifting between us until Jasmina opened her eyes and gave me a questioning look.

"Can you see anything?"

I shook my head. "I'm afraid to even close my eyes."

She squeezed my hand. "It's OK. I'm here with you."

After glancing at the nodding Remmy, I did as told and was greeted with…nothing.

"I so don't understand," I protested. "I totally can't see anything. Can you?"

I felt her shrug. "No." There was a pause as she squeezed my hands again. "Maybe it's because you have a direct connection to him and that's keeping me out of the loop."

My eyes still closed, I looked around again. Though I couldn't see anything, I sensed motion.

"I think he's walking, but it's dark." I started seeing vague shapes that blurred then came into soft focus then blurred again. "Oh God, the sun has set and they're walking in the dark."

"The mission has started?" Remmy whispered anxiously.

Keeping my eyes closed, I nodded and imagined Remmy on the edge of her chair, body leaning forward, green eyes wide, mouth open.

"We're running out of time," she added anxiously.

"Wait! I see the moon…and stars."

I heard Remmy shuffling in her chair as she groaned.

"There's no one around," I assured her. "We're totally alone out there."

"It's dark. How do you know there isn't someone waiting along the trail?"

I felt my head shake as my other persona looked at the ground. "I don't think there's any trail. We're, like, wading through tall grass and right now it kinda feels like we're climbing a hill."

"Can you read his thoughts?" Jasmina asked, her hand squeezing mine.

I felt my head shake. "Not really, but I'm sorta getting a sense of how he's feeling."

"He's Chinese," Remmy protested in a loud whisper. "He won't be thinking in English."

"Do you think he is aware of you?" Jasmina asked.

"No. He's totally focused on what he's doing."

"Is he nervous?" Remmy asked.

"Oh yeah, but he's not freaked out by it. It's kinda like he's done this kind of thing before."

Afraid to open my eyes, I watched for whatever was to come. A moment later, I heard Remmy typing on her laptop.

"What are you doing?" I asked.

"I'm Googling it. Maybe I can find out something about this battle."

"But we don't know much more than this guy is an ancient Chinese soldier."

"Which doesn't help much," she sighed dejectedly. "According to this, they fought all the time."

I shrugged. "Not much different than any other part of the world during that time."

"Wait a minute," Jasmina said excitedly. "You mentioned a general earlier. Sun something or other."

Though the name was at the edge of my consciousness, her mentioning it pushed it into oblivion.

"Argh," I cried. "I so totally had it, but now it's gone."

"Surely you can get something from his thoughts."

I concentrated, trying to get a sense of what he was thinking, or feeling, or anything, but it was all a jumble until...

"Wait! I've got something."

"What?" Remmy cried, her excitement sounding slightly hysterical.

"A word," I answered slowly. "Some kind of distance." I shook my head slowly as the thought formed. "He has to travel ten *li* to get where he's going."

"Li?"

Keeping my eyes closed, I listened to the sound of Remmy's fingers scrambling over her keyboard.

"Got it," she finally announced. "A *li* is about half a kilometer. He has to go five kilometers in the dark?"

"No," I answered hesitantly. "He's got the moon for part of that."

"You're into his thoughts now?" Jasmina asked.

"Yeah. I think so."

"Then give me something more concrete," Remmy demanded, "like the name of a general or an emperor."

"People don't go around thinking about their leaders at a time like this."

"Well, he might be wondering why his general sent him on such a dangerous mission."

"The general probably doesn't even know about...wait!"

I held up a hand, wondering what would make me think of someone important and then it occurred to me to just ask.

Who am I?

For a long moment, I sensed a flood of confusion, shame, despair.

"Something's got him really upset. He's, like, crying and there's a name...a general. Yeah. I think I've got it...he's leaving the camp of General Sun Ce or Tse."

Chapter 16

He marched through a darkness lit only by the faint glow of the waning moon, his troopers plodding along behind. Even though their eyes should have adapted to the meager light, it seemed as though this clumsy group managed to stumble on every loose stone, stick, and imaginary object in their path.

An-Chi had memorized the map, but had few reference points to navigate by. Because the sky was clear, the moon's glow hid any light from the encampments on his left, and though the celestial stars kept them moving in the right direction, they were of little use in knowing which hill they were passing, what object in their way might make them trip or stumble, or where a stream might cross their paths. To avoid getting lost, he paid careful attention to their pace to get a sense of how far they had travelled, and kept the moon over his left shoulder.

Upon leaving the trees, they waded through a wide meadow of waist-high grass. Feeling more comfortable as they proceeded, he increased their pace while paying careful attention to the amount of noise his men made. At first they were clumsy, and that brought on more grunting, gasping, and occasional equipment noises. When they finally settled into the new pace and quieted down again, he increased their speed again.

On the far side of the meadow, they skirted a hill, and crossed a smaller meadow. As they approached the next hill, An-Chi looked up at the moon floating just above the horizon, and realized there would be no moonlight on its eastern side. Not wanting to risk travelling in the dark so early in their journey, he led his stumbling, grunting troopers up the hill's gentle slope.

As the ground leveled out, he studied the memorized map and realized they were close to the first enemy patrol camp.

"Stop here," he whispered as loudly as he dared. "I will scout ahead."

While moving away, he could hear his troopers collapsing where they stood: the butt of their spears scraping the ground, their shields smacking small rocks, and faint groans issuing from their parched throats.

"Ssss," he hissed without turning to face them. "Quiet! Stay alert for attack."

He resisted the urge to rush back and use his rod on these lazy louts, knowing they would cry out, and alert anyone who might be nearby.

Continuing on as quickly and quietly as he could, he proceeded until the terrain started to slope downward. After a few more paces, he saw light from a campfire. Though not burning brightly, it was a beacon to his dark-adjusted eyes.

In fact, the fire was brighter than it should have been, revealing half-a-dozen prostrate soldiers lying around it, and two more hunched close to its glowing flames. Even at this distance, he could see hands stretched out to absorb the heat, heads bobbing and shaking in concert with what An-Chi hoped was a very absorbing conversation.

"Our first encounter," a soft voice announced as An-Chi jerked around, hand on sword.

"Doctor?"

"Sorry," Mei-Xiu apologized. "I did not mean to sneak up on you."

"What are you doing here?"

He heard a sigh. "My apologizes, Troop Leader, but I feel safer with you than your…soldiers."

Realizing what her hesitation meant, he looked first at the soft shapes that represented his reclining troopers then again at the glowing camp fire.

Who is the bigger fool? he wondered. *The leader of these misfits, or that sentinel below us with such an obvious campfire?*

Stifling a sigh, he turned to Mei-Xiu. "This is the first of three outposts. It is probably near a stream, but they appear to be confident that no one would dare venture out on such a dark night. Those two hunched up around the fire may be the only ones awake. If so, they will not likely see us if we are quiet."

"Not an easy accomplishment for your men."

His eyes on the fire, An-Chi patted the map in his shirt pocket. Though he could not read it in the faint moonlight, just knowing it was there gave him an odd sort of comfort.

"If I recall correctly, this whole area is covered with a kind of prairie grass to dampen the sound of our footsteps."

"That leaves only clattering equipment and grunting soldiers."

Thankful she could not see his frustrated expression in the dark, An-Chi needlessly pointed back toward his troop.

"Let us go back and get them moving."

Chapter 17

"I see a light," I cried.

"Bogus," Remmy barked so loudly I almost opened my eyes. "They found him."

I felt my head shaking. "No. This is a camp fire and it's some distance away."

"Is he going to attack them?"

"I don't think so. There's no telling how many are down there."

"Down?" Jasmina asked.

"Yeah. We're on a hill above them, but he doesn't have much confidence in the soldiers with him."

"They sent him on a dangerous mission with rejects?" Remmy cried. "What were they thinking?"

I shook my head. "Maybe someone doesn't want him to make it."

"That's it," Jasmina cried.

"What?"

"Someone on his side wants you dead, and this is their way of doing it."

"But why?" Remmy cried.

"Maybe we're looking at this the wrong way."

Unable to stand it anymore, I opened my eyes to look at her. "What do you mean?"

"The last time you were connected to a past life, it was because you both shared the soul of another being, but that isn't the case this time because we released that soul and sent him back to his own universe."

"Yeah, but his mortal enemy, the *Tsabbat* is still…"

I stopped when Remmy barked a laugh.

"What?"

"Mortal enemy?" she responded. "That's so like a comic-book villain."

"So? That's what he is."

Jasmina's cough pulled my attention to her. "Regardless what we call him, we also know the *Tsabbat* can't come to Earth, so there has to be another party involved."

"Any idea who?"

Her smile vanished. "We don't even know who all the players are in this timeline. We need to figure out how An-Chi's death will affect history."

"I'll work on that," Remmy announced.

"I've already seen the assassin," I said. "He almost killed me last time."

"And he's going to try again."

"But who is he trying to kill? This Chinese guy or me?"

Jasmina shrugged. "If the *Tsabbat* is involved, it is most likely both of you."

Chapter 18

"But Troop Leader, we cannot go past them." Chong Dai protested in a loud whisper, his finger pointing at the enemy campfire.

"We have no choice," An-Chi argued. "Those are our orders."

"We go back. Tell commanders we not find cave. Nobody know better. Yes?"

"Not the way it works, Soldier," An-Chi countered as he heard the footsteps of his other troopers approaching. "We return without the commander, we die."

"I wish to go back, I think, and have head cut off, not belly slit open by enemy." Chong Dai announced.

"Are you serious?"

"Very much so. Chop, chop. Quick death. Less pain."

"Is that what they told you?"

"Not told," Chong Dai said hesitantly. "Just think it so."

"Cowards do not get their heads cut off. The punishment has to be worse than anything you will experience in battle."

"Worse? What can be worse?"

"They force you to eat a pound of salt."

"Ugh! Make really sick. Throw up big time!"

"Worse than that, Soldier, it makes you very thirsty, and you can drink as much water as you like. That much salt stops the water from coming out. It takes many agonizing days to die."

"Yaa," Chong Dai cried. "You not serious."

"Very serious, and do not think that deserting will help. The other side is honor-bound to do the same thing. That is, after they have tortured you to extract every bit of useful information."

From the groans behind him, An-Chi knew they understood.

"Line up, Soldiers," he whispered loudly. "I am your only hope of salvation."

Chapter 19

"I have to go," I announced as my phone chimed, its screen flashing, "Get back to school".

"But we haven't solved anything," Remmy protested. "We need to keep working on this."

"I can't," I argued while grabbing my backpack and jerking to my feet. "I have a mid-term in twenty minutes and I can't miss it."

"You're not serious."

The events of the last few days were overwhelming me, and though even to me it sounds irrational, I wanted to get things back to the way they were. More than anything, I wanted to take this exam and forget about someone trying to kill me.

"Yes. I need to do this."

"No!"

Unwilling to waste time arguing with her about it, I headed for the door. Before I managed two steps, Remmy had a grip on my arm. I tried to keep going, but she refused to let go and the move pulled her into me. When I tried to step away, her right foot hooked my left, throwing me off balance. As I tried to pull my foot free, both of them entangled with hers and I went down, my right cheek crashing into something hard.

"Gaaa," I cried as my injured cheek slammed the floor, and pain exploded in my face.

Overwhelmed by agony, I threw hands over my face, and rocked from side to side on the floor until I realized Remmy was tugging on my arms, crying, "Let me see! Let me see!"

Pushing her hands away, I shouted, "Leave it, will ya?"

After my hands reflexively covered the wound again, I looked up to see Remmy leaning over me, but her attention was now on her aunt.

"Give him a minute," Jasmina insisted while gently pulling her niece back. "He took quite a knock to the head."

I gingerly touched my right cheekbone to find it tender and sticky, the bandage covering the cut now gone. Though it still hurt like the dickens, I took a deep breath, lowered my hands, and looked up at the two women.

My mind filled with tons of biting, rude things to say, but before I could bring any of them to my lips, Remmy cried, "Shit! You're bleeding."

"Ya think?" I said angrily while looking at my blood-smeared hands.

"I'm so totally sorry," she cried while sitting back on her haunches, hands over her mouth. "I never meant to..."

"Yeah, well, you did and it hurts."

"I'll get my first-aid kit," Jasmina announced. "We'll patch you up in no time."

Closing my eyes again, I was once again thrust into the disorienting darkness, but also felt a sense of alarm and fear. I could tell the Chinese soldier had dropped into a squat, and heard the faint sound of water and whispers.

Ohh that hurt, I thought, hoping he might hear me.

I suddenly felt his anxiety.

Who spoke?

I was momentarily at a loss for what to say until the throbbing in my cheek gave me the answer.

Does your cheek hurt?

Where are you?

I was struggling to answer because I didn't want to say the wrong thing and totally freak him out. Of course, I was nearly freaked out myself, and had no real idea of how this should go, so I finally decided to tell the truth.

This may sound weird, but I'm in your head.

What do you mean?

I hesitated again, wondering what I did mean. The connection really wasn't my choice and I had no way of knowing how it worked. Was I in his head, or he in mine?

Think of me as a spirit from the future.
You speak in riddles. Show yourself!
I can't, but I want you to know, I'm in as much danger as you are.

Ssss! Silence!
Don't worry. No one else can hear me.
How is that possible?
I'm not really sure, but you have to trust…

My eyes popped open when Jasmina touched my hand. Both excited and disturbed by what just happened, I looked up and saw the alarm on her face. Lowering my hand, I looked again at the blood on it.

"It hurt him too."

At the sound of dual gasps, I looked up to see both women staring at me opened mouthed.

I nodded at their unasked question. "When it happened, he nearly fell down."

"Did you speak with him?" Remmy asked excitedly.

"Yeah. I guess so. At least I think we're sharing thoughts."

"Awesome," Remmy cheered as Jasmina opened the first-aid kit I was unhappily familiar with. "Did you tell him to go back to his camp?"

My head aching, I gingerly shook it. "It was all…too overwhelming. I didn't even think to mention that. I suppose, if I'd been in his shoes, it'd have scared the shit out of me too."

"But you've got to, like, tell him what's happening. He needs to know the risk he's taking."

"He knows the risk," Jasmina said while carefully touching a damp rag to my throbbing cheek. "It is doubtful he has a choice."

I couldn't stop myself from flinching, and the painful distraction almost made me miss Remmy's response.

"What do you mean? Everybody has a choice."

"Not everybody," Jasmina argued. "Soldiers are expected to follow orders no matter what the risk."

I closed my eyes when Jasmina spoke the last sentence, and suddenly felt myself falling forward. Catching myself, I opened my eyes as Remmy responded,

"But surely, when he tells them what's happening, they'll let him go back."

"You're not serious," I countered. "Who will believe him?"

While removing the wrapping from a large bandage, Jasmina slowly shook her head. "My husband, Tim is researching this. In ancient China, a soldier had to follow orders to the letter. The penalty for not doing so was death, even if that disobedience won the battle."

"So what can we do?"

After carefully pressing the bandage over my wound, Jasmina straightened. "We have to let this play out until we see who's pulling the strings. In the meantime, Gerry should take his midterm."

When I rose, Jasmina put a hand on my arm to steady me.

"I will look for someone else connected to that timeline. Hopefully, they'll have another perspective on this."

"What about me?" Remmy asked.

"Have you been connecting with anyone?"

"No."

"Then we have to keep looking, because right now I'm flying blind and I don't think Gerry can do this on his own."

"I'm going to be late," I complained, though still unsure if I could even make it out the door without crashing into something.

"We'll keep working end until we find someone," Jasmina assured me as she handed me some Advil and a glass of water.

Quickly downing the medicine, I returned the glass and pushed through the back door, setting a brisk pace in the direction of school, my head spinning, mind reeling, both my cheek and chest throbbing. My world was being pulled apart again, and my family seemed to be working against me. There were only two people I could turn to for help and I wasn't sure if involving them wouldn't put them in danger as well.

Reaching the street, I looked back at Jasmina's house and felt a tinge of guilt. How was I going to keep them from harm?

"Maybe I should just run away."

Chapter 20

When pain exploded in An-Chi's cheek as though he had been struck, he clamped his jaw to keep from crying out and dropped into a squat to regain his balance.

His eyes scanning the darkness, he reflexively pulled out his sword and tried to locate his attacker. To his surprise, he saw no one nearby. Fearing the enemy was hidden in the brush bordering the creek bank, he was preparing to call out a warning when a strange voice said,

"Ohhhh. That hurt."

This was not a statement he would expect from an attacker, and the confusion sent his heart racing.

"Who spoke?"

"Does your cheek hurt?"

The voice seemed to come from everywhere and as he twisted around to find the source, he became disoriented, feeling as though he were lying down as he reflexively pulled up a hand to cover the painful injury.

"Where are you?"

After a pause, the voice answered, "This may sound weird, but I'm in your head."

"What do you mean?"

There was a long pause before the voice said, "Think of me as a spirit from the future."

The statement made no sense. Spirits came from the past or the present. There was no such thing as a spirit of the future.

"You speak in riddles. Show yourself!"

While waiting for a response, An-Chi attention was drawn to his troopers crossing the nearby stream. Their path had taken them within sight of an enemy patrol's camp, and he had moved a short distance closer to the camp to listen for sounds that might indicate they had been detected. He was preparing to take on a perimeter guard, if necessary, but not a talking spirit.

"I can't, but I want you to know, I'm in as much danger as you are."

Frustration and fear made his anger flare.

"Sssss!" he hissed while lowering his hand and again searching the area around him for the source. "Silence."

"Don't worry. No one else can hear me."

"How is that possible?"

"I'm not really sure, but you have to trust…"

"Troop Leader?" Chong Dai whispered loudly. "You OK?"

Dropping back into his defensive squat, An-Chi turned toward the sound of footsteps in the soft grass. "Did you hear that other person?"

"I hear no one, but you, Troop Leader."

Desperately searching the dimness around him, An-Chi listened for a moment more before stowing his sword and turning to Chong Dai. "Cross the stream. Hurry. Hurry. The spirits do not want us here."

"Spirits, Troop Leader?"

"Be quiet! Go quickly!"

The entire side of his face throbbing, An-Chi followed Chong Dai across while struggling with the distracting pain and the overwhelming confusion created by the strange encounter. Upon reaching the other side, he pushed through a wall of brush, his hand on the hilt of his sword until he spotted the others.

Moving close, he whispered, "Are you all here?"

"We stay together, Troop Leader," Chong Dai announced softly. "Nobody get lost."

"Good. Now follow me."

Still reeling from the bizarre encounter, he marched into the lead before looking back to make sure his troopers were following.

Once they were off the stream bank, the ground leveled out again, and they moved from low brush into soft grasses high enough for An-Chi to touch without bending over. While he was relieved not to hear the strange spirit's voice again, he also realized the moon was nearly behind the western hills, and what little light they had would soon be gone.

He felt an annoying tenseness as his troopers continued to stumble in the dim light, cursing under their breaths, heading in the wrong direction, and forcing him to repeatedly hiss to keep them in line and quiet.

Unable to take it any longer, he stopped and faced them.

"The moon is nearly gone, so we must practice walking without light. Form a line, grab a belt, and close your eyes."

Starting slowly, An-Chi felt the doctor tugging on his belt, and heard the hushed voices of his troopers forming up behind her. The start was jerky, with plenty of pulling and pushing as the soldiers struggled to keep pace. However, after a dozen or so steps, they matched each other's stride, established a rhythm, and allowed him to gradually increase speed, though he knew he could not maintain more than a steady, walking pace before someone's toe kicked a heel, made the follower stumble, and threw off the whole line.

Picking out his guiding star, he headed toward it, being careful to walk deliberately, keeping his body balanced, and feeling each step in the hope of staying upright, even if he stepped into a small hole or onto another muddy stream bank.

As they marched on, An-Chi was beginning to think they might just make it when a female voice exploded in his head.

Soldiers are expected to follow orders no matter what the risk.

The intrusion so surprised him, he missed a step. When the doctor kicked his heel, he stumbled, but quickly caught himself, regaining his stride. As he resumed his even pace, An-Chi looked around, listening for sounds of approaching enemy, but heard only the footsteps of those behind him.

The last statement by the strange voice both scared and perplexed him, not only by its intensity, but because he knew the maxim well. A general must have the absolute loyalty of his troops. Soldiers who are concerned only with their own welfare will never hold together as a unit. But he also remembered that statement used in another context: one only appropriate if your father was a general.

You are a disloyal son!

The words were like a slap in the face, interrupting his concentration, forcing him to struggle to maintain his pace. Tears filled his eyes as the shock of the statement reverberated through his body, even though several years had passed since his father spoke those hurtful words.

Why would he think me the one who had been disloyal? He repeated the question he had asked many times since that day. *It was not I who killed his aide.*

Giving his head a sharp shake to ward off the distracting thoughts, he focused on the nearly invisible path ahead and pressed on.

But he could not stop the memories.

You have been betrayed, his father's assistant had said as he lay dying in that dark alley, his clutching hand smearing blood on An-Chi's sleeve, the same blood he saw accumulating in a black pool beneath the body.

Who was it?

His question went unanswered as the assistant's eyes slowly closed, and his hand dropped away. When shouting voices echoed off alley walls, he looked at the blood on his tunic, and the weapon lying beside the body. Even in the dim light, he recognized the inlaid ivory dragon on the ebony handle. It was the knife his father had given him on his promotion to squadron leader. Though he shouldn't have, the sudden panic of knowing his weapon had been used to commit murder made him run.

Though he was an experience soldier, trained to avoiding capture, this was different. He was not running from a pursuing enemy, but from the threat of facing his father. He ran in blind panic, his mind empty, heart pounding. He had no plan of escape, no objective to pursue, no thoughts whatsoever, except to get away.

Not surprisingly, he had gone only a short distance before they caught him, and though his father should have put him to death, he did far worse: banishment from his family, his friends, his ancestors.

The shock of the unbidden memories, combined with another sudden pain in his forehead, made him stumble again.

"Troop Leader," the doctor whispered. "What is the matter?"

"All stop."

After the command was passed down the line, he turned to listen for whomever, or whatever was speaking to him. The voice had been female this time, and definitely did not come from the members of his troop.

The silence was as disturbing as the voice. Not even a cricket chirping.

How can this be?

The achingly lonely howl of a gray wolf pierced the darkness, its sound eliciting gasps from his men and a nervous tug on his belt by the doctor. Though he knew the animal was some distance away, and no immediate threat to them, the guttural fear produced by the haunting sound flushed the questions and doubts from his mind, and brought a sense of focus lost since the voices haunted him. Before he could take a breath, the faint but distinct sound of a spear clacking against iron-plated armor reached his ears.

"Down!" he whispered.

His attention now completely forward, he heard footsteps coming their way.

One? No, two people. A patrol?

As he strained to hear more, a foot splashed water, and one of his troopers gasped. Unable to chastise the fool, An-Chi kept his attention on the approaching soldiers, unsure if they would be coming directly at them or passing on a different path.

"Ahhhh," a high-pitched male voice protested. "Water cold. Not want to wade stream."

"Troop Leader say, check ridge," a second voice demanded. "We go."

"What we find on ridge? Snakes?"

"No snakes on ridge, you foolish girl."

"You wade stream, fight snakes. I stay here. Guard rear."

"Coward!"

"I see no one on ridge. Why bother?"

"You see nothing from here. It too dark."

"It dark up there too. Snakes see in dark. You see."

As An-Chi held his breath, he heard a soggy foot squishing out water as it plopped back onto solid ground.

"Not worth trouble. We go back."

"You good soldier."

When the sound of their rattling gear faded into the background noise, An-Chi finally let out a breath.

Still listening, he took a moment to compose himself before turning back to his troopers.

"Follow close and keep silent. There is a stream ahead, and their camp may be nearby."

He moved carefully to the stream, and stopped to remove his shoes. When he was sure those following had also done the same, he moved into the water, feeling the cold as his foot slipped into the water; the muscles in his legs tensing, and twitching against the chill. As he proceeded, the water rose to his waist before he reached mid-stream and started the climb to the far side. Once on dry land, the evaporating water made him shiver as he stopped and turned back to help guide the others. To his surprise, the doctor was standing beside him. She had moved so quietly he had not known she was there.

Unfortunately, this was not the case with his soldiers. They gasped, grunted, splashed, gently bumped spears against shields, and mumbled curses as each one labored to make their way across in the dark. After the first of them reached dry ground, An-Chi moved further inland to focus his attention in the direction the enemy patrol had gone, listening for pounding feet, cries of alarm, or any sign they had been discovered.

After the soldiers were finally across, he hissed them silent and listened again for sounds of alarm. When he was sure the enemy remained unaware of their presence, he turned to his troop.

"Put your boots back on," he whispered, "and be quiet about it."

When they were finally ready, he formed a line and started forward, again feeling the doctor gripping his belt, hearing the footsteps of the soldiers behind as they whispered quietly to each other, a violation of his order that, under different circumstances, would have earned them rod across the face. However, as before, they finally achieved a rhythm, their whispering stopped, and the scattered sounds of their many footsteps became one.

Scanning the nearly invisible path ahead of him, he gradually increased the pace, and continued on, with occasional stumbles, and hushed curses, but mostly a steady pace that made An-Chi think they might defy the odds and make it to their destination.

Despite his effort to stay focused by blocking the distracting thoughts, they kept slipping back in, pulling his attention from the task at hand. It was not enough to make him stumble again, but it kept him from realizing how noisy his troopers had become. They covered another *li* before he shook his head to clear it and focused his attention enough to hear their feet scuffing the ground, spears occasionally clapping against something hard.

He was preparing to order a stop to chastise them when a movement only a short distance ahead made him slow and peer into the darkness. Seeing nothing, he was preparing to resume his pace when more activity made him realize what was happening. An instant later, he heard a foot softly scuff the ground ahead, the slight tap of wood against wood, and someone sucking in a sharp breath.

"Spears at the ready," he cried. "Spread out."

The cries of his own men were met with a barked order from his left. A flash of light briefly blinded him as he pulled out his sword and squinted at the shadowy figures rushing at them.

A lantern flared to life, its brilliant light silhouetting a dozen moving figures. The nearest soldier was less than twenty paces from An-Chi, his spear barely visible as he howled at the top of his lungs and charged. More voices joined the first as demonic shadows split up to take them on.

An-Chi heard several of his men cry out, but focused his attention on the lead soldier, who was leaning too far forward and slightly off balance. He waited until the man was close enough to make contact, then quickly stepped to one side, knocking the spear away with his sword. Twisting his body into a counter-clockwise spin, he did one complete rotation before bringing his sword down hard on the back of the soldier's neck.

As warm blood gushed onto his hands, An-Chi let his dying enemy crash to the ground and jerked back to avoid another spear tip aimed at his chest. Unfortunately, his sword was below the spear, and when he reflexively used his free hand to grab his opponent's weapon, the attacker yanked it back, cutting his hand with the blade as it pulled free. The move threw An-Chi off balance, and he dropped into a half-squat to keep from falling over. As he struggled to regain his balance, he looked over to see his attacker preparing for another thrust and knew he would not get his sword up in time to block it.

In the harsh light, the soldiers eyes were intense, his mouth open, teeth gleaming as he put all his effort into delivering the killing blow. The soldier's arms pulled back and as he started to push the spear forward, his expression changed to one of uncomprehending shock when the blade of a different spear pierced his side, its penetration stopping only when the T-like extension behind the blade hit his ribs.

Stunned by this sudden change in events, An-Chi turned to see the doctor's intense face, her eyes focused on her opponent as she gave one more push to send the man over sideways before yanking her spear free. As the dying soldier fell to the ground, their eyes met only briefly, giving An-Chi no time to react before his savior turned in the opposite direction to deflect a spear aimed at her head.

Hearing footsteps behind him, he reflexively ducked down and did a quick spin to see someone taking a swing at him. Squatting so the blade passed over his head, he lurched forward, dropped to one knee, and thrust upward so the tip of his sword slipped under his attacker's armor. The soldier grunted as An-Chi pushed hard to drive the blade into his heart. When his opponent dropped his weapon, An-Chi rotated, yanked his sword from the dying man's belly, and hurried past him.

The move put him behind the line of charging enemy, allowing him to briefly assess their strength. Five were on the ground, but the remainder were aggressively attacking his men, and driving them back. Only the doctor and Chong Dai were holding their ground, fighting bravely, but unless something changed, they would be overwhelmed.

Put out the light!

Picking up a spear, An-Chi took two quick steps to gain momentum and heaved it at the soldier holding the lamp. While it was in flight, he closed his eyes and charged at the nearest attacker. Now blind to the world around him, his ears took in the sounds of clanging weapons, grunting soldiers, scuffling feet, and his own breathing until he heard the solid thud of the spear hitting its target. The resulting scream was his signal to open his eyes. Though the light did not go out, with its holder down it was dimmed by tall grass. The short time his eyes were closed made them better adjusted to the suddenly-dimmer light than the other combatants and gave him a brief, but valuable advantage.

"*Móguǐ*," he screamed as he hacked into the neck of the first soldier he came to. "I am a demon!"

As his gurgling victim fell, he turned his attention to a soldier fighting one of his own. Since the enemy soldier's chest and waist were protected by armor, An-Chi hacked the man's exposed upper arm, his blade slicing deeply into flesh and nearly through the bone.

As a compliment to his opponent's scream, An-Chi howled, "*Móguǐ!*"

In the dimmer light, his invocation of demons was making his superstitious opponents hesitant, but unfortunately his own men also paused.

"Owl Troop attack and drink blood!"

The nearest enemy soldier swept his spear around to take him on, but An-Chi hacked it with such force, the impact severed the spear's shaft just behind the blade. His opponent staggered back, dropping the headless spear, which made two of his comrades retreat as well.

With over half of their number down, the remaining enemy went on the defensive, backpedaling, and looking around for someone to take the lead. Only then did An-Chi notice their troop leader lying motionless on the ground behind Chong Dai.

"Drink their blood!" he howled while snatching up a spear to heave it at the nearest enemy.

Light from the lamp was nearly gone as a screaming An-Chi jerked his sword over his head and followed the spear.

Though the soldier's ghostly figure jerked to one side and avoided being impaled, An-Chi was on him before he could regain his balance, aiming his blade for the soldier's head. Unfortunately, his opponent moved too quickly, and the blade clanged ineffectively against his iron-plated shoulder. Still off balance, the soldier swept his blade around, forcing An-Chi to pull back, but the tip still caught his left cheek, making him to turn his head as the razor-sharp weapon sliced through flesh and split the tip of his nose.

Running high on fear-driven adrenaline, An-Chi pushed off his opponent, but the enemy's heavier bulk left him standing as An-Chi stumbled back, off balance, and managed only two steps before his foot struck a body on the ground. The wounded soldier screamed, An-Chi toppled backwards, and the standing opponent scooped up a spear and charged, his weapon high, mouth clamped, eyes squinting, body leaning forward.

An-Chi tried to roll away, but the thrashing person under him made it hard for his feet to gain purchase. When he tried to dig in his heels, they slid on the bloody grass, leaving him flat on his back, his eyes on the spear tip bearing down on him.

A cry nearby made the attacking soldier hesitate long enough for An-Chi to somersault backward and rise to his feet.

Though his spear now gave him an advantage, the soldier still hesitated, continuing to hold his weapon with both hands while nervously glancing at the fighting around him.

Finally, seeming to make a decision, he scowled at his opponent and charged forward, flying over his prostrate comrade only to slip on a pool of blood and drop to one knee. When he released a hand from his spear to steady himself, An-Chi charged, pushed the spear aside, and stabbed his blade into the side of the man's neck, the razor-sharp edge slicing in until blood spurted.

An-Chi turned quickly to look for another opponent, but to his surprise, Chong Dai held up the lamp, flooding the chaotic scene with light. Nearly a dozen bodies lay on the ground, some still thrashing, most inert. The bulk of the fighting had moved to his right, with the now-retreating enemy trying to get away from his troopers.

As he relaxed, he spotted an enemy soldier on hands and knees, his head down, breathing short and loud. Almost without thinking, An-Chi moved to him.

"I will be merciful," he said while bringing his sword down onto the man's neck.

He heard a gasp as the headless body thumped to the ground, making him jerk around to see the doctor staring at him, her mouth open, eyes wide.

"I might have saved him," she stated angrily.

The statement briefly confused An-Chi. "You are no longer safely behind our lines, Doctor. Our mission is to retrieve the division commander." He pointed his sword at the fallen soldier. "Not to take prisoners."

"We don't have to murder them!"

Huffing loudly, he wiped blood from his blade and sheathed it. "He would gladly have killed you, wounded or not." Picking up a spear lying near the body, he moved to another enemy soldier who was holding both hands over his stomach, his breathing rapid, eyes pinched shut. Without hesitating, he stabbed the tip into the man's forehead. "The battlefield is not a civilized place, and we have no need for mercy. You either kill or be killed."

He started to walk away, but stopped when he realized she was still looking at the soldier's body.

"Doctor," he shouted, and nodded when she jerked around to look at him. "We must move quickly now. Those who escaped will soon be back with a much larger force." He pointed at the corpse with the spear jutting from his forehead. "Do not think they will treat you any better."

When she continued to stare at him, he stabbed a finger in the direction he was walking. "Now, Doctor!"

Looking stunned, she walked in a wide path around the corpses before falling in behind him. Though he listened to her footsteps to make she was following, An-Chi kept his eyes ahead, watching for stragglers as he marched toward his troopers now standing in a huddle around a person lying on the ground.

When they reached the cluster of soldiers, Chong Dai broke from the group, holding up the lantern as he approached. "Troop Leader. One captive. He speak plenty."

"Where are his comrades?"

"No more soldiers. Maybe two escape. Long way back to army."

An-Chi shook his head. "Even if that is true, their reinforcements may well arrive before the sun rises."

"By then we be in cave. They not find us."

Shaking his head again, An-Chi looked around before settling his attention on Chong Dai. "They failed to find the division commander's hideout because they did not know he was there. Now they will be more thorough. We must get him out of here tonight."

Chong Dai looked back at the crowd of troopers. "What about captive?"

When the soldier faced An-Chi again, he scowled. "What captive?"

"Do we have time before we leave?" Chong Dai asked with a malicious smile that turned An-Chi's stomach.

"No. We leave immediately. Be quick about it."

The look of disappointment on Chong Dai's face was obvious, but the trooper bowed quickly.

"Yes, Troop Leader. We be ready to march very soon. Quickly, quickly."

As his number two hurried back to his comrades, An-Chi turned toward Mei Xiu and saw her turn away from the troopers and stare into the darkness.

"Why does this bother you so? You see death every day."

"I am trained to save lives, not take them."

"That didn't stop you from killing when we were first attacked."

"I had no choice then, but this is different."

An-Chi sighed. "It is no different. I have been ordered to get to the division commander quickly. Taking prisoners and tending to the wounded only slows me down, especially now that we must outpace reinforcements."

"You could have tied him up and left him for them to find."

"To reveal my strength and direction? Why not post signs along our way, 'Enemy troops in this direction'?"

She opened her mouth to respond, but stopped when a scream erupted from the small crowd. Though he fought not to show it, their resulting laughter bothered him.

Stifling a sigh, he looked back at the doctor to see she was wiping her eyes.

"You may think me heartless, Doctor, but war takes a toll on us all. To survive, we must accept its reality and fight on. To fail to do so will bring dishonor and shame to our family and our ancestors."

She pointed at the laughing troopers. "And this brings honor?"

"If I had taken him captive, he would have been considered a traitor to his own people. If the division commander's men didn't kill him outright, our leaders would be honor-bound to execute him as a deserter."

"We ready to leave, Troop Leader," Chong Dai announced as the seven remaining soldiers lined up behind him.

"We must now march at double-time, and hope the directions I have to the hideout are accurate. Put out the lamp, no talking, keep your gear quiet, and follow close. We will not stop for stragglers, and you know what the enemy will do if they catch you."

"Yes, Troop Leader," Chong Dai responded. "We stay close."

Visualizing the memorized map, An-Chi took off at a fast jog, hearing the footsteps and breathing of those behind him. If his reckoning was correct, he had less than two *li* to the cave, but he knew that even if they ran like the wind, the moon would be gone before they arrived. It did not matter how quickly the doctor worked, they would have no choice but to return the division commander in daylight or risk being trapped in the cave.

I should have set a faster pace, he fumed silently. *We would be there by now.*

Chapter 21

While checking my cell phone's clock, I jogged around the last street corner, and despite a lingering headache, breathed a sigh of relief when I realized I'd make it to my class in time.

Punching a speed dial button, I waited for a response, and felt a flare of irritation when Remmy's voicemail message played.

"Remmy, this is Gerry. Tell your aunt I'll be at her house about three."

I was preparing to pocket the phone when squealing tires drew my attention to a black van stopping just ahead of me. I didn't really give it much thought, and was looking down at my pocket when the side door of the van opened and an attractive blond woman jumped out, her light blouse coming nowhere close to hiding the motion of her large, bouncing breasts, her tight miniskirt emphasizing narrow hips and slender legs.

The fact that her attention seemed to be totally on me was unsettling, and when my toe snagged a bit of the sidewalk, I nearly dropped my cell.

Clutching the phone, I was struggling to get it into my pocket when she announced, "You're the one."

I looked up, surprised to see she had covered the distance between us more quickly than I had anticipated. She was nearly jogging, and coming down hard on her heels which sent her blouse bouncing, hips swaying, hair flying. It was all too much for my teenage hormonally confused brain. I stopped and stared like a deer with his eyes on some fantastically jiggling headlights.

"Give us a kiss, handsome," she said while lifting her hands, as though to wrap them around my neck.

All rational thought ceased when instant fantasies overloaded my brain. I didn't even see what she had in her hand until she slipped the black bag over my head, and cinched it tight around my neck.

The sudden loss of vision brought on an instinctive reaction. Dropping my phone, I started to push her away, but only until something hard slammed my groin.

"Gaaa," I screamed, doubling over as a different pair of hands grabbed my other arm and both people yanked me forward.

The pain making me want to throw up, I stumbled along until my shins slammed painfully into a hard ledge. Crying out, I toppled forward, but before I reached the ground, a hand grabbed my belt and heaved me forward, painfully slamming my head into the far wall. I crashed to the floor, my scrambled brain not even thinking of shouting before a knee jammed into my back, painfully slamming my chin to the floor as a sliding door banged shut.

Before I could even think of how to react, I heard the squeal of tires and the van lurched forward.

"What's going on?" I cried while my hands were yanked behind my back and bound together.

When I tried to resist, something cold and hard pressed painfully into my neck.

"One more word," a male voice warned, "and I blow your fuckin' brains out."

Chaotic thoughts filled my head as a rope was wrapped around my ankles and synched tight.

My vision totally blocked by the bag over my head, I was desperately struggling to understand what was going on when a hand pushed my head down, forcing my face against the floor.

"Hold still," the male demanded as the gun barrel dug into the back of my neck. "We're going to lift the bag, but don't move a muscle. If you try to look up, or shout, I'll pop ya right here and now. Got that?"

I resisted automatically for a brief moment before relaxing as much as I could and jerking a nod.

"Yeah."

Clumsy hands fumbled the knot loose and the bag was slowly lifted. Try as I might, all I could see was the floor of the van, and purple toenails poking out of a woman's green, open-toed shoes.

Still gripping my head, the man pulled it up just enough for the woman to slide a blindfold over my eyes, which she tied tightly at the back.

"Help me get him onto the seat," the man ordered.

"What are you gonna do?" she asked as I was lifted up to sit uncomfortably on my bound hands.

The seat sagged as a person sat next to me and laid something over my shoulders.

"A coat?" the woman asked.

"And a hat," the man announced as he pressed it onto my head. "And the last touch: dark glasses. We prop him up, buckle him in, and anybody who sees him will think he's just another happy passenger."

As I felt the sunglasses being pushed onto my face, I tried to reason this out.

This must be some kind of bizarre prank, but I can't believe anyone I know would...

My thought froze when the angry face of a Chinese soldier appeared in the blackness and I realized he was preparing to shove a spear into my chest. I stiffened, but my other self jumped to one side and barely avoided being run through. Though my bound hands could not move, I saw a hand reach out to grab the shaft, gripping it tightly, but not tight enough as my opponent cried out and yanked it away, the sharp blade slicing into my thumb.

"Shit!" I cried in response to the biting pain.

"Shut it!" the man demanded, his hand gripping my arm.

"Something cut my hand."

"Maybe you'd fuckin' like it better if I just hacked your damned tongue out."

OK. This definitely isn't a prank.

I no longer felt the pain in my hand because my other self was falling backwards, his opponent lifting his spear high then oddly hesitating as he took a quick look to his right. I felt my body jerk as my other self did a backwards roll to reach his feet before his opponent could get to him.

"Drink their blood," I heard myself shout while seeing my alter ego charging in to attack.

"What was that?" the woman cried just before pain exploded across my entire left cheek.

"Yaaaa!"

"Jesus!" the man protested as warm blood flowed down my face. "Where'd that come from?"

I tried to pull away when something pressed into the wound, causing even more pain.

"What are you doing?" the man demanded.

"Gotta stop the bleeding," the woman shouted defensively. "We don't want this prick dying on us."

"Danny," the man called. "Give me your damned handkerchief."

"It's all snotty," a nasally, higher-pitched male voice responded.

"I don't give a shit what's on it. Just hand it over before I put a bullet in yer fat fairy ass."

Suddenly pulled back into the present, I felt the van swerve one way and then the other.

"Here, Ronny" Danny stated angrily.

"Stupid shit," Ronny complained. "You're gonna run off the friggin' road. We don't deliver this package safe and sound, we don't get paid."

"Stop swearing," the woman protested. "He's just a kid."

"You called him a prick. What's that? Pillow talk?"

More pain in my cheek.

"This is going to need stitches, and antibiotics," the woman said anxiously as she lifted the cloth and announced, "God this is ugly."

"And how do we do that?" Ronny asked. "You wanna take him to the emergency room and ask them to patch up a kidnapped kid, but please don't tell the cops he's here?"

"Maybe we could stop and Charisa could go get something," Danny offered.

"Shiiiit! We ain't stopping until we get him to where he's gotta go. Let them stitch him up. It ain't our job."

"Let me out and I'll walk to the hospital," I offered.

Pain exploded in my cheek again.

"Keep yer yap shut," Ronny shouted. "Or I'll stick my gun through that cut on yer cheek and blow yer gawd-damned tongue out."

The pain knocked me into a sort of nether world: partially in the present and partially in the past. Voices seemed to be coming from both timelines, but I could make little sense of either.

In the present, Charisa was protesting, her words sounding harsh, but indistinct and hollow. Since the blindfold blocked any sight of the present, my vision was filled with faintly lit people standing around a badly injured soldier. It felt like I had been fast-forwarded from a fight outside to a more subdued scene in a cave.

Someone I recognized as a doctor was rushing to the person's side as my alter ego thought,

A man without courage dies a thousand times, while the brave die but once.

My captors in the present went suddenly silent when I heard myself ask out loud,

"What have I to lose?"

Chapter 22

His troopers jogging along behind, An-Chi scanned the dark space around them and fought down his angst. Though the moon had disappeared behind the hill on their left, a faint glow radiated around it, giving him some sense of what lay ahead. Thankfully, they were now jogging down a narrow patch of grass between two hills, and except for an occasional bush tangling his legs, he managed to keep their pace up while still hoping he was heading in the right direction.

He was about to call a halt to allow his troopers to rest when three ghostly shapes appeared in front of them, their crossbows at the ready.

Stopping, An-Chi sucked in a desperate breath before whispering, "I follow the Son of Heaven."

The troopers following piled up behind him, grunting as each bumped into the person ahead, their whispered protests seeming to bring even more ghost-like figures from the darkness to surround them, their images so faint An-Chi wondered if they might really be spirits: spirits with crossbows.

"Who is the Son of Heaven?" a voice demanded.

"I bow to Emperor Xian, the only true Son of Heaven."

"Why are you here?"

"I bring a doctor for your commander."

An-Chi struggled to contain his sigh of relief when the soldiers lowered their weapons.

"Follow me," the leader whispered while waving them forward.

"We must hurry," An-Chi warned. "Danger is near."

The soldier nodded and led them up a steep rocky slope. Their guide set a brisk pace, only stopping at intervals to call out a passphrase and wait for a response before hurrying on. An-Chi could hear his men gasping for air as they slowed again. The soldier whispered one more passphrase before pushing through a clump of bushes to enter a low cave.

"Keep your head down," he warned, "or teeth in the ceiling will take a bite out of it."

An-Chi looked up to see dozens of stalactites glowing softly in a dim light emanating from the interior. He stumbled on an uneven floor, but only after they moved closer to the light source did he realize that someone had hacked away stalagmites from the floor to create a passage.

After moving down a twisting tunnel, they entered a large cavern. In the middle, a figure lay on a pile of grass. Light from a nearby lamp revealed blood on his armor, and a large, blood-soaked bandage strapped to his shoulder with a ribbon of leather.

An-Chi slowed when the doctor rushed past, watching as she announced herself in hushed whispers. The soldiers next to the grass bed bowed, none challenging her credentials, all appearing eager to see whether she succeeded or failed. Their duty was clear: protect their leader in life, or follow him in death. An-Chi also knew that if the commander died, he and his remaining troopers would also be given the "privilege" of accompanying them to the afterlife.

Oddly, the thought did not bother him. After all, his banishment meant he was already dead to his family.

A man without courage dies a thousand deaths, while the brave die but once.

"What have I to lose?"

Chapter 23

"Gerry's going to be here soon," Remmy announced as Jasmina opened her front door to let her in. "He should have finished his midterm ten minutes ago."

"Then let's get started," her aunt responded. "There are some things you and I need to discuss before he gets here."

"What?"

Motioning toward the back of the house, Jasmina smiled. "It would be helpful if we knew what your part is in this, if any."

"How could I not be?"

"Have you been having any flashbacks, dreams, or strange memories?"

"No, but that doesn't mean I'm not involved."

After they entered Jasmina's office, she motioned for Remmy to sit on the couch and sat next to her.

"What has he told you about the situation back then?"

"Not much more than you already know. It's totally a jumble to him right now. He's hardly..."

A ringing doorbell stopped her.

"There he is now," she announced as she pushed off the couch and rushed to the front door.

Yanking it open, she said, "We were wondering when..."

The sight of two frowning men in dark suits stopped her.

"Missus Jasmina Maxell?" the huskier of the two men asked.

"Uh, no," Remmy answered hesitantly. "She's my aunt."

"Who is it, Remmy?" Jasmina asked as she appeared from the hallway.

Remmy looked from her aunt to the two men and back.

"Missus Maxell? Missus Jasmina Maxell?" the man asked again.

"Yes, and who are you?"

"Ma'am, I am Special Agent Evans, and this is Special Agent McCarthy from the Federal Bureau of Investigation. We'd like a word with you, if we may?"

"What is this about, gentlemen?"

"May we come inside, Ma'am?"

After a moment's hesitation, she stepped back and motioned toward her front room. "Please do."

The women locked eyes for a moment before following the special agents into the room where the men stopped, turned as one, and faced them.

"We understand you know a Gerald Patterson," Special Agent Evans stated.

"Yes, I do."

"We were wondering if you know where he is right now."

Shaking her head, Jasmina heard Remmy gasp as she prepared to answer. "I assume he is at school taking a midterm exam. Why do you need to know?"

"Have you seen Mister Patterson today?"

"What has happened to Gerry?" Remmy cried.

The agent glanced at her before returning his attention to Jasmina. "Have you seen Mister Paterson today?" he repeated without emotion.

Nodding, Jasmina glanced at Remmy as well before answering. "He was here about noon. We visited for a while and he went back to school. Is he OK?"

The two agents looked at each other for a long moment before Special Agent McCarthy nodded and his partner turned back to Jasmina.

"It appears he never arrived, Ma'am, and we were wondering if he mentioned where he planned to go after leaving you."

"As far as I know, straight to school. He's a freshman at Marion County Community College."

"Yes, Ma'am, we know that, but…"

"What's happened to him?" Remmy interrupted.

"And you are?"

"I'm his girlfriend, Remmy Reed. I was here when he came over."

"Why didn't you return to school with him?"

"I don't have a class until later this afternoon. Jasmina made me a sandwich and we had lunch."

"Didn't Mister Patterson eat with you?"

Looking down at her hands, Remmy sighed, "No."

"And what did you talk about while he was here?"

It was Jasmina's turn to sigh. "Gerry has been having nightmares and he wanted to talk to me about them."

"Why you, Ma'am?"

"Because we're friends and he needed someone to talk to."

"He couldn't discuss it with his parents?"

Jasmina barked a dry laugh. "He's a teenager, Special Agent Evans. He's not getting along with his parents right now."

"What were these nightmares about?"

"The stress of being a teenager: parental problems, fears about his future, stress about the deteriorating state of our planet. Normal teenager angst, I suppose."

Special Agent Evans turned to Remmy. "Did he mention problems with anyone in particular?"

"No."

"He part of a street gang or dealing drugs…anything like that?"

"God no! Not a chance. Ever!"

"Wait a minute," Jasmina interjected. "If Gerry's only been gone a short while, why are you involved in this?"

The two agents looked at each other again before Special Agent McCarthy said, "Someone saw Mister Patterson being shoved into a dark van, apparently against his will. From details we can't discuss at this time, there is a possibility it might be terror related."

"You're not serious."

"Yes, Ma'am. We are," McCarthy responded.

Her hands flying to her mouth, Remmy screamed, "Gerry? No!"

"Did they get a license number?" Jasmina asked.

"Yes, Ma'am, but it has been reported stolen."

When Jasmina looked at her, Remmy's eyes were so wide it looked like they might pop out of her head. Moving to the girl, she wrapped an arm around her shoulders and gave her a squeeze.

"Ransom?"

"Not yet, but if it is a terrorist act, there won't be one."

As Remmy began sobbing, Jasmina held her tight and sighed. "I was afraid this might happen."

"Ma'am?" Special Agent McCarthy asked. "You have some idea of what is going on?"

"Sit down, gentlemen," she said while guiding Remmy to the couch. "You're going to find this hard to believe."

Chapter 24

An-Chi turned to see his troopers standing at attention, or at least as close an approximation as they were capable. He felt his own back automatically stiffen when a tall, sturdy figure approached. The expensive steel plates covering his red and blue uniform were splattered with dirt and blood, and though his black hair was somewhat disheveled, and his hands dirty, his bearing and demeanor projected the rank of captain even before the *zhang* patch on his right sleeve confirmed it.

"What is your status, Troop Leader?"

"We were attacked about two *li* from this position, Sir," he heard himself responding, while feeling strangely disoriented.

Though he stood at attention, it felt as though he were sitting, his hands bound behind him. Fighting off the sensation, he pulled the map from inside his tunic and opened it.

"Here is the approximate location," he said while pointing at the map. "At least two of the enemy escaped, so I marched double-time to find you. We must leave as soon as the doctor can stabilize the division commander."

"Why did you not pursue them?"

"My orders were to find you and bring the division commander back. There wasn't time to chase those who escaped and also accomplish my objective."

"How much time do you estimate we have?"

"If our intelligence is correct, there are no other troops near the unit we engaged. By now, those who escaped are probably halfway to their base camp. If we start moving soon, we will be nearly to our own camp before they can organize their return."

"Unless they send cavalry," the captain growled.

"With all due respect, Sir. With the engagement so near at hand they will not waste such a valuable resource on us. It is most likely they will simply reinforce their left against a flanking move."

The captain scowled at An-Chi for a moment before nodding. "You seem quite knowledgeable for a mere troop leader."

Bowing, An-Chi struggled to keep from showing a disrespectful smile. "I have read the great works of Sun Tzu. His wisdom is timeless."

"From the way you speak, I should have known you were not an illiterate peasant farmer."

"Thank you, My Captain. I am originally from Chang'an."

"The capital? I trust you are also not from the family of a merchant."

Shaking his head sharply, An-Chi did not try to hide his disgust. "No member of my family would tolerate such a disgrace."

The captain eyed him for a long moment before nodding. "Then I will plan our escape. Have your troop ready. Since you have no armor, your soldiers will be bearers. Carry him well."

"Yes, My Captain," An-Chi responded but his superior was already marching away.

After waiting a respectful moment to make sure the captain would ask no more of him, An-Chi hurried to his troop.

"Chong Dai," he called when he was within earshot. "We are to carry the division commander."

"Troop Leader?" Chong Dai asked, his expression one of surprise and dismay. "Maybe better if he go on horse?"

"Do you see a horse?"

"No, Troop Leader, but we only eight. No can carry such heavy man all way there."

"Captain's orders. We will do as told."

When Chong Dai opened his mouth to protest, An-Chi needed only to scowl at him.

"As you say, Troop Leader."

"The doctor should be finished soon. Have the men eat a small meal and be ready. We will not stop once we have started."

"Yes, Troop Leader."

After Chong Dai shuffled away, An-Chi moved closer to the doctor, but quickly realized she was too occupied to be disturbed. He was impressed by how quickly, but carefully she worked: eyes watching; nose sniffing; hands quickly stitching up a long gash in the division commander's arm before applying a cooling poultice; her concentration absolute as she mixed herbs into a cup, added water and tried to feed it to the nearly unconscious commander.

Of course, at this point, An-Chi thought she was a he, but as he watched her move, saw her slender fingers working, noticed her head tilting in a feminine way, he felt a disturbing longing. The sensation made him turn away, his body shuddering reflexively. Sexual attraction between two men was something he was aware of. He also knew it was encouraged in some circles of society, but for him such feelings were strictly forbidden.

He started to leave, but stopped when Mei-Xiu called, her voice slightly panicked. "Troop Leader. Could you assist me?"

He wanted to pretend he hadn't heard her and keep walking, but before he took another step, a warrior next to the injured commander called in a loud, clear baritone,

"Troop Leader. The doctor wishes you to attend him."

His disgust now under control, An-Chi turned to find Mei-Xiu staring at him.

"Please help me, Troop Leader," she pleaded while holding up a ceramic cup. "I cannot get him to drink this."

When he reached her, she motioned toward the commander's mouth. "Pull his lower jaw down and hold it while I pour this in."

"He will choke."

Mei-Xiu's head was shaking as she learned toward the commander. "He will swallow it just fine. Please be quick. I am told we must leave as soon as possible. This will take but a moment to bring relief."

Reaching over to grab the commander's jaw, he felt Mei-Xiu's shoulder pressing against his, and even over the smell of blood, sweat, urine, he caught the scent of something unfamiliar, yet repulsively arousing.

His desire to leave was checked by the sight of the commander's soldiers lined up in a circle around them. He saw nervousness in stern faces, tension in hands gripping and releasing whatever they held, fierce determination in straight backs and unwavering eyes. These were elite troops who lived by rules as distinct and inflexible as the steel blades hanging from their waists. There was no question in An-Chi's mind that the division commander would leave this cave alive, or none of them would.

The realization banishing his revulsion, An-Chi gripped the commander's jaw and slowly, firmly pried his mouth open. He nervously watched Mei-Xiu's steady hand as she deftly poured the milky liquid in, and saw the commander react as promised: swallowing hard, occasionally choking, but finally getting it all down. The moaning quickly subsided and her patient soon sighed and relaxed onto his bed.

"We can go now," Mei-Xiu announced to the nearest guard. "He will sleep quietly until the sun sets again."

Remaining silent, An-Chi stepped away from her and walked toward his own troopers, his head shaking as he strained against the urge to look back while muttering,

"But will *I* ever sleep again?"

Chapter 25

"What did he say?" Charisa asked.

I heard Ronny spit on the floor. "This kid is crackers. How long before we get there?"

My throbbing cheek made time seem disjointed, but it still felt like a long moment passed before Danny squeaked, "A little longer than we thought."

"What the hell do ya mean?"

"Uh," Danny said hesitantly. "I think I left the map to our destination at the hotel."

"You did what?"

"I can't find it in my bag. Did you take it, Charisa?"

"No. The map was your responsibility."

"I must have dropped it when I was getting the van's keys."

"Wait a minute! Keys?" Ronny cried. "This van is stolen. Where'd ya get keys?"

"Uh…well, it *is* stolen. Sort of."

"What do ya mean, *sort of*?"

"My uncle doesn't know we have it."

"Ya took this van from yer *uncle*? What were ya thinking?"

"Well," Danny whined. "I tried hotwiring his neighbor's van, but the steering wheel locked and I couldn't get it out of the driveway. You need keys to steal a van nowadays."

Ronny's knee bumped me as he shouted, "You stupid shit!"

"Ow!" Danny cried and the van swerved. "That hurt."

"Keep this damned thing on the road, or I'll smack ya again."

Charisa huffed angrily. "You didn't have to hit him."

"Stupid *should* hurt," Ronny growled. "So let's get back to that hotel and find the map."

"But what if we can't find it?"

"You'd better hope we do, 'cause otherwise, we waste this kid and dump him in a forest somewhere. At least ya got plenty of that around here."

"Not like Chicago, eh, Ronny?" Danny asked.

"What the mother…"

"Ow!" Danny cried as the van swerved again. "Why'd you do that?"

"'Cause obviously yer momma didn't do it enough while ya was growin' up, ya dumb shit."

"But…"

"Just shut up and drive, or I'll hit ya with my gun next time."

"But Ronny," Charisa protested. "You don't have to…"

"Shut it, Bitch. Let's just get to the hotel. The sooner I'm free of you two the better."

The van swerved again as Danny whined something I couldn't make out. Knowing I had only a little time, I tried to ignore the pain and count the number of turns they made, and how many times they stopped at lights, but lost count when I started jumping between the past and present, my senses filling with the unpleasant smells and muffled sounds of a small cave filled with soldiers.

When the van took a wide, slow left, I snapped back to the present, feeling my body shift as the vehicle turned, but what surprised me when I reflexively stuck out a foot to balance myself, was that the rope around my ankles was loose.

I quickly pushed my feet back together, listening for familiar sounds as the van slowed, made several sharp turns, and stopped.

"Give me the receipt for the room," Ronny demanded.

"I…uh…I don't have it," came Danny's nervous response.

"What did ya do with it?"

"You said not to keep anything that could ID us, so I tossed it just before we left the hotel."

Groaning, Ronny slid the van's side door open.

"Come on," he demanded. "Let's go get it."

"Me?" Danny squeaked.

"You checked us out, right?"

"No. Charisa did, and then she gave me the receipt."

Snorting angrily, Ronny spat. "OK then, Charisa comes with me. You stay in the van."

I felt Charisa clumsily step past me and then the van's side door slid closed. A moment later, an electric motor whined, like a window was being lowered.

"What do I do if a cop shows up?" Danny asked anxiously.

"You sit tight and act norm...shit. Just sit tight, don't play the radio, or honk the horn. OK?"

"Got it."

The window stayed down, and after a minute, I heard Danny moan.

"I need a smoke," he muttered as the driver's side door opened and closed.

Pushing my feet apart, I kicked off the rope, twisted around to release the seat belt and then pulled my knees up to slip my hands under my feet. Now that they were in front of me, I pushed up the blindfold to find myself in a dark van with no windows behind the driver's seat.

I leaned forward, held my breath, and listened carefully for sounds of my captors. Hearing none, I peeked around to find the front seat empty, but cigarette smoke drifting in through the open window told me Danny was just outside.

Realizing this gave me a momentary advantage, I tried to free my hands, and felt near panic when the plastic ties binding them would not give. After struggling a moment more, I took a deep breath, forced the panic down, and looked around for something to cut them with. Failing that, I searched for a weapon, but the sight of keys dangling from the ignition made it clear there was a third option.

"Damn, these people are stupid," I muttered while crawling into the driver's seat.

Adrenaline pumping, I reached over with bound hands and managed to turn the key enough to engage the starter, but my fingers slipped off before the engine caught. I'm sure I swore while struggling to turn it again, but the engine had only started to turn over when the door flew open and Danny grabbed my arm.

Chapter 26

They set off at such a fast pace, An-Chi wondered how long his troopers would last. His first concern had been finding their way in the dark, but the sound of marching feet gave them a sense of direction, and whispered warnings of obstacles were quickly passed back.

Though he would have preferred to have all eight of his remaining men carry the stretcher at one time, without time to practice, it was simply too difficult for that many men to maintain a steady rhythm. He settled for having four carrying while the others rested.

They made excellent time, and covered the first four *li* with little trouble. While the warriors were getting organized, he had his men practice swapping places, and thankfully, they did well enough, which meant they probably would not drop their precious cargo.

If the warriors had not been slowed by the litter, they might have made it to camp before the sun rose, but as it was, they were still six *li* from their destination when first light glowed on the eastern horizon.

"Hurry, hurry," An-Chi urged when increasing light made it possible to see where they were going, but also made them easier to spot.

He had just finished overseeing a change of litter carriers when the captain moved up beside him.

"We have neutralized the first encampment," he announced. "Those lazy worms died in their sleep."

"I assume the last one will not be so easy."

Looking ahead, he jerked a nod. "Our advance team has already reached their camp. The entire lot ran off before we arrived, and it appears the ones you fought have already alerted their leaders."

An-Chi glanced over to check on his men, but when he looked back, the captain was pointing at a man and his prancing horse on top of a far hill. Since he made no effort to hide himself, the statement was clear and unequivocal: he was not alone and they could not outrun him.

"Cavalry," An-Chi stated flatly.

"It would seem you misjudged the enemy on that point," the captain said firmly with the stony face expected of one with his high rank.

Pushing down a rising panic, An-Chi focused on the rolling hills ahead of them. When he saw no clouds of dust churned up by charging horses, he realized they had a little time.

"If I may offer a suggestion, My Captain."

"Let's hear it."

"I would guess they did not send their best riders at such a critical time, so this person is leading an auxiliary troop with less experienced riders." An-Chi pointed at the hill ahead of them. "We crossed this hill on our way here. The ground is quite rocky."

"You are suggesting we take the hill and fight from the top?"

"Not from the top, My Captain," An-Chi answered while visualizing the upcoming fight. "We meet them on the western side, where the ground is steep and their horses are at a disadvantage."

"And what would make them take such an inferior position?"

An-Chi struggled to suppress a laugh, keeping his face neutral as he faced his superior.

"Greed."

Chapter 27

"No you don't, asshole," Danny growled through a cloud of cigarette smoke as he grabbed my arm and pulled me toward him.

Desperate to get away, I yanked my arm free and slammed an elbow into his nose.

"Christ," he cried as he fell back, his hands flying to his face.

Reaching for the keys again, I twisted with all my might, feeling elated as the engine roared to life.

Since there was no car in front of the van, I pulled the shift lever down as far as it would go and stomped on the gas. My hope of an easy escape vanished when Danny grabbed my arm and pulled me toward the door. I tightened my grip on the steering wheel, but couldn't hold on as his feet flew out from under him and the weight of his body nearly yanked me out of the seat. Bringing my right thigh up against the steering wheel gave me enough leverage to pull back, but not break free of his grip. With my foot now off the accelerator, the van slowed, giving Danny the advantage. As he started to regain his footing, I pulled with all my strength until I was able to hook my hands inside the steering wheel, pull myself upright, and stomp on the gas.

Locked in a tugging stalemate, we raced through the nearly-empty parking lot, me unable to steer, the stumbling Danny refusing to let go. The impasse continued until the van slammed into a parked car, throwing Danny into the open door, and whacking my head against the steering wheel. The van's horn blared, a car alarm whooped, and the engine died.

A stunned Danny crumpled to the ground. Terrified and disoriented, I tried to scramble out, but my foot snagged something, sending me head-first into Danny's stomach.

"Oooph!" he exhaled as I did a clumsy somersault over him to bang my head on the pavement.

Totally knocked for a loop, I tried to jump up, but the world around me was a rocking, spinning carnival ride, and the vertigo forced me back to one knee. Panicked, I forced myself to rise, but when I tried to run, my knees wouldn't lock, and the pavement kept rolling one way and then the other.

My stomach cramped, sending me staggering forward to lean against the nearest car, and desperate to regain my balance before the moaning Danny recovered.

"Help," I gasped while struggling to keep my lunch down.

Knowing time was running out, I swallowed hard and tried again to walk before the sound of squealing tires made me turn to see an elderly couple waving their arms and shouting. When a copper-colored blur disappeared behind a large van, I turned and staggered between two parked cars, bouncing off one then the other until I was in the open. Before I could take another step, the Cadillac screeched to a stop in front of me.

"Get him," Ronny bellowed as Charisa erupted from the front seat.

I tried to change direction, but couldn't even mange that before Charisa had an iron grip on my arm.

"No!" I screamed while desperately trying to push her hands away.

"Stop it," she growled, "or I'll knee your nuts again."

Panic kept the threat from registering as I yanked free, and tried to run, but was so disoriented, I managed only a couple of steps before crashing into the side of a car. Charisa was on me again, the heel of her hand hammering my chin. My already-scrambled brain lost track of up and down until my body slammed hard pavement.

"Thought I was a pushover, didn't ya?" she screamed while towering over me. "Do that again and I'll put you in permanent time out."

Feeling thoroughly defeated, I rolled onto my side to see Ronny leading a staggering Danny toward us.

"Inta the fucking car, Bitch," Ronny bellowed as he heaved the gasping Danny into the back seat.

I felt a foot kick my leg.

"You heard him," Charisa snarled. "Move it."

My head, legs, and shoulder were all throbbing as I tried to think of what to do, but hadn't even finished with my first thought when strong hands grabbed me by the arm pits and yanked me up. I stumbled along on rubbery legs until a hard push sent me crashing onto the Caddie's floor.

Squealing tires and the push of acceleration made it clear I was no better off than when I started.

Then Danny threw up on my legs.

Chapter 28

Captain Yin Bohu sat on his prancing war horse, his colorful steel-plated uniform glowing in the morning sun as he watched the small group of foot soldiers ahead of him split up. He was eager to engage the enemy, as he had only recently been promoted, and this was his first taste of battle.

A distant nephew of the General Lü Bu, he had spent much of his military career as an auxiliary in the emperor's elite guard. After his relative rebelled against the emperor, he joined Lü Bu's army, but his lack of actual battle experience kept him in the rear guard where he did everything but fight. Only recently had he been ordered to join the main army, and now after much practice and parading, he would finally get the chance to lead his men against the enemy.

"I will show my uncle that I am general material," he muttered conspiratorially while watching the small enemy force.

To his surprise, the bulk of the enemy ran behind a hill opposite his position. Of the dozen or so remaining, six were supporting a litter which had to be carrying a wounded officer, because a common soldier would have either followed under his own power, or been quickly dispatched rather than allow him to fall into enemy hands.

"What idiots has General Sun taken into his army?" he asked rhetorically as his horse snorted and shifted under him. "Only a fool divides his forces against a superior enemy?"

He laughed while squinting at the litter-carrying group as they started climbing the hill. "What good will higher ground do them?" His horse shifted again, matching his eagerness to get into the fight. "Maybe they think I am only a single rider."

Laughing, he moved to the southern-most edge of his position, and looked down at the twenty-eight horsemen standing in perfect alignment, crossbows at the ready; highly polished armor sparkling like glittering diamonds; their similarly armored horses shifting impatiently, but not breaking formation.

"Wait until they see my deadly jewelry," he laughed while attaching a red flag to his spear, waving it once over his head, and pointing at the group climbing the hill opposite.

"I will deal with the small group first," he growled as he spurred his horse forward. "We will have them all on the ground and be back in camp for breakfast."

Riding down the gently-sloping face of the hill, Yin Bohu moved to the front of his advancing riders, feeling smug and confident. He started off at a trot, gradually increasing speed over the flat ground, his eyes sweeping the area for a surprise attack. There had been no reports of other troops in the area, and these were all on foot: no chariots, or horsemen, and to make it easier, the idiots split their forces. He would not be so foolish.

As they neared the hill, he could see the enemy looking back, and though they were obviously aware of the size of his force, they stayed together and kept their pace steady.

They have no bows, he was thinking as they drew near enough to see the enemy soldiers were carrying only spears and swords. *Take the bulk of them with arrows, and finish the rest with swords. This promises to be more an invigorating morning ride than a skirmish.*

"They will not reach the hilltop before we have them," he shouted to the men galloping behind him.

The grass thinned as they climbed the hill, and Yin Bohu could hear his horse's hooves clattering over gravel. It did not slow the animals, as they too were eager for the engagement.

"*Jinji!*" he cried as the slope increased, forcing the horses to lengthen their strides and push harder to maintain their pace. "Attack!"

Yin Bohu scowled when some of his riders let out a whooping cry and fired off their arrows too early. They were still half-a-*li* from the enemy and the shafts fell far short of their intended mark, shattering when they struck the rocky ground.

His scowl deepened when he realized the slope was steeper and rockier than he had anticipated. Dust-covered rocks had blended into the soil, making the hillside appear smoother than it was.

He listened to his horse's heavy breathing as he struggled with the increasingly steeper ground, but they had been over far worse terrain together.

These fools will still be obliterated.

Yin Bohu leaned forward in his saddle and looked more carefully at the fleeing enemy. They were jogging along at a steady pace, but did not seem as anxious as he would have expected. Their odd behavior made him cautious, but with no trees or outcrops to hide behind, and the rest of their troops on the other side of the hill, there was no one to reinforce them.

Gripping his reins tightly, he shook his head. "Even if they try to resist, it will be a slaughter."

When they finally came within range, he was preparing to give the order to fire when his horse stumbled, caught himself and pressed on. Looking at the ground again, he realized that the further up the slope they went, the larger the rocks were. Several more horses stumbled, and though they quickly recovered, Yin Bohu could see their riders were struggling to load their weapons.

Returning his attention to the enemy, he was surprised to see they had stopped, lowered the litter and were opening the blanket to reveal its true contents: composite bows.

"Attack," he bellowed over the increasing clatter of horse hooves.

Lifting his crossbow, he pulled the trigger, only to have his horse stumble again just as the arrow was being released. To his dismay, the bolt barely missed his mount's left ear before thumping into the ground a dozen paces ahead of him. Swearing, he fought to stabilize himself before looking uphill to see a second group of enemy appear about thirty degrees to their left, their heads and shoulders covered with dried grass, making them nearly invisible until they rose up and started running toward his position. He sucked in a sharp breath upon seeing they were also carrying composite bows, which had more than twice the range of his smaller, more compact crossbow.

A scream on his right made him jerk around to see a hole in his line. Even if they managed to take out the soldiers directly ahead, his horsemen would be fodder for the second group, as they were beyond the range of his men's more limited weapons.

The discovery confused him, but only for a moment. He was, after all, a cavalry troop captain.

"Right turn," he bellowed while yanking his mount in that direction.

As his horse turned, he reloaded his crossbow and fired at the closer group.

Their path took his horsemen further from the second group, giving them time to deal with one enemy force at a time. Unfortunately, fire from the first group had already taken out two of his men. To make it worse, their pace was beginning to slow as the horses struggled to move over increasingly rockier ground.

To his advantage, only half of the soldiers in the first group had bows, and now his men were close enough to reach them with their own weapons.

"Stop and stand," he commanded, watching as his men wheeled their horses around to form a line facing the enemy. "Fire at will."

Arrows streaked away from their line, forcing the litter bearers to hit the ground or be pin-cushioned as the missiles landed all around them. Two of them fell in the first volley, and those without bows seemed unwilling to risk rising up to take their weapons for themselves.

"They are overcome by fear," he scoffed as he watched the cowering soldiers. "They need not fret for long. Death will come quickly."

Chapter 29

"We gotta dump this car," Ronny growled angrily as Danny's warm barf soaked into my pants.

"You're telling me," Charisa moaned. "Danny puked all over the floor back there."

"We can't take long. That couple was probably calling the cops before we were out of the parking lot."

"This isn't going like we planned," she whined.

"Nothing ever does."

"But all we had to do was grab this kid and drive him to Portland. It shouldn't have been that hard."

"We're gonna make it," Ronny shouted. "I ain't going through all this grief fer nothin'."

"Where are we gonna find a car without someone else calling the cops on us?"

Danny's moaning blocked Ronny's muttering until the latter barked a laugh.

"We don't need to steal a car. We just need different plates."

"Huh?"

"Don't worry your pretty head. I'll take care of it."

"But we gotta ditch this car or I'll be tossing *my* cookies."

"Open the damned window and shut yer trap. I've got this under control."

I felt the car swerving, but could see nothing from my position on the floor. Worse yet, Danny looked like he was going to soil my pants again. When Charisa peeked into the back seat, I closed my eyes, pretending to be unconscious as Danny groaned,

"Oh God."

And let loose another round.

Squirming, I looked up to see Charisa glaring at me.

"You could'a killed him, ya know."

I lowered my head, closed my eyes, and didn't respond.

"You're just lucky you're worth more alive than dead," she growled.

I found that statement puzzling. For starters, who would want to kidnap me in the first...? The question was cut short when I found myself scrambling up the side of a sunlit hillside covered with large rocks.

What the...?"

A shout from behind made my other self turn toward what I realized was an impressive line of glittering soldiers on horseback. My awe was interrupted by the sound of an arrow rattling over rocks.

A distant shout and the horsemen moved a short distance to our left, before reforming their line.

Seeing a litter crash to the ground just uphill from me, I ran up and tore open a large bundle on it. As arrows landed all around, I grabbed a bow and quiver of arrows, passed it to another soldier, and reached for the next. My heart was beating a mile a minute as I emptied the litter of all but one bundle.

Grabbing it, I looked up at the impressive line of horses and men facing us.

Oh shit! I really am going to die.

The sound of Danny puking again brought me back to the present, but when I looked at my legs, the gooey slime covering them was peppered with red.

"Oh God," Danny gurgled. "I'm dying."

"We gotta do something, Ronny!" Charisa whined. "He's spitting up blood."

"Damn," Ronny howled just before the car swerved sharply and stopped.

"Ya gotta get me to a hospital, man," Danny sobbed. "I've ruptured a spleen or something."

I looked up to see Ronny's head shaking. "We can't take ya to no hospital, Danny. You'll have to get there on yer own."

"Huh?" his two companions said at the same time.

"Just go over to that store," he said while pointing out the window. "Walk far enough inside so someone can see ya and fall down. When they ask what's wrong, tell 'em ya got hit by a car and need an ambulance."

"But I'll get arrested."

"Fer what, ya stupid shit? Nobody knows yer with us. Ya were in the van when we stole this car."

"But what will I say?"

"Tell them it was a hit-and-run and give a vague description of the car."

"What car?"

"Any car, ya idiot! Hell, describe this Caddy. By the time the cops get around to speakin' with ya, we'll have dumped it and be in the next county."

"But what about my money?"

"Don't worry about that. We'll settle up after ya get out of the hospital."

Danny looked from Ronny to Charisa and back. "Really?"

"As God is my witness, we will. Right, Char?"

It took her a second to get the look of shock off her face, but she finally jerked a nod. "Absolutely. I'll see to it personally."

Danny blinked slowly, his brain seeming to work even slower than usual. After a moment, he wiped a sleeve across his mouth and looked at the blood smear on his sleeve.

"OK. I'll go."

"Help him out, Char."

The blond gave Ronny a long look before slipping out and opening the back door. Though she helped Danny to his feet and started him on his way, her eyes stayed on Ronny until she was safely back in her seat.

"Thought I was gonna take off and leave ya, Doll?" Ronny asked teasingly.

"Let's just go," she snapped angrily.

"What's the matter?" he asked playfully as the car accelerated.

There was a long pause before she spoke. "You're not going to give Danny his share, are you?"

Ronny grunted a laugh. "If it weren't for that dumb fuck, we'd have already delivered this kid and be celebrating naked in some hotel room."

"You think I'm going to get it on with you?"

I noticed the slight pause, and envisioned him giving her a lecherous look.

"The thought had crossed my mind."

"Well think on this. We're business partners and that's it. Find someone else to get naked with."

The car turned sharply and accelerated, pushing me into the seat, the movement reminding me that my legs were covered with Danny's barf and I was still a tied-up captive being delivered to an unknown person for unknown reasons. However, it stood to reason that since kidnapping was a serious offense, regardless of what Ronny and Charisa were after, the person or persons who ordered it were not likely to let me share my experience with the police.

Even if my other self survived to fight another day, I needed to get away from these whackos or I wasn't going to.

Chapter 30

While scrambling up the rocky hillside beside his men, An-Chi looked back at the approaching horsemen. Though the doctor's poultice made the pain tolerable, the exertion was making his cheek throb. At least now he could keep pace with his men without the cut being so painful he couldn't think.

Turning back, he could see the riders were still a safe distance away, but it was disturbing how quickly they were closing the distance.

My plan must work, he thought while urging his men on.

At this distance the wrapped bundle on the litter was obviously not a person, and doubt made his stomach clench.

Will they be fooled?

He looked back again, dismayed to see the charging soldiers had already cut the distance between them in half.

At least the doctor is safe.

The thought surprised him, but it was quickly replaced by self-doubt. What kind of fool would risk everything on the hope that his enemy captain would be too cocky and self-assured to believe that mere foot soldiers would think of a clever plan to defeat him?

The brazen cock crows in the morning, his father once told him, *and draws the fox to his home. His cocky assertion that he is king makes him vulnerable to attack.*

"Be cocky," he muttered just before he heard the clatter of an arrow striking rocks behind them.

"NOW," he screamed, throwing all his strength into climbing the final distance to the litter as his men let it fall to the ground.

Grabbing the cloth, he yanked it open, snatched up a bow and bundle of arrows and tossed them to an approaching warrior. The soldier caught them and moved away in one swift move, allowing An-Chi to toss a second bow as quickly as he could grab it.

The fox only succeeds if he is stealthy and nimble. An alert rooster will not be easy prey.

An-Chi was tossing out the third bow when an arrow smacked into a large stone behind him. Splinters harmlessly pelted his back, making him duck reflexively before he grabbed another bundle and threw it to waiting hands.

Another bundle went out before An-Chi grabbed the last one.

Has it been too long? filled his head as he grabbed the arrow bundle and threw its strap over his shoulder.

The bow was a natural fit for his hands, evenly balanced and light. He briefly enjoyed the feel of it until an arrow embedded itself into one of the litter's handles, and pulled his attention back to the horsemen. Yanking out his own arrow, he was already lifting the bow as he brought the missile down to nock its end in the string. He felt his chest swell as he pulled back on the arrow, found a target, instinctively adjusted for range, and let go.

His eyes on the arrow, he reached back for another, and was already nocking it when the dark streak hit a rider in mid-chest and bounced off.

Higher, he chastised, and adjusted his range before his bow string twanged, sending the second arrow on a slightly higher arc.

As his target rolled off his mount, the horse kept going, undeterred by the loss of his rider.

The horse is a larger target, his sergeant had screamed. *Shoot for its chest.*

It was an order An-Chi found nearly impossible to follow. During his first battle, his arrow pierced the foreleg of a beautiful chestnut stallion. The collapsing leg threw the screaming creature forward to smash its nose into the hard ground. The experienced rider flew from the tumbling horse, ducked into a practiced roll and was quickly on his feet. While the poor creature thrashed on the ground, his rider charged ahead on foot without even looking back.

The scene so appalled An-Chi, he vowed to never again kill such a majestic beast. He had practiced for days on end, using every spare moment to improve his skill at shooting from the ground, on horseback, even while running. He had no trouble killing a man in battle -- it was a necessity of war -- but something deep within made it impossible for him to do that to a horse.

Releasing another arrow, he immediately grabbed for the next one, hardly hearing the scream before he took aim on his next target. He fired as quickly as his hand could nock an arrow, upset only because the majority of his arrows either struck armor or missed the moving rider entirely.

Their leader bellowed a command and his riders shifted virtually as one to his left.

Good, he thought while reaching back for another arrow, and sucking in a sharp breath when his fingers grasped nothing but air.

He yanked the quiver around to find it empty, and a quick check showed his comrades were also out or nearly so. Further up the hill, ten of the division commander's warriors were howling at the top of their lungs and shooting at the horsemen, their arrows just reaching them until the enemy moved further to the left and out of range.

The slight break in action allowed An-Chi to relax and when he did, he became acutely aware of the pain in his cheek. It had throbbed while they ran up the hill, but the stress of the moment kept his mind off it. Now it was becoming a distraction, something he didn't need at this critical moment.

"Get down!" he shouted while crouching behind a low bush.

When safely out of sight, he pulled a bundle from his pocket and unwrapped it. With a finger he scooped out a small amount of the salve Mei-Xiu had given him, and pressed it into the wound on his cheek. The sudden pain forced out a groan before he re-wrapped the bundle and stored it away.

"Eyes ahead," he called as he peered around the bush and reminded himself not to look at the spot behind and slightly uphill from the horsemen where the last part of his plan was unfolding.

Timing would be critical. They needed to keep the horsemen focused on them, because if they guessed An-Chi's reason for leading his men to that exact location, he and his troopers would soon be rotting corpses on this dry, rocky hillside.

Chapter 31

The increased throbbing in my face made the puke on my legs a non-issue. Even before the adrenaline rush of Ronny's assault wore off, my cheek felt like it was on fire. I couldn't pay attention to where we were going, or what people were saying. Everything in my universe was bound up in that pain. Each time the car hit a bump, swerved around a corner, stopped at a light, or accelerated, my body shifted and produced so much pain I was literally seeing red.

Ronny said something I didn't even care to listen to and the car took a painful right turn, the light dimming as we hit a bump that bounced my head off the floor.

"Gaaa," I cried.

"Shut your trap, Asshole," Ronny growled.

I didn't respond. Didn't even want to try opening my mouth, and yelling was definitely out of the question.

"That cut on his face seems to be hurting him pretty bad," Charisa said anxiously. "He's crying."

"I don't care if he shits his pants," Ronny snapped back angrily. "He only needs to live long enough for us to make the delivery. After that, I hope they burn his ass to the ground."

The car took a sharp left and came to an abrupt stop, all of which was making me nauseous. Out the windows I could see the concrete ceiling of a parking garage, but little else.

"Here, take this," Ronny demanded.

"What? Why?" Charisa cried.

"If Asshole so much as looks like he's trying to escape, ya put two slugs in his head and get out of here."

"Shoot him?"

I heard Ronny laugh knowingly. "This ain't a squirt gun, Honey."

"But that's...murder."

Another laugh, only louder. "It don't matter what we do now, murder and kidnapping are both life sentences. We don't leave no witnesses behind. Got it?"

There was a long pause before Charisa answered hesitantly, "Yeah...I...guess...sure."

"There's no 'I guess' about it, Babe." Out of the corner of my eye I could see Ronny leaning over the back of the seat. "This guy talks, we ain't never gonna see the light of day again as long as we live."

"OK, Ronny. I get it."

The car shook, a door slammed, and a moment later I looked up to see Charisa leaning over the seatback, pistol in hand, but thankfully not pointed at me.

"Why did you have to cause so much trouble?" she whined. "We weren't going ta hurt ya."

At that moment, the pain in my cheek started to diminish, like someone had given me a pain killer. Even so, I could think of nothing to say to the woman because I had the impression she knew what her employers had in mind for me. Knew, but just hadn't thought about before now.

Taking a deep breath, I slowly stretched my jaw, feeling a strong ache in my cheek, but nothing like it had been only a moment earlier. Grateful for the relief, but having no explanation for it, I turned my attention to more pressing matters.

How can I convince her to let me go?

I struggled to come up with something, but drew a complete blank.

Give me the gun and I won't tell anyone about you, I thought lamely.

"If you help me out, the cops will go a lot easier on you," I said hoarsely, not realizing how dry my mouth was until I tried to speak.

"Shut up," she moaned. "I need to think."

I had to believe that was going to be a new experience for her, one in which I would not fare well, but before I could open my mouth, screeching tires made her look out the back window.

"He's back," she announced, the gun now pointing at me. "Looks like we got new wheels."

I was suddenly overwhelmed with fear, but it didn't seem like it had to do with my current situation. Though my alter ego didn't seem to be as afraid as I was, it hardly mattered. I had enough problems of my own and was thankful that the feeling vanished an instant before Ronny pulled the door open, grabbed my feet, and dragged me out onto the concrete.

"Get up, Stupid," he growled as I slammed onto the concrete, biting down hard to keep from screaming, "or I'm gonna kick your ribs in."

"He can't, Ronny," Charisa protested. "His feet are tied."

I looked up to see the gun pointed at me, Charisa's index finger twitching dangerously as Ronny grunted angrily,

"No Problem!"

A moment later, I was being lifted up by my belt and shirt collar before being heaved onto the seat of an idling SUV.

"Get in the back with him and make sure he don't try to get anybody's attention."

After a slight pause, Charisa opened the other back door and pushed me into a sitting position. As she pulled the seatbelt around me, I was unhappy to see she no longer had the pistol, and even more disappointed when Ronny twisted around in the driver's seat and pointed the weapon at me.

"I so want an excuse to pop you," he growled. "Maybe somewhere where it won't kill ya, but will hurt like hell." He waved the gun dismissively. "Sit up nice and straight, and stay quiet or that's exactly what I'll do. Understood?"

We all three froze for a long moment until I jerked a nod. Seeming happy with my response, Charisa buckled herself in next to me, but Ronny continued his angry stare until I nodded again. Swearing under his breath, he turned around, slammed the car into gear and raced through the parking garage. As we squealed around corners, I was alternately thrown against the left door then Charisa, and the door again.

When we finally bounced out of the garage and onto the street, Ronny announced, "We'll be there in about an hour, less if the traffic ain't bad. You got that map we recovered from the hotel?"

Charisa pulled a bag off the floor, yanked a folded piece of paper from it and waved it over the seat back. "It's right here."

"Keep it close, Doll. We're on the right track now."

Chapter 32

Captain Yin Bohu swore as his horse stumbled on the rocky ground.

Something is not right here.

The small force ahead of him was not retreating even though his men were now close enough to wipe them out.

He watched as arrows from the second group of enemy soldiers hit the ground a dozen paces short of their mark.

Are these men so inexperienced they would not know the range of their weapons?

He lifted his red flag, and prepared to point it forward as a sign to charge, but another thought stopped him.

There are not enough of them.

He scanned the top of the hill again, seeing nothing.

Are the others hauling away something or someone more valuable?

The sound of an arrow shattering nearby made it clear that he had more immediate concerns. The approaching soldiers would soon be in range, shifting the odds in their favor. The closer group seemed to be out of arrows. Better to take them out quickly and then deal with those who remained.

He lifted the red flag again. "Company at the ready!" He waved it in a tight circle, pointed it at the closest enemy group, and screamed, "Charge!"

He quickly realized the command was not a wise one. The war horses, trained since birth to act aggressively on command, lunged forward, but their hooves slipped on the steep, rocky ground. Yin Bohu's charger stumbled again, and an instant later he heard the wild cry of another stallion as it fell. His mount swerved, caught himself and slowed along with the rest of his troop, but the action was uneven, with those behind bumping up into the leaders.

Horsemen tried to move away from those pushing into them, but the quick turns caused more horses to go down, crushing their rider's legs and arms. Looking down, he realized the ground was simply too rocky for their mounts to stay on their feet.

A trap!

When the riders tried to maintain their charge, things only got worse. Their formation was now badly deformed, diminishing its effectiveness. Warriors were being unnecessarily injured without a shot being fired by the enemy.

Swearing angrily, Yin Bohu started to reach for his red flag when his horse shrieked and pulled to his left. He looked back to see an arrow sticking from the horse's flank. The assault initially angered the captain until he realized the angle of the arrow meant it could not have come from either group of soldiers. A quick look behind made his heart stop.

"Enemy at our rear," he bellowed.

The outburst was a mistake, and the resulting confusion it caused sent more horses to the ground. Struggling to maintain his seat as his injured mount fought to stay upright, Yin Bohu looked around to see that the third group was made of at least two dozen archers standing in a row, their weapons held high. His men were in nearly total chaos now with more of them tumbling off their mounts, horses screaming, legs flying, men crying in pain.

A loud grunt drew Yin Bohu's attention to his left as one of his riders fell forward, an arrow in the back of his neck. He jerked around to see the second enemy group were now also within firing range, combining their firepower, and sandwiching his people in a deadly hail of arrows.

He started to lift his lance to signal a retreat, but an arrow sliced his forearm, sending the spear to the ground. His horse stumbled again, nearly ejecting him from the saddle as yet another arrow zipped past his head.

"To the right! Retreat!" he cried, his horse lunging to move clear of the rocks, and dangerously close to going down as they moved down the slope in search of better footing.

Looking back, Yin Bohu saw others breaking in the same direction, but did not bother to shout at them again.

You cannot help them now, screamed in his head as he fought to stay on his pitching mount.

When his horse finally reached better footing, he leaned forward and spurred him to a limping gallop. After a dozen or so hoof beats, he looked back to see less than ten riders following him. Twisting further around, he saw a few more fleeing in a different direction: half of his original force. He knew he should have rallied those remaining for another attempt at the enemy force, but most of those following were injured. Shaking his head, he hunkered down, and urged his mount on.

Chapter 33

"I'm sorry," Charisa whined for about the tenth time, "but I seriously gotta pee."

"Son of a bitch," Ronny protested angrily as we approached the Woodburn exit. "Just hike up yer skirt and pee on the seat. It's not like we have to worry about getting our cleaning deposit back."

Charisa gave me a shocked look before shaking her head. "Not in front of the kid."

"Kid," Ronny yelled as he glared at me via the rearview mirror. "Look out the window. Yer too young to see this."

"No!" Charisa protested. "Just find me a gas station. I'll only be a minute."

"A damned minute will be the difference between getting there and getting busted."

"Ronny!"

"Crap-a-hoola," he moaned. "I gotta get a whore with a tiny bladder."

"I'm not a whore."

"Ooooo," Ronny crooned sarcastically. "You're a *call girl* with a tiny bladder. Big fuckin' difference."

Her face flushed, Charisa glanced sheepishly at me before turning to look out the window. "Just pull over, and shut up, OK?"

Releasing an exaggerated sigh, Ronny jerked the car into the far right lane, raced up the exit, and drove into the first gas station he came to. Charisa was pushing open the door before the car was completely stopped, and I saw tears on her cheeks as she gave Ronny a glaring look on her way out.

The car was still jiggling from the slammed door when Ronny slumped in his seat and exclaimed, "Crap almighty!"

Looking out the window, I saw a State Police cruiser driving by. It took a second for my brain to jump back into gear and reach for the door release lever. Unfortunately, as my fingers slipped under the lever, I heard the electronic door locks slide into place with a heart-dropping thunk.

Before I could raise my hands to try to get the officer's attention, Ronny growled, "Don't even think about it, Mister Asshole. It'll be the last thing you do."

Wanting to scream, I watched the cruiser slowly roll past, turn at the next street, and vanish from sight. My heart racing, breath coming in short puffs, I pushed back into the seat and closed my eyes to be instantly transported into the soldier's body as a cloth was being pressed against his cheek. Though the pain was terrible, he barely reacted, but I could also feel a strong sense of attraction and revulsion that had something to do with the doctor working on his wound.

The doctor was speaking, but the soldier's mind was now filled with a confused mix of anger and joy, disgust and relief. Not wanting someone else dumping their messy emotions into my own boiling mental soup, I tried to return to the present, but could not seem to pull away.

What do you want from me? I asked, not really caring if I said it out loud in the present.

Chapter 34

Mei-Xiu dabbed a more powerful numbing agent onto An-Chi's swollen cheek. Though the pain was excruciating, he did his best not to flinch, thankful that the pain quickly decreased.

"I will use acupuncture once we get back to the surgery," she announced while standing back to look at his face. "Most of my equipment was lost in the attack before we arrived at the cave, so I cannot stitch up your wound, but I will wrap it up and..."

An-Chi stood abruptly. "I will not be trussed up like a prisoner. It will be fine."

"The wound is infected and it will only get worse. The pain must be terrible."

He shook his head. "Your poultice is working well enough. We will be in camp very soon. You can deal with it then."

When Mei-Xiu started to protest, he lifted a hand, palm out. "Thank you for the help, Doctor. We must gather our gear quickly and be gone before the next wave of General Lü Bu's soldiers arrive."

When the doctor bowed in acknowledgement, a small lock of black hair slipped out from under her cap. The movement drew his attention to her face, and he felt his breath catch when he saw the small T-shaped scar on her chin.

By the souls of my ancestors!

It shocked him that he had not noticed it before, but he simply assumed this doctor was a *he* not a *she*. The sudden realization of what was going on brought a flash of mixed emotions: anger, fear, concern, and even lust. The sudden tension made his face hurt and he quickly turned away.

The captain should know, he thought angrily before looking again at Mei-Xiu. *They will kill her.* The thought produced such feelings of anguish, he turned away and shook his head. *That will delay us,* he reasoned desperately, *and any delay favors the enemy.*

In an effort to regain his focus and self-control, he held his breath for a long moment before softly releasing it as he turned back to Mie-Xiu, thankful that she did not appear to be aware of his confusion. When she finished packing up what remained of her medical kit, he looked around to see if anyone was close enough to hear him.

"Your cap is askew, Doctor," he said. "You should tuck your hair back up before we continue."

He glimpsed Mei-Xiu's surprised expression as he turned to see that his men were gathering in preparation for their upcoming task. When he looked at her again, he felt a certain pleasure in seeing that though she had straightened her cap, she did not hesitate to meet his gaze.

"You know who I am?"

He waited a moment before responding, not to taunt her, but because he was caught between the need to do his duty and something else that would put him in extreme danger: kiss her. Despite the overpowering longing to do the latter, he kept his composure and gave a curt nod.

"What do you plan to do?"

He tried his best to give what looked like a casual shrug. "Gather my men and get this litter back to camp."

"And then?"

Though he did not want to, he could feel himself smiling. "Maybe then you will be kind enough to stitch up my face so I can heal properly."

He watched her shoulders sag with relief as she looked at the division commander lying again on the litter.

"I must check my patient," she said while stuffing her medical kit into a large pocket in her tunic. "He must not awaken before we arrive in camp."

"How is he doing?" An-Chi blurted almost desperately as she started to walk away.

The statement shocked and humiliated him. He had never acted this way toward a woman. How was she so different? He felt even more embarrassed when Mie-Xiu stopped and faced him, her expression quizzical, as though the question was absurd.

"We must get him to surgery as soon as is possible. It may already be too late."

He felt his face warm, and suddenly wanted more than anything to be somewhere else.

"Yes. Of course. I will get my men ready immediately."

Despite the humiliating moment, when she turned away, he was suddenly overcome with the unbearable urge to say something to bring her back. The resulting confusion made him angry with himself.

You are a warrior, not a love-sick bird.

The mental rebuke stopped him.

Enemy territory is no place to court a woman.

"Troop Leader," Chong Dai called as An-Chi approached him. "We near camp. Must flee."

Snapping out of his confused state, An-Chi turned to his subordinate, and asked, "What?"

The cowering man shook his head. "Much sorry to interrupt, Troop Leader, but I overhear soldiers. If division commander not survive, they kill us."

"But the commander is doing well."

Walking toward a nearby cluster of bushes, Chong Dai waved for him to follow. "Yes, but there is plot to kill him. Follow me. I show."

"Tell me now."

Turning back, his subordinate waved more urgently. "I must show. Come please. Hurry. Hurry!"

After taking a cautious look around, he followed Chong Dai behind the bushes, but when he arrived, the soldier was nowhere to be seen. The situation put him on alert, and movement on his right made him jump back, barely avoiding the tip of a sword passing only a hand's-width from his throat.

The attack put An-Chi on automatic pilot, his own sword instantly in his hand as he did a quick spin away from his attacker.

Bringing his weapon up as he rotated, he completed the turn in time to block Chong Dai's blade, but could not react fast enough to avoid the boot slamming his thigh.

He staggered back a step as Chong Dai lunged at him, hacking at An-Chi's neck and forcing the troop leader to jerk to one side as the tip of the blade sliced through his outer coat. Reacting instinctively, he brought his own sword around, slashing at Chong Dai's belly, knowing the move would be anticipated, and force his opponent back.

Holding his sword at the ready, Chong Dai snarled, "Degenerate son of a turtle. You were not supposed to survive this mission."

"What?"

"We know what your father is trying to do."

The statement startled An-Chi, both because he had no idea what Chong Dai was talking about, and he was no longer speaking like a simple peasant.

"You have it wrong," he protested. "I am not here because of my father."

"I would expect you to say that," Chong Dai growled. "Lies will not save you."

Yanking up his weapon, he lunged forward, his sword slashing down as he attacked, forcing An-Chi to react defensively to counter the attempt, and keep on reacting to rapid blows that came with such fury, it was all he could do to anticipate and block them.

He jerked back from a thrust at his neck, but not fast enough to stop the blade's tip from piercing his left shoulder. Unfortunately for Chong Dai, the attempt left him vulnerable, and An-Chi shoved his sword toward his attacker's side just below the rib cage. Crying out as he stumbled back, Chong Dai slashed down with his sword to knock the blade away. The impact was so forceful, An-Chi barely held onto his sword, and the power of it made him stagger.

Regaining the offensive, Chong Dai stabbed at An-Chi's belly, but his feet were not squarely planted, and his blade pierced only cloth. When An-Chi jumped sideways to avoid the thrust, he pulled the blade with him, making Chong Dai stumble forward, his belly exposed. Dropping to one knee, An-Chi thrust his weapon deep into his attacker's diaphragm.

His face awash in shock, air rushing from his lungs, Chong Dai still tried to free his weapon, but before he could manage it, An-Chi pushed his blade in to the hilt. Though the excruciating pain froze the dying man's body, he continued to glare defiantly at An-Chi, his lips stretched tightly over gritted teeth.

The two opponents remained in that pose for a long moment before An-Chi gave Chong Dai a push, and he slowly fell backwards.

Catching himself, so he would not fall with his opponent, An-Chi watched Chong Dai slip off his sword to fall onto his back, and release a loud groan that was nearly drowned out by a cry of alarm from beyond the bushes.

Barely aware of footsteps pounding the ground beyond the bushes, An-Chi dropped to a knee beside his gasping opponent.

"Who wants me dead?" he demanded, his hands grabbing the man's coat and shaking him. "Tell me!"

For his part, Chong Dai did nothing but glare at his killer until life slowly faded from his eyes and his head flopped backwards.

The sudden disconnect with his now-dead opponent sent An-Chi's mind into turmoil.

I am disgraced. My father has disowned me. How can my death possibly impact what he is doing?

Though Chong Dai could no longer provide answers, An-Chi was still gripping the corpse's jacket when other soldiers rounded the bushes, their weapons drawn, faces tense.

"What happened here?" the captain demanded as he pushed through the crowd to step up to the still-kneeling An-Chi.

Rising, An-Chi let his bloody sword hang by his side as he snapped to attention.

"He attacked me without explanation, My Captain."

"One of your own men?"

"He said he was sent to kill me."

"Kill you? Why?"

"He said only that my mission was supposed to fail."

Hesitating only a moment as he looked from An-Chi to the prostrate body and back, the captain sheathed his own sword with a snap.

"Then we must move quickly." He waved for An-Chi to follow as he walked away. "Get your men to the litter. We will run the rest of the way."

"At once, My Captain," An-Chi responded while squatting to wipe his blade in a clump of grass.

Slipping his sword into its scabbard, he hurried to follow his superior, but could not resist a last look at Chong Dai's body, his head back, mouth open, arms splayed out.

What is my father planning? he wondered before turning to gather his men for the arduous journey back to camp. *And why would it involve his disgraced son?*

Chapter 35

By the time we pulled back onto the freeway, my panic level was so high I was having trouble breathing.

"I feel really sick," I finally gasped.

"Puke all ya want, Kid," Ronny responded unsympathetically. "I ain't pullin' over fer nothin'."

"I have to pee."

"Puke, pee, it's all the same to me. This ain't my car."

"He can't pee here," Charisa protested. "The car will smell like a toilet."

"Don't care."

"There's a rest stop up the road. We can stop there."

"Are you serious? Ya think no one's going to notice me draggin' a kid around trussed up like a rodeo calf?" He huffed out a derisive laugh. "What *are* you smokin' woman?"

"So what we gonna do, Ronny? Let him pee his pants?"

"I'm good with that. Go ahead Kid."

"You've got a gun," Charisa argued. "He knows you'll shoot him if he causes trouble."

"I don't give a rat's ass what he knows, it's not gonna…shit!"

I looked up to see Ronny's eyes locked on the rearview mirror, but he wasn't looking at me.

"What's the matter," Charisa whined.

"This damned state is lousy with cops." Ronny's head dipped for a moment before he looked back again. "We're in the slow lane and I'm not going that fast."

"Maybe he knows this is a stolen car."

"They wouldn't have gotten word out this fast."

"What're you gonna do?"

"Take the next exit," I said, hoping that at the very least, it would get us off the freeway and maybe give me a chance to escape.

"Shut the fuck up!" Ronny shouted as we passed a sign announcing the Aurora exit.

"He's right, Ronny," Charisa argued. "It's the only way to know for sure whether he's after us."

Ronny slumped down in his seat, I heard the click-click-click of the turn signal, and felt the car slow.

"Shit," he moaned. "He's following."

"So don't turn off," Charisa argued.

"Na. That'll just make him suspicious."

We stopped at the end of the exit ramp, and to my dismay, I looked up to see Ronny smiling.

"He's turning left, so we're goin' right."

As we sat at the stop sign, the cruiser pulled in beside us. I looked over to see the officer watching cross traffic until he pulled out. Since he didn't look my way, there was little I could do to catch his attention.

Turning right, Ronny let out a heavy sigh. "Let's get our ass turned around and get back on the freeway."

He was pulling into a driveway that lead to a gas station when an alarm sounded.

"Oh, fer Christ's sake. This damned thing's out of gas."

"Good thing we pulled off then," Charisa sighed. "I think God's watching out for us."

I was stunned by the absurdity of her statement.

God protects kidnappers?

Ronny barked a derisive laugh. "I think it's more like the horny guy with the red suit and pointy tail. God pretty much don't give a shit about the likes of us."

"Can I pee now?"

"Sit still, and be quiet," Ronny shouted, his eyes glaring at me in the mirror. "Yer not leaving the car. Got that?" He looked back at the road, and added, "Charisa. Throw a coat or something over his hands, so the attendant can't see they're tied up."

Get your hands free.

The thought came from nowhere. I didn't get the sense that An-Chi was tied up, but the fear gripping my chest seemed to dissipate as the car rolled to a halt.

When he saw the attendant approaching, Ronny pushed his door open and stepped toward the back.

"It'll be cash," he announced before walking around the car to tap on Charisa's window.

When she rolled it down, he passed her a large knife.

"I'm goin' to the head. He tries to draw attention to himself, poke him somewhere vital with this a few times and then come get me."

"Take him with you."

Ronny gave his head a sharp shake. "Not gonna happen."

"Yes, but…"

She stopped when Ronny abruptly walked away.

"God! He can be such an ass," she cried, her face flushed, body shaking as she turned toward me.

I suddenly felt outside myself, as though someone else was in my head. A groan erupted from my mouth, my head thumped against the window, and I felt my hands straining against the nylon ties.

"What?" Charisa asked anxiously.

Pulling my hands out from under the jacket, I could see they were now red and swollen. I held them up, hoping the attendant might see, but he had already moved off to help another customer.

"This tie dig into wrists," the other self inside me moaned. "I almost pass out from pain."

Her expression turned puzzled. "Why are you talking like some kind of Chinese Cooley?"

I see where you're going with this, I thought. *Let me do the talking.*

"Sorry," I sighed. "It's the pain. I can hardly think."

"What are you playing at?"

I felt my mouth open, but held my tongue until I was sure it was me speaking.

"I'm losing circulation in my hands. If I don't get relief soon, the damage will be permanent."

Her eyes wide, Charisa looked toward the bathrooms for a moment before turning back to me.

"You're trying to trick me."

I shrugged. "You have the weapon. Just cut this loose and then put on another that's not so tight. I promise I won't try anything."

After glancing toward the bathrooms again, she stared cautiously at me for a moment more before saying, "Hold up your hands."

When I did as instructed, she sawed on the straps until I heard a snap and felt sudden relief. The rest was all An-Chi.

Charisa barked a startled scream as my right hand grabbed her wrist and twisted hard. Her fingers seemed to automatically open and my left hand stripped the knife from it before she could react.

Don't kill her, I was thinking as my right hand grabbed her behind the neck, yanked her head towards me. I dropped the knife and slammed the heel of my free hand into her forehead. When she collapsed back onto the front seat, I picked up the knife and cut my ankles free.

Feeling suddenly back in control of my body, I dropped the knife again, and jumped out to search for the attendant. Seeing him on the far side of the bay, I started to move in that direction, but the sight of the bathroom doors just beyond stopped me.

Afraid Ronny might come out before I could get to the attendant, I gave the area around the station a quick scan, only to find the nearby restaurant dark, and its parking lot empty. I was near panic when I spotted a chain-link fence, and beyond that a cluster of white camper trailers.

Glancing once more at the gas station's bathrooms, I gulped in a deep breath and ran like hell.

Chapter 36

They were passing through a patch of low brush when a soldier sprang up in front of An-Chi, his sword above his head. Reacting instinctively, An-Chi jumped to his right, did a quick somersault and came up with his own sword out. The attacker hesitated only briefly before changing direction to follow, but the move threw him off balance. Before he could recover, An-Chi leapt forward, shoving the tip of his blade between the attacker's ribs and straight into his heart. His eyes wide with terror, the assailant lost his grip on his sword, and it clattered to the hard ground an instant before its owner.

An-Chi turned to see his troopers stopped in their tracks, the litter still on their shoulders, their wide eyes on the fallen enemy soldier.

"What is happening?" the captain demanded as he rushed to An-Chi, his warriors instinctively spreading out to form a defensive perimeter.

Still breathing hard, An-Chi shook his head. "He was in the bushes, but I don't think it was an ambush. He seemed unprepared to fight."

Squatting next to the body, the captain pulled a leather pouch from inside the fallen soldier's jacket. "He was a messenger."

Opening the pouch, he pulled out a piece of paper and unfolded it. After a moment, his eyes narrowed.

"This is for the bandit leaders to the west of us," he said with disgust. "General Lü Bu is asking them to attack our rear." He shook his head slowly. "What kind of person does such a dishonorable thing?"

An-Chi also shook his head. "Since we are almost to camp, it will do him little good."

Jerking a nod, the captain turned to face his men. "To the camp, quickly."

Jogging alongside his captain, An-Chi looked at the camp's northern sentry post, little more than a *li* away. Further on, he also saw a cloud of dust stirred up by soldiers marching west toward enemy troops gathering just beyond the valley's small stream.

Though his cheek and hand still ached from his recent injuries, he longed to be in that conflict. Beyond keeping him from being demoted, this mission would do little to improve his status. He was but a troop leader. If the division commander survived, the higher-ranked officers would get the credit for saving him. To him it seemed salvation could only come on the battlefield.

There is no honor in surviving a battle you did not fight.

"Hurry! Hurry!" he shouted at his troopers. "We must get there before the battle is fully engaged."

You do not absolve disgrace by wishing it.

Chapter 37

My mind spinning, I sprinted out of the gas station, and through the deserted restaurant's parking lot.

Please have someone there to help me.

I crossed a narrow access road, and scrambled over the chain-link fence surrounding the RV park, all the while searching for a place to hide. Unfortunately, the park was just an expanse of concrete slabs, widely spaced trees, and a menagerie of variously sized RVs and pickups.

Is anybody home?

Ronny's angry bellowing reached my ears as I ran between two large RVs. A scream from Charisa made me put on a burst of speed that sent me into the middle of a small cluster of campers.

"Help," I cried. "I've been kidnapped."

Realizing that Ronny could also hear me made my chest tighten with panic. Not knowing what else to do, I ran to the next cluster of four trailers, beating on walls and doors as I went. Just before I reached the third RV, I heard a swearing Ronny scrambling over the fence.

"Please," I moaned, my fists banging the camper's door. "Help me."

I jumped back when a gray-haired, heavyset woman appeared in the doorway, still straightening her long flowery skirt.

"Why all the ruckus?"

"I've been kidnapped," I gasped, my head spinning, lungs aching. "Please call nine-one-one."

"What's going on, Marta?" a male voice asked.

The woman looked back into the RV. "There's a boy out here who says he's been kidnapped, Willie. He wants us to call the cops."

"Really?"

Feeling desperate, I pointed back in the direction I'd come. "Please hurry. He's got a gun."

"You're shitting me," Willie said skeptically as he leaned over his wife's shoulder.

"No. There really is someone after me. "

Willie shook his head slowly, but Marta nudged him with her elbow. "Go get the pistol," she said. "Just in case."

I was still trying to catch my breath when Ronny's voice completely froze my lungs.

"I know yer in here, Kid. If ya come out now, no one'll get hurt."

"That's him," I gasped while looking around for a place to hide.

Marta turned back into the RV. "Hurry it up, Willie. There really is someone out here."

"Call the police, Ma'am. This guy is really dangerous."

"Oh right," she said, her hand already probing the large pocket of her skirt.

Feeling blind panic at the sound of approaching footsteps, I ran in the opposite direction, cut left in front of Willie and Marta's trailer, and ran as fast as my legs would carry me. I had no clue where this led, but I only wanted to keep my distance from that maniac until for the cops to arrived.

Above my own desperate breathing, I could hear Marta saying, "Don't shoot, you dummy. You might hit somebody."

"I thought that was why I got the gun," Willie countered.

"Are you totally wacked out? I was talking to..."

My heavy breathing blotted out the rest, but when I heard Ronny shouting again, I put all my energy into running.

I was passing a cluster of port-a-potties when the roar of an engine made me look back to see the Caddy leaning heavily as it rounded a corner.

"Crap!"

The RV park was a twisting maze of blacktop and staggered parking slots, many shaded by trees. I could run a fairly straight line, but the Caddy had to weave around the spaces, giving me a small advantage. My disadvantage was that I didn't know where I was going, and was already gasping for air.

Cutting down a path between two RVs, I made a sharp left, but two strides later my foot snagged a garden hose and I went down hard, slamming my head on the pavement. The impact added a new pain and my already battered balance was knocked completely off kilter. Though I managed to reach my feet, my clumsy legs would not cooperate, and after only a few steps, they tangled with a lawn chair and I went down hard.

A blur of white, green, brown, and black filled my vision as I struggled to get up, but though I could hear tires squealing, my efforts to rise were wasted.

I was rolling over for the umpteenth time when a figure blocked the sun.

"Don't move," Charisa commanded.

My vision cleared enough to see a small silver revolver pointed at my face.

"Where did you get that?" I asked stupidly as I visualized Ronny's big black automatic.

"Get up," she demanded, the fear in her voice obvious and confusing. When I didn't respond, she reached down and grabbed my arm. "Hurry! He's coming."

"But I thought…"

She yanked on my arm, helpless to lift my dead weight, but apparently desperate to try.

"Ronny's insane," she moaned while continuing in her futile effort to pull me up. "He's gonna kill both of us before this is done. We go now or we're dead."

Suddenly realizing what she was saying, I rose to my feet, but a sharp pain in the knee almost sent me back to the ground. Grunting, Charisa kept me upright, and the two of us hobbled to the car, where I literally fell onto the passenger seat. Still loopy from the impact to my head, I was struggling to sit up when she slipped behind the wheel, dropped her pistol on the seat, and slammed the door.

"Keep your head down," she ordered as she gave the steering wheel a quick spin.

She stomped on the gas, and the sudden acceleration slammed me against the door, but I still had the presence of mind to ask, "Where's your cell?"

Her eyes wide with panic, she cried, "Who the hell cares?"

"I'll call the cops, and let them know…"

The front windshield cracked, forcing a terrified squeal from Charisa as I twisted around to see a similar hole in the back window.

"Shit!"

Two more holes in the glass sent stinging shards into my skin, and forced me to slump down, knees pressing the console, back still against the door. I looked up to see Charisa holding her head down and blood oozing from her right ear. An instant later the Caddy slammed into something solid, throwing us both into the dash. Charisa bounced off the steering wheel but the impact smashed me into the foot well.

I was wedged in tight, butt down, feet under me, knees pointing at the ceiling, shoulders wedged between the seat and the dash. I looked up to see a hysterically angry Ronny at the driver-side window, his gun pointing at Charisa, his screaming incoherent. Charisa's face was toward me, and in addition to the chunk missing from her ear, I could see blood oozing from her nose and a cut on her forehead. Her mouth was open, eyes partially rolled up into her head.

Ronny was screaming and pounding the butt of his gun against the driver-side window, creating spider-like cracks in the glass with each impact. I tried to get up, but was hopelessly wedged in with one shoulder under the dash and the other pressed into the front of the seat.

An enraged Ronny yanked open the door and grabbed Charisa's arm. When he pulled, the unconscious woman tumbled out to sprawl on the ground. Figuring he was going to shoot me then and there, I fought to get my body un-wedged, working my left shoulder out from under the seat, and grasping desperately for a handhold until my fingers wrapped around something cold and heavy.

"You're dead, Bitch," Ronny bellowed as he gave the prostrate Charisa a savage kick then took a step back to point his weapon at her.

When his gun popped, I lifted the silver pistol, pointed in his general direction, and squeezed the trigger again, and again, and again, and again, and again. I was so terrified, my finger continued to jerk, even when all I could hear was the hammer snapping against empty shell casings. I didn't stop until a surprised Ronny toppled like a felled tree and vanished from sight.

Chapter 38

Long Gang adjusted the silk jacket covering his broad flabby chest, shifted his wide butt in his comfortably padded chair, and looked up from a steaming cup of aromatic tea to watch his servant, Toilet Face approaching. He didn't know the man's real name, but as far as he was concerned, the one he had given him was well deserved. The creature dressed shabbily (peasants always did), had terrible personal hygiene (smelled like a toilet), and ate -- well, by any cultured-person's taste -- shit. Despite these revolting habits, Long Gang employed Toilet Face because he was infinitely submissive, had no qualms about doing dirty work, and was very easy to read.

Unfortunately, at this moment the quickness of the scrawny wretch's pace, and his pained expression broadcasted news of failure, and that made Long Gang scowl, his dangling earrings tinkling as he angrily tapped long fingernails on the table top.

"Master," Toilet Face announced, though he could easily see Long Gang was staring directly at him. He stopped the required distance necessary to protect his master's delicate senses from his disgusting body odors. "I bring news of rescue."

"Not the news I wish to hear, I would guess," Long Gang snarled.

"Good news, Master. Yes. Emperor's cousin back in camp. Everybody happy!"

"I care more about the flies on a donkey's ass than I do for news about the division commander, you fool. What of Chong Dai's mission?"

"Ah," Toilet Face sighed sadly. "Your friend very dead."

"And?"

Long Gang did not think his servant's shoulders could droop more than they always did. Toilet Face surprised him.

"He not dead, Master," he sighed again. "An-Chi…"

"Stop!" Long Gang barked angrily while jerking up a pudgy, bejeweled hand, palm out. "Do not mention that name to me again."

"But Master, how I…"

"He is scum, and scum is what we will call him."

"Scum, Master?"

"Yes. From this moment forward, his name is Scum. Is that clear?"

The wretched man jerked a bow. "Yes, Master."

"And the other person?"

"She not dead either, Master."

Long Gang let out a sigh of relief. "I don't want *her* dead, you fool." Half-a-dozen rings clacked against the side of his porcelain tea cup, as he snatched it up, but stopped halfway when liquid slopped over the side. Remaining still until sloshing tea no longer threatened his silk jacket, he carefully wiped the wet cup with an embroidered napkin before setting it back down, and waving the servant away. "Go watch Scum and report back when he has settled in."

"Yes, Master," Toilet Face responded before quickly bowing and scurrying away.

Yes, Long Gang thought, his grimace mounding the fat on his cheeks as he watched his servant leave. *He actually does scurry.*

When Toilet Face was out of earshot, he took a sip from his cup, carefully lowered it to the table, and leaned back.

"Did you hear that? Our nemesis lives."

Getting no reply, but also unwilling to lift his overweight body from its comfortable perch, he turned his head to peer into the tent opening behind him.

He had never actually seen the face of his benefactor, because the man kept in the shadows, and always masked his face. The prospect of wealth and power beyond imagining excited Long Gang, but he was still nervous about how mysterious he was: the fact that he could almost instantly appear and disappear without a trace, that he seemed to know more about the future than was reasonable, and the incomprehensible idea that he would simply give Long Gang such power without asking for anything in return had him thoroughly perplexed.

"Hello? Are you still there?"

When no response came, he released a disappointed sigh. "Some people are too impatient."

"I do not lack patience," a deep gravelly voice countered. "But your incompetence would try that of the emperor himself."

Barking a yip of alarm, Long Gang protested, "My incompetence? I hire perfectly good assassins and they fail me. What more can I do?"

"They were obviously not *perfect*. You need better ones."

"That is not as easy as it sounds. The general is much loved by his soldiers. It is not easy to find one who will kill his son. Even so, I do have one more still trying to make it happen."

"Find more, Fool," the deep gravelly voice demanded. "Very few here know that An-Chi is his son. Tell them he is an enemy spy and they will gladly slit his throat."

"And when word gets back to the general that his son has been murdered, he will find and interrogate his killer to learn that I ordered the attack." He shook his head. "No. For your sake as well as mine, it must be someone who has no loyalty to the general, and an overwhelming love of money."

"Then offer more!"

"Are you sure?"

An angry sigh drifted to Long Gang's ears before the other growled, "You have the crystal. Why worry about petty things like money?"

Long Gang's shaking head made his whole body quiver. "But it is broken."

"Even so, according to the hag you foolishly killed, the two pieces will permit you and that worthless servant of yours to travel through time."

"Yes, yes, I know, but how am I to find An-Chi's spiritual counterpart in the future? Surely he isn't going to just announce himself so I can…"

"You idiot!" the other shouted so loudly Long Gang knocked his tea cup over. "The stones will find him for you."

While wiping up the spilled tea, the merchant whined, "But I am not clear on how that will happen exactly."

"Did you not listen to anything that old woman told you?"

Letting out a terrified whimper, Long Gang protested, "She was so *boring*, prattling on endlessly about how I had to do this, and then that, and then this. I just want to be emperor of the world. Can't we do it without all that useless ritual?"

"You are even more of an idiot than I thought, Long Gang," the other growled. "The stones offer power beyond imagining, and yet you prattle on about how difficult they are to use?"

"Well," the merchant pouted. "They are."

"Then let me make it simple. You only need one half of the crystal to travel through time where you will find the future manifestation of this miserable soldier. Once you have him, you cut open both An-Chi and his future self at the same time and smear blood from their livers onto the broken ends of each crystal. When you press them together, the two parts will bind into one again, and you will have all that you desire."

"That is all?"

"Yes, you simple idiot, but we must have this business concluded soon. An-Chi must be dead before you kill his father."

"But why is the father of this disgraced son of any interest to you?"

There was a long pause before a deep-throated chuckle made Long Gang cringe.

"You ask too many questions, Merchant, but rest assured, if you fail, the general will become emperor, and he will learn of your scheming to destroy his son. Instead of being emperor for all time, you will die a very slow and agonizing death."

"Ew!" Long Gang cried, his face scrunched up in disgust. "Surely it will not come to that, will it?"

Hearing no response, he turned, and flinched noticeably when he realized the tent was empty.

He had his answer.

Chapter 39

Coughing from the overpowering smell of burnt gun powder, I dropped Charisa's gun onto the seat and was suddenly overcome with the intense need to get out of that car, which still took some doing, since my feet were behind my butt, shins pressing painfully into the console, and my only free hand could barely reach the steering wheel.

By the time I worked myself free, clusters of people were cautiously approaching the car, their cries of alarm echoing wordlessly in my ears. Ignoring them, I crawled to the open driver-side door to see blood coming from both Charisa's mouth and a neat hole in her left breast. I tried to exit the car gracefully, but since I was on hands and knees, and she was lying directly below the door, it took some effort to get out without stepping on her.

"What happened?"

The familiar voice made me look up to see Marta and Willie running toward me. When they were only a few feet away, Marta slapped both hands over her mouth, and stared down at the bodies while her husband towered over her and watched from behind.

Turning my attention back to Charisa, I dropped to one knee next to her and reached a hand out, but stopped just before I touched her.

"They tried to kidnap me," I muttered, my eyes locked on the gasping woman and somehow knowing she didn't have long to live. "Actually, they did kidnap me, but…"

I froze when Charisa started coughing, and then her body convulsed several times. Helpless to do anything, I continued to gawk until she released a long, raspy breath and went limp.

Tears warped my vision, making it appear as though she were still moving. I felt myself gasp in the hope that…

"Someone call 911!"

The shout pulled my attention to the inert Ronny, spread-eagle on his back, blood and urine spreading in a pool under him.

There's no need to rush, I thought, but couldn't vocalize it because of an unmovable frog in my throat. *Why does the death of these two bother me? They kidnapped, abused, and threatened to kill me. I should cheer their passing, not cry.*

"Come on, Sweetie," Marta cooed as she patted my shoulder. "Why don't you come back to our place until the police get here?"

I tried to resist, but Willie took my arm and the two of them pulled me to my feet. Scenes from my ordeal flashed in my head, and before I knew it I was climbing into their trailer.

"This should do it," Marta cooed as she guided me to a table. "Sit yourself down and I'll get you something to drink."

Numb beyond belief, I did as told, leaning heavily against the table as I slipped into the tight space behind it. When Marta opened her refrigerator, I felt the table shift, and the other side of my brain, the side that really wasn't me at all, became agitated and made me ask,

"What was that?"

"Oh, don't you worry none about that," Marta answered soothingly. "We was preparin' to leave when you banged on our door. Willie'll finish up the packing so we can be on our way once the cops are through with us."

"Someone called them?"

Pulling a container out of the fridge, Marta laughed. "We took care of that before we ran after you."

An engine started outside, and I looked out to see a large pickup slowly backing towards us until I felt a slight bump.

"He's real good with that truck," Marta said as she handed me a glass of orange juice. "You should drink this all up, and I'll get you another. Orange juice is good for just about anything that ails you."

An agitated bee buzzed in the back of my head as I took the glass but I was so confused I didn't know what to make of it.

"Mmmm," I responded when the tangy liquid tingled on my tongue. "Yeah."

Marta snatched up the glass after I put it down, but made no move to refill it. When I looked up, her eyes were on me, her face expectant, mouth tight.

"What?" I asked, but when I heard Willie connecting the trailer to the pickup truck, I knew what the buzzing was about.

Starting to feel dizzy, I tried to rise, but Marta rushed in to stop me. My arms felt heavy, and my attempt at knocking her hands away threw me off balance.

"What did you give me?" I demanded as I crashed back onto the seat.

"Don't you worry about that none, *Dear*. You and us are goin' on a little trip."

"Who *are* you?" I moaned as her face blurred.

Marta's laugh gave me the chills. "You might say we're the luckiest people in the whole wide world."

My head involuntarily slumped forward, but I could hear her slam the refrigerator door.

"Haven't you figured it out yet?" she snarled. "We're Ronny's backup."

Chapter 40

While jogging along with the others, An-Chi felt a powerful sense of anxiety as his left index finger twitched repeatedly. He shook off the strange sensation, but still kept alert for signs of another attack, even though they were almost to the guard post.

Beyond the sentries he could see the large cloud of dust raised by the fighting armies, and felt an aching disappointment that he was not among them.

"We rest now?" one of his men gasped as they entered the perimeter of the camp.

"We must get the division commander to surgery," An-Chi responded. "Hurry! Hurry!"

He wanted to jump in and help, but strict protocols forbid a troop leader from doing his subordinate's work. Just the same, he also realized his men were close to collapsing.

"Captain," he called. When his superior turned toward him, he waved at the surgery, still nearly a *li* distant. "Would your men like the honor of carrying the division commander the rest of the way in?"

Though he initially scowled, the captain's expression softened when one of the sweating litter bearers stumbled. Without a word, he waved his men over, and one-by-one they replaced An-Chi's.

As his staggering troopers slowed and appeared ready to fall to the ground, An-Chi hurried to them.

"Do not stop," he demanded. "Fall in behind the litter and keep up with it."

One of his men started to protest, but An-Chi's angry glare kept him quiet.

"Hurry! Hurry!"

Marching along with his men, he was surprised to realize the doctor had moved up beside him.

"How is our patient, Doctor?"

Mei-Xiu shook her head. "I pray to the Three Sovereigns to give him the strength to make it."

They marched in silence for a moment before An-Chi asked, "What is your real name?"

When she did not respond, he looked at her, and was surprised to see her smiling knowingly.

"I might ask the same of you, Troop Leader. You are far too self-assured to be a simple foot soldier."

"And you are far too confident for a mere woman," he fired back, almost immediately regretting the observation.

"Then maybe it is best we remain ignorant," she answered stiffly.

Unable, and unwilling to beg her forgiveness, An-Chi looked ahead as the litter stopped in front of the surgery tent and Doctor Chu Gao pushed through the opening.

"Doctor," the captain announced as he approached Chu Gao. "Our commander is gravely injured."

An-Chi noticed Chu Gao's eyes quickly search the crowd, and realized from his expression when his gaze locked on Mei-Xiu that she was his daughter.

Without comment, Chu Gao waved the litter bearers into the tent, leading them inside and through the maze of cots of those recovering from the previous engagement.

"We are preparing to clear these people out," he explained needlessly as he went. "We will soon be overwhelmed with a new group of wounded."

Reaching his destination, he moved behind a table and indicated that the commander be put on it. As carefully as they could, the warriors lowered the stretcher and did as instructed.

"Now, leave," he said offhandedly before leaning over the commander and preparing to remove his bandages. Realizing the soldiers had not moved, he looked up and shook his head. "You can only get in my way. Time is of the upmost importance in these cases. Go and rest yourselves. I will send word when I know more."

After a moment of hesitation, the captain nodded and motioned his men out. When An-Chi turned to follow them, Mei-Xiu grabbed his sleeve and pulled him aside.

"Your cheek needs tending," she said matter-of-factly, though her eyes did not reflect her disinterested tone.

Though it hurt to do so, he shook his head and waved a hand at Chu Gao. "There will be no point in fixing me up, if the commander dies."

Her look of surprise made him pause, and though he should have left it at that, something deep inside reasoned otherwise.

Nodding at the division commander, he smiled at her. "Help your father save his life and I will tell you my story."

He was pleased to see her eyes widen with surprise, but bBefore she could react further, he marched to his men still clustering just out of earshot.

"We have a war to fight, gentlemen," he announced while waving a hand toward the exit. "We must eat now and recover our strength so we can make the Son of Heaven proud."

As he followed his soldiers out, An-Chi could not resist turning back to see Mei-Xiu speaking with her father. His mental image of long black hair caressing her shoulders, her narrow waist, and light skin aroused something in him he had thought lost to his dishonor.

Honor lost is the path to ruin.

Yes, he thought as he turned to follow his men out of the tent. *But with the right incentive, one can find salvation.*

Chapter 41

Muffled voices weaved in and out of my consciousness and it felt totally weird. I couldn't open my eyes, my arms and legs would not move, and my brain was so muddled, I couldn't remember what put me in this sorry state.

What happened? I wondered until an attempt at moving brought everything back big time. My head ached, cheek throbbed, and the cut on my hand stung when I made a fist. It was all I could do to keep from crying out, but knew that was something I didn't want to do.

The pain cleared out the cobwebs, and I finally managed a semi-coherent thought.

Why am I...An-Chi!

I now remembered being kidnapped, but also knew I was connected to a soldier whose violent life required him to be totally aware of his environment. Apparently, his way of thinking was seeping into my consciousness because I kept my eyes closed, took a deep breath and listened for a reaction to my stirring.

Hearing nothing but the hiss of air-conditioning, I slowly opened my left eye and looked around. Seeing no one, I opened the right to confirm that the room was unoccupied. Turning my aching head, I took in the sparsely furnished space that reminded me of a doctor's exam room, and the sight made my chest tighten.

Revenge is most satisfying when it is slow and painful, flashed in my head.

"Oh boy," I tried to mutter, but tape over my mouth turned it into a muffled grunt.

The drugs Marta had given me still dulled my senses, but the pain made me clear-headed enough to realize I was on a cold, hard table. When I tried to sit up, a strap across my chest set off panic-driven struggle that accomplished little more than confirming that my wrists and ankles were also bound to the table.

A faint alarm beeped outside the room's only door and seconds later, it swung open.

The man who entered was tall and slender with oriental features and black hair. For reasons I could not explain, I instinctively knew was Chinese, and the sight of him sent my heart racing. He stopped in the doorway, his thin, angular face looking smug, his dark eyes focused on me, but the action seemed mechanical: his eyes jerking from one part of my body to another while his face remained frozen. It couldn't even tell if he was breathing.

"Good afternoon, Mister Patterson," he said with accented English. "I trust you slept well."

Marta's head appeared next to his left shoulder, her tightly curled gray hair hugging her head like an oversized Brillo pad.

"See," she exclaimed, her wrinkled face the picture of excited glee. "I told ya, Doc. I told ya I didn't give him too much."

"Can we get our money now?" Willie asked from somewhere behind them.

The doctor briefly closed his eyes and frowned, though from her position behind him, Marta would not have seen his reaction. He hesitated only long enough to mask his disgust with a pleasant smile before facing her.

"My assistant will be happy to help you," he said as he ushered Marta out of the room. "Just go with him to the next room and he will provide your payment."

"The full amount?" Marta asked cautiously. "Ronny and the girl are dead, so the full amount should come to us. Right?"

The doctor's head bobbed. "The full measure of your worth will be paid."

I was puzzled by his response until he spoke in Cantonese. I'm sure Marta and Willie didn't know I had a built-in translator, and his words made my heart stop.

"Kill them, Toilet Face."

Desperately yanking on my restraints, I fought to free myself while Marta barked a laugh and said something I didn't catch. Her tone was gleeful, as though she had won the lottery. Knowing the doctor's intentions, I tried to call out, but could manage little more than muffled M's and Ah's.

I stopped struggling when the doctor reentered the room and the door closed behind him with a nerve-rattling snap.

"Ah," he said, his smile malevolent. "You understood me. Excellent! That means you are fully connected to the one who calls himself An-Chi." He moved to the side of the table and leaned close, his eyes squinting, lips pulled back to reveal two perfect rows of pearl-white teeth. "It is most auspicious that we meet at this exact moment, Mister Patterson. Most auspicious indeed."

I heard a loud thump, as though someone were being slammed against a wall. I glanced in the direction of the sound, but he didn't flinch.

"My name is Doctor Long Gang, from Anhui Medical University, in Shanghai." He took two precise steps back from the table, straightening as he went, but kept his hands behind his back. "I have been many years waiting for this moment, Mister Patterson." His malevolent chuckle made my scalp tingle. "Actually, as you must now know, it has been many, many lifetimes."

I tried to say, "I don't know," but it came out, "I ohn no."

Smiling, he jerked a nod. "Ah yes, I know this will be a one sided conversation, but your input is not necessary for what I am about to do."

Another muffled thump drew my attention to the door, but Doctor Long kept his attention on me.

"Why?" I cried, trying my best to enunciate without the use of lips.

He started to say something, but hesitated, his eyes on me, expression uncertain.

"Yes," he finally sighed. "After all this time, I guess talking would be good." When he lifted an arm to look at his watch, I could see long, perfectly manicured fingernails, their length unusual for a man of our century. "And we have some time before I begin."

"Huh?"

His eyes softened as he looked at me. "Do not be alarmed. The procedure is very much painful, but will not last long."

If he thought that declaration brought me comfort, he was sadly mistaken. However, as I struggled madly against my bonds, he moved back to lean on the wall-mounted counter, speaking softly as though I were an apt listener.

"As you may not know, during Han dynasty, merchants like me not viewed in very good...light. Unjust, surely, but it was family occupation. What was I to do?"

Exhausted by my useless struggles, I slumped back onto the table, trickling tears cooling my face as they slithered down to pool in my ears. He went on as though he didn't notice.

"It was, most certainly, a minimalist existence, but I struggle on until pitiful servant, Toilet Face, bring me even more wretched creature: an old hag covered with dirt and dung, smelling like maybe she live in sewer, her teeth rotted away, eyes milky, clothes in tatters. By the Souls of my Ancestors, she such disgusting sight, my first impulse is to strike her dead right then and there."

Hardly listening to him, I strained to hear what was going on in the other room. Had Marta and Willie escaped? Would they call the police? My heart sank when it occurred to me that they weren't likely to turn themselves in just to get revenge.

"Do you know, it was good thing I spare her, because she had deep, dark secret. One which give her great power and long life." He grinned wickedly. "You can imagine my surprise when she claim to personally know Yellow Emperor. That make her over twenty-five centuries old when I meet her."

His statement sounded ridiculous, but upon reflection, he knew of An-Chi, something even I hadn't known of until recently.

"At first, as you can understand, I not believe her, but she quickly provide proof. I not bore you with details, because you already know I speak truth." He barked a laugh. "Stranger than her having magical powers is that she not want to give secret to her descendants. She say it is more curse than blessing, but I do not find it so."

I tried to say, "What's this gotta do with me?", but it came out a's and o's. Oddly enough, he nodded as though he understood.

"I did not understand at time, but I not only live forever, it is possible for me to go forward and backward in time. You see, not only will I be able to settle old scores, but my revenge will change Chinese history...*world* history."

I shook my head, trying to grasp the magnitude of what he was saying, but he continued on as though it didn't matter.

"If I go back in time and kill certain people, I make sure the father of soldier you know as An-Chi will not become Emperor of all China. Instead, it will be I who become Sun of Heaven. Imagine possibilities. With old hag's secret, I become emperor that live forever. Not just of China, but entire world. My ancestors will be very proud."

Stepping away from the counter, he held up a finger. "But there is one problem." Lifting a pouch from his pocket, he slid a green crystal out and held it up. The thing seemed to have a light of its own, but more so at one ragged end. "You can see it is broken, which dramatically reduces its power. I cannot make my changes permanent until I make crystal whole again."

When I shrugged, he smiled and started to return the crystal to its pouch. "That where you come in."

He was so preoccupied with shoving the pouch back into his pocket, he didn't see Willie until he slammed through the door, bounced off the doctor, and both men crashed to the floor. The more agile doctor was up in a flash, but before he could do more, Marta appeared, her gun pointed at him.

"I'm guessin' this won't kill you either, Doc, but all the same, it'll sure hurt like hell."

"What you do with Toilet Face?" Long Gang cried.

Rising clumsily to his feet, Willie spat on the floor. "I stabbed that bastard chink a dozen times and he kept coming at me. If Marta hadn't whacked him on the noggin' with one of those microscopes, he'd a like ta have killed me."

"Even that didn't do him in," Marta snarled angrily. "What's with you crazy Chinamen, anyway. Don't you know how to die?"

I can't describe the relief I felt at seeing Willie and Marta, though it was short lived. After all, they had kidnapped me and brought me here. I had no clue as to how this was going to play out.

"What you want?" Long Gang asked angrily. "I give twice what I promise."

"Don't trust him, Marta," Willie cautioned.

Shaking her head, Marta huffed a derisive laugh. "I ain't stupid. I just haven't figured out what to do yet."

"How about eternal life?" Long Gang asked expectantly. "I make it so you live forever."

"That's pure bullshit," Marta shouted. "No one can live forever."

Nodding slowly, Long Gang smiled. "I am eighteen-hundred year old." He nodded toward me. "Ask him."

After glancing at me, Marta gripped the gun tighter and focused on the doctor.

"He's just a stupid kid. He don't have a stinkin' clue about anything."

Shrugging, Long Gang said, "Come to my house. It not far. I have safe. Give you twenty-five-million in gold."

When Marta hesitated, Willie cried, "We want fifty million, and not a penny less."

Scowling, Long Gang shook his head. "I have twenty-five only. You take or leave."

Willie opened his mouth to respond, but Marta beat him to it. "We'll take it, but I ain't goin' to your place. It's probably full of all kinds of traps." She motioned to Willie. "Cut the kid loose, and let's take him back to the RV." She looked at Long Gang. "Give me your cell number. I'll tell you where to bring it."

"That a lot of weight to carry."

"Don't give a rat's ass, shit face. You work it out."

I could see Long Gang glaring at me as Willie cut away my restraints. He kept that pose for a moment before reciting a phone number.

"Got it," she snapped as Willie helped me off the exam table. "And don't think about followin' us. If I see anyone on our tail, I shoot this kid and you can do whatever you want with his corpse."

"I wait for call," Long Gang said between gritted teeth.

"You got half-an-hour to get the gold together. I'll call then and arrange the meet."

The doctor nodded. "One half hour. I be ready."

Keeping her gun on the doctor, Marta motioned for her husband to escort me out of the room. With me stumbling along beside him, Willie hurried to a door at the end of a short hallway. I looked back to see Marta running toward us as Willie cracked the door slightly to peek out.

"Clear," he whispered while yanking the door open and pushing me through.

"Try to run away and I'll shoot you in the balls," Marta gasped before running ahead to open an outside door.

"Trust me, Son," Willie said solemnly as we left the building. "She's just mean enough to do it."

Chapter 42

Long Gang pretended to ignore the passing cluster of soldiers, but could not help hearing their insults: slimy dog, worthless slag, donkey urine, gutter life.

As a member of the merchant class, he was used to derogatory comments, disgusted looks, and occasional assaults, but he still wanted to thrash the lot of them until they pleaded for his forgiveness. Just the same, there were five of them, and one of him, not to mention that he was decadently fat, and disinclined to take on even one dog-breathed soldier, let alone a whole pack. He knew they would have no qualms about gutting him and leaving him to bleed out in the street. No one but another merchant would come to his aid. In fact, it was more likely that anyone passing would give him a swift kick in the ribs, and spit on him, if they paid any heed to him at all. He made a mental note to hire a burly eunuch the next chance he got. He shook his head because he knew that would not be easy. Even lowly eunuchs looked down on merchants, and few would consider working for one.

He heard Toilet Face call, "Master," and turned toward the scurrying peasant, thankful that he had at least one person, no matter how pathetic, he could count on.

"What have you learned?" he asked sullenly.

Gasping as though he ran all the way from the soldier's compound, Toilet Face stopped the prescribed distance from his employer and jerked several quick bows.

"An-Ch..." he started, but bit off the name with a regretful whine. "Sorry, Master. I follow Scum to soldier barracks. Great surgeon Chu Gao work on division commander. Everybody think maybe he survive. Emperor be very happy. Soldiers be very happy. Ohhh," the pitiful creature moaned as Long Gang scowled at him. "You not be very happy."

"How insightful of you," Long Gang growled. "I do not care one bit about the division commander. It is Scum, that offspring of slime, who is supposed to die disgracefully, but he didn't, did he? From what I hear, he heroically masterminded a defense that saved the entire mission. HOW is that disgraceful?"

"Not disgraceful, Master," Toilet Face whined. "Soldier Scum very bad person. Very bad!"

"What more do you know?"

"Good news, maybe," the servant said uncertainly. "Soldier Scum go into battle soon. Maybe he die and make Master happy?"

Long Gang took a deep breath and let it out slowly. "I'm not sure you will ever understand, my cretin of a servant," he said sadly. "I don't want this particular soldier to die in battle. For my plan to work, he must be disgraced."

"Maybe he run away. Lose face."

"Did he shy away when offered a suicide mission? Did he run when confronted with overwhelming enemy cavalry? This soldier will never disgrace himself, at least not without our help."

"What we do, Master?"

"It would be best if he were a deserter."

Long Gang noticed his servant had bowed his head, hunched his shoulders, and squatted slightly, as though he were trying to hide in plain sight. What if he could do that with...

"Yes!" he exclaimed while shaking a fist next to his head.

"Master?"

Long Gang scowled. "When does his troop deploy?"

Still bowing repeatedly, Toilet Face whimpered, "They be in lead squadron in morning."

Rising slowly from his comfortable chair, Long Gang stepped to the middle of the dirt walkway and turned one way and then the other before facing his servant.

"Find me a witch," he declared.

"A witch, Master?"

Moving to his tent, he stopped at the entrance, and turned slightly. "I need a potion that will paralyze but not kill its victim."

Chapter 43

My feet and hands once again bound, I sat in Willie and Marta's camper-trailer, my chest cramping with fear as I watched this pissed-off woman muttering angrily and fiddling with her pistol.

"What're we gonna do now?" Willie asked, as his head poked through the trailer's door.

Marta's whole body shook as she turned toward him. "Well, we can't just sit here and wait for him to find us. Get this rig movin'. We'll drive around until it's time to get the gold."

"You really think he will?"

She shrugged. "He seems desperate enough, but if he tries to play us, we can just pop this kid and keep on driving."

"What about the gold?"

"Either he brings it or he don't. Either way, we can't wait forever."

Nodding anxiously, her husband pulled his head back and closed the door. From where I was sitting, I could see his shadow on the curtains as he moved toward the truck. However, my heart rate jumped when I looked to see Marta pointing her gun at me.

"I sure hope I don't have to pop you, kid," she said calmly. "There's nothing I'd like more than being a rich woman."

Feeling totally dumbstruck, I stared at her, my mind blank, gut aching, and heart heavy with the hopelessness of my situation. I was so desperate, only one thought came into my head.

Please help me, An-Chi.

I felt stupid for the thought, so you can imagine my surprise when he pushed a question into my mind.

"What will you do with all that money?" I blurted.

The truck's engine strained as the trailer jerked and we started moving. Since Marta had closed all the curtains, I could see nothing of the world outside that might give me a clue as to where we were headed.

Giving me a cautious look, Marta shook her head. "I'd tell ya, but that might give you some clue as to where we'll be, and I don't want that perverted Chinaman trackin' us down."

I shrugged. "I don't think he'll care one bit about you or the money once he has me."

She shrugged back. "Just the same. He seems like the vengeful type, and I ain't takin' no chances."

"But you're taking an even bigger chance giving me to him."

She shook her head. "I don't see how."

"Because you don't know what's at stake here."

"What are you talking about?"

I looked over my shoulder, or rather An-Chi made me do it, like I was going to reveal something no one else should hear. When I looked back at her, she was frowning.

"He really is eighteen-hundred-years old."

Her head jerked back as she puffed out a laugh. "Bull shit!"

I nodded. "He was a merchant during the Han Dynasty."

"Not possible."

"I can prove it," I heard myself say, having absolutely no clue as to how I was going to make that happen.

Marta's wry expression made it clear she would need some serous convincing.

"Please do."

I held up my hands. "Can't do it all bound up like this. I need to stand up and move my arms."

Shrugging, she let out a knowing laugh. "You must think I'm stupid as a stink bug."

Feeling my head shake, I was suddenly overcome with the immediate need to rise. Pushing off the chair, I somehow managed to reach my feet and take several hops before a turn in the road sent me to the floor. I tensed when Marta laughed again and stood. Her slippers shuffling across the carpet, she walked over and kneeled next to me.

"You aren't going to prove much by…"

Jerking around, I put all my strength into smashing my bound fists into her nose. The gun thumped to the floor as she fell back, howled in pain and threw her hands over her face.

In one fluid move, I did a quick roll and grabbed the pistol.

"You son of a bitch," Marta moaned as she staggered to her feet. "I'm gonna cut your little..."

I pointed the weapon at her thigh and pulled the trigger. The action was as much a shock to me as it was to her, but she was the one who screamed when the bullet zipped through muscle to embed itself in the refrigerator door.

"God damn!" she howled and fell backwards onto the floor. "God damn!"

Gritting her teeth, she grabbed her leg just above the wound, and screamed, "Why did you do that?"

Pulling the hammer back, I pointed it at her contorted face. "Get up."

Whimpering between short, choppy breaths, she shook her head. "I'm fucking bleeding you little shit."

I kept the gun on her face, and held it surprisingly steady considering that my mind was in total turmoil.

"Get up or I shoot again."

Her eyes wide, she continued to moan as she pushed herself up to lean against the kitchen counter.

"Get a knife and cut my legs free!"

She gave me an angry-desperate-confused-questioning look, but didn't move. I shifted my aim to her other leg.

"I won't ask again."

Swearing, she yanked a drawer open and pulled out a long kitchen knife. Teeth clenched, and grunting with each step, she hobbled over, and sawed at the tape binding my feet.

When they were finally free, she looked up at me, and I could tell she was trying to make a decision.

I took aim at her face. "Drop the knife."

A long, stressful moment passed before her shoulders slumped, the knife thumped to the floor, and she staggered back to collapse into the nearest chair. Holding the gun with one hand, I grabbed the knife, and more nimbly than I knew how, sliced the tape binding my wrists.

Throwing the knife behind me, I moved to the nearest window and peered out. The rig was stopped, and it didn't take me long to realize we were at an intersection. I was trying to decide what to do when I heard a drawer slide open and turned to see Marta lifting an even larger knife over her head.

Aiming quickly, I fired into her left side. She was still screaming when I bolted through the door and raced around the back of the trailer. Running across two lanes of traffic, I sprinted down a tree-lined street filled bumper-to-bumper on each side with parked BMWs, Volvos and Mercedes.

At the second house, a seriously overweight man, grotesquely outfitted in a too-small T-shirt, baggy sweat pants, and slippers was standing at the top of his driveway. His eyes went wide, mouth open as he dropped a small, plastic garbage can and stared at my waist. Only then did it dawn on me that I was still holding Marta's gun.

I threw the weapon onto the grass and held up my hands, palms forward.

"Please call the police," I pleaded. "I've been kidnapped."

Saying nothing, the man stumbled back a few steps before jogging to his house. Moments after he ran inside, he was peeking through his front curtains, cell phone against his ear, mouth moving while he pointed at me, as though the police operator could see what he was looking at.

Lowering my hands, I sighed and looked back at the intersection to see the truck and trailer were gone.

Chapter 44

Sitting on a stool in her small tent, An-Chi gasped involuntarily as Mei-Xiu pressed a cloth into the swollen cut on his hand. Gritting his teeth, he tried to give no further indication that he was feeling pain, but knew from her reaction that Mei-Xiu could see his muscles tense as he struggled to keep from crying out.

"Hold still, Troop Leader," she said almost automatically. "I must clean this wound before I can apply stitches."

"Why are you not using needles to stop the pain?"

She shrugged. "The wound is badly infected and this ointment is needed to fight it. It will also numb the pain." She gave him a mischievous smile. "An experienced soldier, such as yourself, should have no problem with pain."

"Just because I am trained to fight through pain, does not mean I enjoy it."

"And yet you are eager to return to the fighting."

It was his turn to shrug. "It is what I do."

Threading her needle, Mei-Xiu moved her face uncomfortably close to his. Despite the pain in his hand, he was strongly temped to kiss her.

Seeming to realize what he was thinking, she pulled back and turned her attention to the task at hand. "Hold still, brave warrior. You will not enjoy this."

Though his hand was numbing, he could still feel a sharp prick each time she pushed the curved needle through his skin. Just the same, he had endured far worse, and kept his silence while she deftly sewed up the gap.

As he watched, he was surprised when a strange flavor exploded on his tongue, and the words, *orange juice* flashed in his mind.

What is…?

His thought was cut off when Mei-Xiu tied off the last stitch, and plastered a cloth over the wound.

"That will take care of it," Mei Xiu announced as she took a step back and motioned for him to rise.

Pushing off the stool, he felt sluggish as he stood, and managed only one step before the room started to spin.

"What is happening?" he cried as Mei-Xiu pushed him backwards.

"Do not be concerned," her comforting voice responded. "This is not unexpected."

He felt her hand on his back as he regained part of his balance, managing two steps while he fought against the dizziness. Though he could feel the doctor guiding him somewhere, he quickly lost control of his legs and crashed to the floor like a drunken recruit.

Mei-Xiu was speaking, but he could not make out the words as everything went dark.

*   *   *

He awoke with a start, seeing only Chu Gao's face glowing like gold in the light from a nearby candle.

"What happened?" he moaned, surprised to find himself on a cot, a blanket over him.

Looking around, he saw the reddish light of the setting sun, heard the rhythmic sound of marching men, along with the cries of wounded soldiers in the nearby surgery tent.

"You lost consciousness," Chu Gao answered, his eyes flicking to the tent's doorway and back.

"How long have I been here?"

"Since early this afternoon."

"What happened?"

"We do not know. You were fine one moment, and then you just collapsed."

"Where is…the other doctor," he asked while waving a hand around the tent.

Chu Gao seemed confused by the question, but quickly recovered. "Doctor Chu Ju had to go out for a moment. I am covering for her...him until he gets back."

An-Chi shook his head, both to clear the cobwebs cluttering his thoughts and as a signal to Chu Gao.

"There is no need to pretend. I know who she is."

Chu Gao's eyes went wide only briefly, but it was enough to make An-Chi chuckle.

"Do not worry, Doctor. I will not divulge your secret."

The doctor's expression remained cautious. "Why would you keep it?"

The question struck An-Chi as odd. Actually, the entire situation did. Before he started his last mission, he was in total agreement with his fellow soldiers: women should not be doctors, especially military doctors. Their place was in the home, not digging through the bloody guts of wounded soldiers. And yet, here he was, concealing a secret that might well get Mei-Xiu, and possibly her father executed.

Only a day earlier, he had faced possible execution himself, and was given a nearly impossible chance to redeem himself. Since then he had seen Mei-Xiu fight as no woman should know how, and heal with a skill that rivaled the famous physician, Hua Tuo.

Why should that matter? he wondered as his head shook. *I should not be protecting a woman who defies our most sacred traditions and beliefs.*

He had no answer, but knew he would protect her just the same.

Sitting up, but still dizzy, he nodded toward the tent's entrance. "I am well enough to take care of myself now."

As An-Chi pushed himself up, the doctor rose quickly, taking the soldier's arm as he swayed.

"You should not be up so soon," Chu Gao cautioned, his eyes searching An-Chi's face for some clue as to what to expect from him.

An-Chi patted the doctor's hand and shook his head. "I must get back to my troop, and you have many patients."

Staggering to the entrance, he pushed the flap aside and peered out to see normal army life: rows of tents, rows of stinking latrines, rows of men marching, rows of soldiers lined up for food. He looked down at his dirty, torn uniform and let out a disgusted laugh. He needed a bath, and though the food line seemed quite long, he desperately wanted to be in it.

Finally orienting himself, he staggered off in the direction of his sergeant's tent, feeling woozy, and paying little attention to the noises around him, until someone behind him grunted. He was starting to turn when a blinding flash of pain turned everything black.

Chapter 45

The police interrogation room looked like the aftermath of a violent flash-mob attack. Everything in the room, including the walls and lone door was nicked, chipped, scuffed, or scratched. I settled into a chair in front of a small table and stared mindlessly at the empty chair opposite me. The simplicity of the room, the fact that there was absolutely nowhere for anyone to hide, and dozens of police officers were just outside the door, gave me an odd sort of comfort.

I doubted the cops would normally have put the victim of a kidnapping in an interrogation room, but I asked them to. I wanted the isolation, to be spared the stress of mingling with murderers, thieves, molesters, drug addicts, and God-knows-who-else involuntarily occupying their holding cells and waiting rooms. I wanted to totally cut myself off from what we pass off as "civilization".

The sergeant assigned to my case was a stocky woman with short brown hair, ruddy complexion, no obvious makeup, and pointed questions. I tried to tell her as much as I could, but kept the past-lives thing to myself. That meant I had to lie about the cuts on my face and hand. She wasn't about to believe I'd gotten them in a battle fought some eighteen-hundred years ago. Just the same, it wasn't that hard. I blamed it all on Ronny, and since he was dead, they couldn't very well ask him, could they?

Picking up a Styrofoam cup of very weak hot chocolate, I gripped it with both hands, more from the comfort of its warmth than its highly-diluted contents. Someone would have called my parents by now, but I desperately wanted to speak with Jasmina because my link to the Chinese soldier had been broken.

He was there when I got into the police cruiser, his stable mind being the only thing keeping me from losing my own. Then, somewhere along the way, it felt like someone smacked the back of my head. It was all I could do not to cry out, but just the same, it left me gasping, and soon after that I realized he was completely gone.

How could this be? He can't be dead if I'm not, can he?

The shock of the impact made me nauseous, and for the rest of the trip to the police station I struggled to keep from puking in the back seat. By the time we arrived, my head was throbbing, and that was why the sergeant had given me this cup of cocoa along with some Aspirin.

Still holding the cup, I lowered my head, pressed my forehead against the cool metal of the table top, and tried to blot out sounds coming from outside the room: a shout, muffled voices, the warble-warble-warble of a ringing phone, and the thump of a closing door.

Even though the headache was fading, I felt totally numb. So much had happened in the last few hours, I couldn't keep it all straight. First there was my unwelcome connection to An-Chi, then Ronny and Charisa kidnapped me, followed by the totally perverse Willie and Marta, and finally, the outrageously insane Doctor Long and his meathead of an assistant, Toilet Face.

Slowly lifting my head, I noticed two ghostly shapes in the one-way mirror on the opposite wall. They seemed to watch me for a moment before one of them moved to the left and a door closed. Shaking my head, I lowered it again, and waited for the inevitable invasion of my semi-private space. I counted to five before the knob turned and I looked up to see a dark-suited man with a serious face, square shoulders, and a totally forced smile. His dark hair was short-cropped; eyes an odd color of blue; rounded nose, slightly off kilter; and a dark scar on his right cheek.

He was followed by a very short, attractive, almost anorexic Hispanic woman in a dark pants suit. When she hurried through the door, her straight, black hair whipped around with such energy, I was afraid it might fly off her head. Unlike the female sergeant I met earlier, this woman wore too much makeup, the effect being almost comedic, though I was in no mood to laugh.

"Mister Patterson," the man said, "I am Special Agent Nichols and this is Special Agent Martinez with the FBI." He stepped to the table and plopped a thin folder onto it, but didn't sit. "We'd like to ask a few questions about your ordeal."

I looked up, wincing as the move intensified the throbbing in my head.

"Do you feel up to this?" the woman asked, her voice much deeper than I would have expected.

Even though I was sitting, the woman was almost eye level with me, saving me the effort of looking up to make eye contact.

"I just want to go home," I sighed. "Ask whatever you want so I can get out of here."

The woman seemed amused by my directness, but exhaustion took away my ability to care.

Special Agent Martinez gave what looked like the first genuine smile I'd seen since this whole thing started. "Your parents are on their way. We'll try to make this as painless as possible."

She looked at her partner, but whatever passed between them was lost on me. Nichols gave her an almost undetectable nod and pulled back the only other chair in the room. Without comment, Martinez sat and opened the file folder.

"We understand you are from Salem. Is that correct?"

I nodded numbly. "Yeah. I'm a freshman at Marion County Community College in Salem."

Martinez did not react, just looked down at her folder before extracting two photographs. When I saw the dead faces of Ronny and Charisa, I pulled back reflexively, as though their bloody bodies were lying in front of me.

"Are these the two who kidnapped you…the *first* time?"

There was more than a question in her voice. Her emphasis on "first" made it sound accusing.

I pointed at each face in turn. "His name is Ronny and that is Charisa."

Martinez tilted her head to one side. "Actually, the guy is Martin Terrance, and the woman we haven't identified yet. Have you ever met either of these two people before?"

My cheek ached as I shook my head. EMTs had bandaged the wound, which thankfully wasn't all that deep, and numbed it with something, but that was wearing off.

"I was on my way to school when the woman jumped out of a van and tried to kiss me, or at least that's, like, what I thought she was doing. Before I knew what was going on, she pulled a bag over my head, kneed me in the…uh…nuts, and pushed me into their van."

Martinez's painted eyebrows shot up as she pointed at Charisa's picture. "This woman? You're saying a woman nearly a head shorter than you, pulled a bag over your head?"

The aching in my cheek increased each time I moved my jaw. It hurt even more when I shook my head.

"She came up fast and said, 'Give me a kiss' or something like that as she reached up to put her arms around my neck. Next thing I know, there's a bag over my head and then there's this pain in my…you know, crotch."

"And then she drags you into her van. Just like that?"

"I tried to resist, but someone else was helping her."

She pointed at the second picture. "Mister Terrance?"

I shook my head. "I don't know. It could have been him, or maybe it was Danny."

"There was another guy?"

"I told the city police about him. I think he was driving the van, but he was injured when I tried to escape at the hotel. Ronny dropped him off somewhere and told him to go to the hospital."

"Do you know where they dropped him off?"

"I was on the floor of the car. I couldn't see anything, but I think it was in Salem."

"How did this person get injured?"

"They had to go back to their hotel to get a map. While Ronny and Charisa were inside, I tried to get away. Danny tried to stop me and while we were fighting, I slammed my head into his stomach. I also hit my head on the pavement, and that knocked me for a loop. Even so, I tried to run away, but they stole a Cadillac and chased me down. A little while later Danny, like, started throwing up." I held up a leg and pointed at the dark splotch on my pants. "As I said, I was on the floor of the car and he totally puked on my legs. When they saw blood in it, Ronny pulled over and told him to go into a nearby store and say he'd been hit by a car."

Without comment, she whispered to Agent Nichols. After her partner left the room, she turned back to me.

"We'll check on that, but I'd like to know how you managed to get a gun and shoot your kidnappers."

She kept asking questions and it wasn't long before I realized she was asking the same question in different ways, breaking each of my answers into parts and probing deeper. I was starting to feel like the criminal and not the victim until Agent Nichols came in and whispered to her.

"Well, Mister Patterson," she finally said with a smile. "The Salem Police found this Danny person at the local hospital and it didn't take them long to get the whole story from him…at least up to the time he was dropped off and left to fend for himself."

Looking at the file folder, she flipped some papers over and held up a photo.

"Is this the trailer your second abductors were towing?"

I shook my head. "I'm not sure about the trailer, but that truck is definitely the one Marta and Willie were using."

Agent Martinez nodded. "The Portland Police found it abandoned in a parking lot. There was blood inside."

At the mention of the blood, I started shaking, tears welling up as my gut spasmmed.

"I sho…" I swallowed hard, trying to hold onto my vanishing self-control. "…shot her."

And then it all went to hell. I pushed back in my seat, struggling to stop the sobs, but they just burst out, releasing all that pent-up pain, fear, and shock. I was mortified, but once the tears started flowing, there was nothing I could do but let them come out.

Wave after wave of sobs wracked my body until I thought I had it under control, but when I tried to speak, another round burst out, to be repeated again and again.

Though I hadn't noticed him leaving, Agent Nichols returned with a paper cup of water. I tried to swallow it, but another sob erupted just as I was doing so, choking me and throwing me into a coughing fit that almost made me throw up.

Surprisingly, that mini-catastrophe ended the sobbing, and once I had it under control, I pulled a handkerchief from my pocket and wiped the tears from my cheeks.

"Sorry," I gasped. "I just…"

My voice trailed off as my mind ran out of things to say.

"It's OK," Agent Martinez said softly. "You've been through a lot, but if you feel up to it, tell me about this doctor."

I shook my head as more tears trickled down my cheek. "He was a Chinese dude, but tall. Nearly as tall as me. And he was a total loon. Like, he wanted to cut me up."

"Did he say why he had you kidnapped?"

Taking a deep breath, I let it slowly out as I tried to recall our meeting.

"He said he needed to kill someone in the past, and was going to do it through me."

"Through you?"

I felt my chest tightening again as I recalled the doctor's cold, calculating face. "I told you he was a nutter. He was talking about becoming emperor of the entire world."

"In the past or the present?"

I felt my head shake. "As far as I could tell, both. He said he would live forever."

"You're not serious."

My head kept shaking. "I didn't say I believed him, but that's what he was saying."

"How did you escape?"

"I was tied to this table as the doctor's assistant took Willie and Marta into the next room to pay them, but in truth, he was supposed to kill them. I heard a bunch of thumping and then Willie charged into the room to tackle the doctor."

"Did they kill this doctor's assistant?"

"No. I think they just tied him up, and then took me to their trailer."

I described how I got away from Willie and Marta and when I was done, I was so weak my head just dropped to the table on its own.

"You haven't explained why they picked you."

Up until now I had been basically telling them the truth, just leaving out my connection with An-Chi. I knew if I lifted my head and lied to her, she'd see it in my face, so I didn't.

"I don't know."

There was a long pause before Agent Martinez cleared her throat.

"Mister Patterson?"

I knew she wanted me to look at her, but I hesitated, trying to think of a lie I could live with. Then I finally realized I didn't have to make something up, and lifted my head.

"The doctor said I was somehow connected to this person in the past he needed to kill."

"How far into the past?"

I took in a deep breath, and let it out slowly. "About two thousand years?"

She gave her partner a questioning look before locking eyes with me again. "You're telling me this guy wants to kill a person who has already been dead for almost two-thousand years?"

I nodded. "I'm just telling you what he said." I sat up, feeling a flash of anger mixing with my fear. "That guy is a total nut case, but there was no question that he wanted to kill me, and I don't think he was..." The thought of him cutting into me made me shudder. "I don't think he was going to, like, be quick about it, either."

Chapter 46

His head throbbing with each heartbeat, An-Chi jerked awake, startled and confused by his inability to see. In the dark, it took him a long tense moment to realize his face was covered with a musty, coarsely-threaded cloth. When he tried to lift a hand to pull the cloth away he discovered his hands were tied behind his back. The floor he was lying on jerked and bounced confusingly until he heard the familiar sound of poorly greased hubs turning on wooden shafts.

"Uhnn. Ohhh," he heard a squeaky voice groan. "My master so unfair. Why I only get crappy job like this?"

His attempt at crying for help was stopped by a wad of cloth in his mouth, something he had not noticed because of his headache.

He tried to straighten his legs, only to realize that a rope around his ankles was tied to the rope binding his hands. Grunting softly, he maneuvered in the tight space until he was on his back, then hunched his shoulders down to pull his knees up to his chest. This uncomfortable position made it difficult for him to breathe, but it also allowed him to slide his hands under his feet.

Groping blindly, he quickly found the knot tying his feet to his wrists. After a long moment, he freed them, and gasped in a breath as he straightened his legs until his feet pressed against the sides of the cart. Hesitating only long enough to take two deep breaths, he turned his attention to the knot binding his hands.

In this case, his captor had tied a knot on top of a knot, so it took a long moment to work his hands free. When he finally managed it, he pulled the blanket off his face and looked out to see a man who was so small he initially took him for a child.

"Why I get scraps only to eat?" the thin, dirty person muttered as he strained to pull the cart. "I work hard. I need food."

After freeing his feet, An-Chi was preparing to leap onto his captor's back when the small person looked back.

"Ayeee!" Toilet Face screamed as he dropped the cart's shafts.

The shift threw the still-woozy An-Chi forward and onto the ground. Screaming again, Toilet Face threw off his harness and scrambled several paces away before turning back.

"I tie up!" he cried in protest as his former captive rose unsteadily to his feet. "You stay in cart."

Struggling to stay upright, An-Chi held his arms out to maintain balance as he turned to face his captor.

"You tie badly," he mocked in his opponent's peasant-like speaking style. "I get free."

He tried to take a quick step forward, but his legs felt like rubber and he found himself stumbling sideways instead. Clumsily stopping, he spread his feet for stability while waving his arms to keep from falling onto his butt. Finally stabilizing himself, he turned to see his scowling captor slip a long, thick bamboo rod from his belt.

"Master not want you free," Toilet Face stated as he started to move forward.

Though An-Chi knew what he would normally do in this kind of situation, the bout of vertigo kept him off balance, leaving him little choice but to stand his ground and try to dodge the first blow.

Toilet Face hesitated only briefly before yanking his weapon up and rushing in. When the rod started coming down, An-Chi clumsily faked a move to his left, but when he tried to cut right, the move was slow and exaggerated, and though the club missed his head, it slammed painfully onto his shoulder, knocking him to the ground.

"Aiiieee," Toilet Face cried as he jerked his club up and charged. An-Chi rolled several times in the dust and managed to reach his feet again, but as he tried to stagger away, the pursuing Toilet Face slammed the rod against his back.

Though painful, the impact was not enough to knock him down. An-Chi staggered for a few steps, but seeing no other recourse, he turned quickly, lowered his shoulder, and charged. The move caught his attacker off guard and sent him sprawling on the grass. Unable to seize the advantage because the vertigo kept him off-balance, An-Chi managed only two long steps before his foot snagged a clump of grass and he also fell.

Uttering a pathetic cry, Toilet Face snatched up his club and jumped to his feet. Despite the vertigo, An-Chi rose as well, and the two men stared at each other for a long moment before An-Chi bellowed a battle cry and charged. Toilet Face was slow to respond and though his club slammed An-Chi's shoulder, the soldier's momentum allowed him to drive his head into the servant's chest. The weapon somersaulted through the air as the pair went temporarily airborne: Toilet Face howling like a wounded cat, and An-Chi slamming a fist into the servant's bony ribs.

When they hit the ground, An-Chi rolled to his right, and rose to watch the still-screaming Toilet Face jump up and disappear into the shadows of the merchant's camp. He was still trying to shake off the effects of the attack when a fat merchant appeared from the darkness. As the obese person waddled toward him, An-Chi heard others shouting from the army encampment.

"What is happening here?" the merchant asked, his eyes wide.

"I was attacked," An-Chi responded while looking at where his assailant had disappeared. "Did you see him?"

Looking lost, the merchant slowly shook his head. "I saw no one."

"He tied me up and put me in that cart," An-Chi explained while pointing at the decrepit-looking vehicle. "I think he was going to kill me."

The merchant played with the long sleeves of his coat and looked around. "Why would he do that?"

Frustrated beyond belief, An-Chi rubbed his sore shoulder. "I don't know, but he tried to crack my skull open."

When the merchant did not respond, An-Chi turned to watch his approaching sergeant leading half-a-dozen soldiers.

"What is all the noise about?" his superior demanded when he was within earshot. "Why are you not with your troop, soldier?"

An-Chi snapped to attention. "With all respect, My Sergeant, I was leaving the medical tent when someone knocked me out and threw me into this cart."

Even though An-Chi pointed at the cart, his sergeant's attention was on the merchant.

"It looks to me like you are consorting with thieves and merchants," he growled.

"Begging your indulgence, Sergeant," the merchant protested. "I only came when I heard this soldier crying out."

Spitting on the ground, the sergeant seemed to ignore the statement and turned back to An-Chi.

"Are you injured, Soldier?"

Despite the terrible ache in his shoulder, An-Chi gave his head a sharp shake. "No, My Sergeant. When the attacker failed to kill me, he ran away."

"The attacker, whoever he was, had left by the time I arrived," the merchant stated, as though that might help in some way.

Ignoring the merchant's statement, the sergeant snorted derisively. "Get back to your troop, soldier and don't make me regret making you a troop leader."

"Yes, My Sergeant," An-Chi barked. "On the double."

Long Gang lifted a silk handkerchief to his lips to cover a smile as he watched An-Chi jogging to the row of tents, but grew nervous when he realized the other soldiers were still glaring at him. His happy mood gone, he stuffed the handkerchief into a pocket in his sleeve and hurried away. He had only gone a short distance when he heard the sergeant order the remaining men to return to their units, the fading sounds of their footsteps giving him the nerve to look back to see the sergeant watching him.

Startled by the soldier's angry glare, he quickened his pace, gasping at the effort of moving his unwieldy body so quickly across rough ground. He regretted having to pitch his tent so far from the soldiers' quarters, but it was necessary, both because of the general's order prohibiting merchants from camping near his troops, and the fear of random attack.

Upon reaching his tent, he summoned the courage to look back and watch the sergeant walk slowly toward his own camp.

"May my ancestors forgive me," he gasped angrily. "I should never have trusted such an important task to that worthless cretin."

Waving a hand dismissively, he took a quick look around to make sure no one was within earshot. "I will have better luck in the future. As for the present, I still have a few tricks yet to play."

He was preparing to enter his tent when he heard panting and an almost imperceptible whimper. Following the sound, he found Toilet Face curled up on the ground next to his tent, still breathing hard from the exertion of his recent encounter, and whimpering because he expected severe punishment for his failure.

Feeling loathing disgust as he glared at the pitiful creature, Long Gang smacked the servant's shin with his walking stick.

"Aiiieee," Toilet Face cried as he jumped up, both hands gripping the injured leg.

"Offal of a degenerate toad. Why is he still free?"

"Sorry master. I beat. I tie up. I carry, but he is spawn of demon. Even my best rope not hold him."

"You are pathetic," the merchants sighed in disgust while smacking him again. "I can't sleep with all your racket. Find somewhere else to sleep, and leave me in peace."

"But I have no blanket."

"What happened to it?"

"Sorry, Master," the thin creature moaned as his head bobbed. "I cover soldier and lose it when he attack. Do you have another?"

Long Gang laughed derisively. "Don't expect me to reward your incompetence," he bellowed. "Go retrieve your blanket from the cart."

"But soldiers watch. If I go, they get me."

Disgusted, Long Gang took another swipe at the servant, but the spry creature ducked under the swing and sprinted into the darkness.

Looking again in the direction of the soldiers' sleeping quarters, he shook his head.

"I have to make that hag's promises come true," he muttered angrily. "Otherwise, I cut her throat in vain."

Chapter 47

I was with the FBI agents for almost two hours before my parents arrived, and though the cops wanted to keep me even longer, my mother was a natural force to be reckoned with. Mount St. Helens did not erupt with more energy, and as soon as Mom had her arms around me, there was no doubt that she would not leave without me in tow.

However, as we were driving back home, my feeling of being saved turned into a sense of entrapment.

"You are not leaving the house until they catch that crazy person," she announced, like it was the eleventh commandment.

"But Mom, this isn't just about…"

"No! I will not put you at risk again. In fact, we're going to pick up your brother on the way home, just in case this wacko is targeting our family."

"He's not interested in Matthew. He only wants me because of some connection I have with an ancient Chinese general."

Turning in her seat, Mom looked back at me, her expression angry. "Will you stop with these fantasies? This is serious."

"I'm totally being serious. This guy believes I'm, like, connected to the son of some Han Dynasty general and he wants to kill me because he thinks it will make him emperor of China."

"That's absurd. China no longer has emperors. It's been a communist country since just after World War Two."

"That's so not the *point*," I argued as my own anger flared. "He's obviously unhinged, but that doesn't mean he won't, like, still try to kill me."

"Well, he won't get the chance if he can't find you, will he?"

"What are you talking about?"

Seeming to ignore my question, Mom faced forward and patted my father's shoulder.

"Alvin, let's pick up Matthew, grab a few things from the house, and drive over to Susan's."

Dad looked as surprised as I felt. "At the coast?"

"They're not likely to look for us there."

"No, Mom," I protested. "I really need to see Jasmina."

Though she didn't turn around, I could see my mother's head shaking. "There's nothing she can do about this. You'll be safer there than here."

"She might have some insight into what's going on."

Mom stabbed a finger at me.

"We'll have no more of that heebee-geebee crap. Your aunt's place will be..." She stopped speaking as her face revealed the surprise of an idea she thought ingenious. "I have a better idea."

Dad looked at her, and though I could not see his face, I could guess he was expressing my doubt. My mother had never accepted Jasmina's ability to see people's past lives, and she was in total denial about the near-death experiences Remmy and I had last year.

"There's an Episcopal church in Rockaway Beach. We'll hide you there."

Her announcement sent my heart into my stomach. "A church?"

"It's a place of sanctuary," she said with an enthusiasm I definitely did not feel. "There's little chance this demented criminal will look for you there."

I started to point out that even in medieval times sanctuary was more a religious myth than a reality, and that it meant absolutely nothing to the murderous fanatic chasing me. However, experience taught me that arguing with her over her religious beliefs was a waste of breath. My mother had the insane idea that she and God were a team against which no evil could prevail. I wasn't as trusting in the power of that relationship, but also knew Dad would side with her, and nothing I could say, no matter how persuasive, would change their minds.

I am so totally a dead man!

Chapter 48

Feeling foggy-brained and confused as he awoke, it took An-Chi a long moment to realize he was in his small tent. An unsettling dream had kept him at the edge of sleep, hiding its details in his subconscious each time he awoke, only to sneak back to attack him when he drifted off again.

Why in the Name of Heaven would I argue with my mother over religion? Father, maybe. Mother? Never!

Crawling from the tent, he rose unsteadily, stretching to feel every cut and bruise his poor body had received in the last few days. He was tempted to crawl back in and sleep the day away, but when he looked around the mostly-inactive compound, a sense of anticipation lifted his spirits.

Turning to the eastern horizon, he saw the faint glow of the rising sun illuminating thin columns of smoke rising from cooking fires. Only two days earlier, the ground around his tent had been muddy enough to squish through his bare toes, but dry weather and thousands of tramping feet had turned it into a flat expanse of fine powder. Now, instead of being brown with mud, his shoes were coated with a light-tan dust.

He knew the sergeants would soon be around to wake their men in preparation for the coming battle, and fourteen of those troopers were his to command. Shaking his head, he looked down at the soldiers sleeping next to his tent: six surviving members of his recent mission, and eight new ones, as green and compliant as fresh bamboo shoots. He'd had no time to properly prepare the newcomers for what was to come, and could only trust that their boot camp training had been sufficient to help them survive the challenge.

As he prepared to wake them, footsteps drew his attention to his approaching sergeant.

"Are you ready for a day of victories for the Emperor?" his superior asked in a low voice.

His aching body reflexively snapping to attention, An-Chi nodded. "Yes, Sir!"

The sergeant pointed at the sleeping men. "Will they be ready?"

Knowing that any sign of doubt would be the wrong response, he repeated the nod.

"We will fight to the last man, Sir!"

"You have hardly spoken with the new ones."

An-Chi pulled his sword partway out of it scabbard. "They may well be afraid of the enemy, but they fear me more."

Nodding, the sergeant looked at the men. "Wake them, Troop Leader. They are to be in the front line."

With only a glance at An-Chi, the sergeant moved on, leaving him with a tight feeling in his stomach.

That they were to be in the front line was no surprise. The rawest recruits were often put in front to kill or quickly be killed, saving the more experienced soldiers to follow and clean up. When wedged between the enemy in front and their own comrade's spears behind, their only hope of surviving would be to attack aggressively, and give no quarter.

Though his "experienced" men were hardly seasoned warriors, they would most certainly give their utmost. As for the new recruits, the only way to find out was to test them in battle.

Moving to his men, he kicked a pair of feet and shouted, "Get up, lazy turtles. The Emperor needs you for battle."

When he was sure all the men were stirring, he turned to briefly take in the glowing eastern sky before looking around to watch other troop leaders waking their own men. He felt his stomach grumble and wondered if today would be his last.

"Troop Leader," one of his men called. "New soldiers not ready for battle."

Shaking his head, An-Chi wanted to laugh. Who would or could be ready for the carnage they would soon face?

"The emperor has no patience for cowards. They will be ready when the time comes."

"But Troop Leader, we do not..."

He cut off the man's protest by lightly slapping his arm with his bamboo rod, the only possession he didn't leave behind after being forced to leave his home in disgrace.

"Hurry to be first in the chow line, eat quickly, and get back here on the double. We will have precious little time to practice before the army marches."

The man's expression was a mixture of fear and puzzlement, but he quickly slipped on his boots and hurried to his compatriots. An-Chi followed them to the nearest food line to discover they were indeed the first to arrive.

Their eyes only half opened, each soldier held out his bowl to receive a watery rice soup, thinly sprinkled with chopped vegetables and a modicum of spice. As the server slopped soup into his bowl, An-Chi shook his head and smiled. He had eaten army food much of his adult life, and was actually looking forward to this meal.

After his men gulped down their portion, he hurried them to an open field to work on their marching. The original six had improved dramatically since they were first assigned to him, but the newer additions were still struggling.

Under normal circumstances, a soldier would go through at least a year of training before being sent into combat. Unfortunately, An-Chi knew these were anything but normal times. Years of civil war had strained the royal army, forcing them to drag clumsy farmers from their fields and rush them into battle with only minimal training. Before his troop reached the parade grounds, An-Chi could see that these poor souls barely knew what his commands meant.

Lining them up on one of the few patches of open ground in the camp, he interlaced the newcomers with his experienced soldiers and marched the whole lot back and forth, again and again until they moved as one entity.

"Raise shields!" he commanded, alarmed that half of the newest members still hesitated briefly before complying, probably because they looked nearly exhausted after only a short time marching in full battle gear.

"Troop halt," he shouted, wincing when he saw several soldiers sag forward, hands on knees.

Running up to the nearest panting soldier, he slapped him with his bamboo rod, growling when the man staggered back.

"Do you think the enemy will care if you are tired?"

Startled, the soldier dropped his shield, his wide eyes with terror.

"We will soon be going into battle." He pointed his rod at the terrified soldier. "Let that terror be your motivation to attack hard and give no quarter."

When the shaking soldier also dropped his spear, An-Chi gave him his meanest scowl.

We are all going to die, he thought, but said, "Pick up your equipment, and never let it out of your hands again. It is the only thing that will keep you alive."

While the soldier squatted to pick up his dropped equipment, An-Chi moved to the front of his men.

"Troopers! Line up!"

Some were still panting, but all stood at attention, eyes forward.

"Right turn!"

Almost as one, the troop jerked in that direction.

"Sānyuè!"

Marching to the front of the line, he led them back to their sleeping area.

"Fall out," he finally shouted, "but keep your weapons close. We can be called up at any moment."

Pretending to be surveying the other soldiers around him, An-Chi watched his men out of the corner of his eye, dismayed when half of them just collapsed where they stood. Seeing his original six troopers clustering together a short distance from the others, he moved to them.

"I would guess," he whispered when he was close enough not to be heard by the newcomers, "that you might be considering going over the wall, but remember the penalty if you are caught."

"With these losers, we die anyway," a dark-skinned trooper complained.

"But dying in battle brings honor to your families. Not only would you be cruelly punished as deserters, but your families and ancestors will be humiliated by your dishonor. Did you risk your lives on our last mission only to erase that accomplishment with such a disgrace?"

"But what are we to do, Troop Leader?"

"Only a short time ago you were as unprepared for battle as these men are now. We will march in three rows of five. Two of you will be in each row, with a new recruit on each side. You must do your best to keep them together and moving forward. Show them how brave you are by fighting with everything you have. Can you do that?"

When the men shuffled their feet and mumbled, he shouted, "Can you do that?"

All six snapped to attention, shouting, "Yes, Sir! Troop leader!"

An-Chi stifled a sigh and nodded. "Good. Then we will make our ancestors proud."

Chapter 49

Sitting on the sands of Rockaway Beach, sun on my face, its warmth seeping into my tired bones, I drew random shapes in the sand with a piece of driftwood, looked at the ocean, and wondered about my fate.

Why is this happening to me?

The steady wind buffeting my ears hid Father Victor's approach so well, I jerked when he appeared next to me, his light shirt and kakis fluttering in the wind, sandals burrowing into sand as he sat. He looked almost nothing like the black-clothed priest I'd met when mom and dad dropped me off at St. Margaret Episcopal Church, except for the crucifix dangling from a golden chain around his neck.

"You look troubled," he said.

I suddenly felt angry, and wanted to tell him to f...errr...buzz off, but Mom's teachings were so deeply ingrained in me, I couldn't even swear at a priest in my thoughts. Just the same, what could he do about the ancient people trying to kill me? Was there a prayer for that?

I bit my lip and decided to clam up.

"Yeah," I heard myself saying. "Life totally sucks."

"Your mother said you've had it pretty rough these last few days. Even terrifying, from the sound of it."

Huffing a sarcastic laugh, I tossed the stick away. "Tell me about it.

"Would you like to talk?"

Yeah, I thought angrily. *Like you'd believe me.*

When I didn't respond, he asked, "You were kidnapped?"

"Twice."

"Really?"

The tone of his voice implied he was interested in my response, but then I had to wonder if this wasn't just a trick to make me open up.

Despite my caution, I felt like two people: the skeptic who knew this was all a scam to win converts, and the anxious kid, separated from his friends, vulnerable, and...well...scared.

Feeling my head shake, I could tell the scared kid wanted someone to talk to, to trust, to hide behind.

"In the last twenty-four hours, I've been kidnapped, beaten up, cut, forced to kill someone, kidnapped again to be delivered to some kind of mad doctor, and then snatched from him at the last moment by the second pair of kidnappers. I even had to shoot a woman to escape, and I don't even know if she's, like, alive now or not."

I slumped forward, chin against my chest.

"And now I'm hiding out at your place, hoping that maniacal doctor doesn't find me again."

The reverend whistled. "That sounds like one hell of a day."

Surprised, I looked at him. "Can you, like, say, uh, hell?"

He shrugged. "I can't take the Lord's Name in vain. Hell is fair game."

I'm not sure why, but that made me laugh, both because of the absurdity of the statement, and its odd rational. Of course, if my mother doesn't complain when I say, "heaven", why should she get upset when I say, "hell"? They're just places.

"So how are you doing now?" he asked.

Turning my attention to the ocean, I watched foamy waves rolling in three at a time, its steady calmness feeling solid, soothing, even safe. I suddenly felt the urge to laugh because I knew now more than at any other time in my life that "safe" was just an illusion: something you believed because not believing would drive you insane.

"I don't know," I finally answered, looking up and down the beach to see if anyone might be sneaking up on us. "It's totally unnerving knowing he's out there looking for me."

When I turned toward him, the priest was looking around as well.

"Maybe you should be inside," he said anxiously. "You know. Just in case."

As his nervous eyes flicked from me to the church and back, the secure feeling vanished. After all, how was this unarmed pastor going to protect me?

He'll just get killed right along with me.

"Maybe I should have stayed in Portland with the cops."

My statement seemed to calm him, and he shook his head. "You'll be just fine here. I'll get you settled in and we can have an early supper. Then maybe we can talk some more."

"Yeah," I said while looking around again. "That sounds like a good idea."

He rose, and I looked up to see him watching me, his face neutral, body relaxed, one hand motioning toward the church behind me. Before rising as well, I scanned the beach one more time, surprised that now everything seemed strange and out of place, like I should be seeing a field of grass surrounded by pup tents. Finding the whole thing unsettling, I shook my head, stood, and followed Father Victor as he walked toward his church.

When we were close to the rectory, I looked back again, shivering at the realization that the people around me -- the cops, my parents, and even this priest -- couldn't protect me.

Where is Beauregard? Why isn't he helping me?

Beauregard was the name of a protecting spirit who helped me in my previous past-life experience. Jasmina had assured me he would be watching over me, but the fact that I saw no sign of him made it clear I was on my own.

I need to reconnect with An-Chi. Maybe he knows why killing a common soldier will help a nutty Chinese merchant become emperor of China.

As we entered the church parking lot, Father Victor looked back and smiled. It was a weak smile that conveyed the uncertainty I was also feeling. Would An-Chi be able to help?

Maybe, I thought as we continued on. *Any maybe not.*

Chapter 50

An-Chi's troop moved into position toward the front of nearly five thousand blue-uniformed, red-capped soldiers, forming three huge human squares. He watched anxiously as his men marched, and was pleased to see they kept pace with their platoon members.

While they marched toward the opposing army, a platoon of cavalry raced around their right. The horses thundered across the hard ground, their heads and tails high, manes flying, riders upright in their saddles, bannered spears pointing at the sky. He longed for the chance to ride again, hoping, as another platoon of cavalry rumbled by, that he would find the cause of his disgrace and regain his rightful place next to his father.

A trumpet sounded, bringing the brigade to a halt with the thunderous synchronized stamping of five-thousand feet. An-Chi could see a sergeant to the right of their formation looking up at the brigade's captain as he signaled their next move, and the order was repeated by the sergeants.

When the brigade rotated as one, An-Chi held his breath until he saw his own men moving smoothly with the others. He knew they were facing certain death, but for reasons buried deep in his psyche, he was more afraid of being humiliated in front of the whole brigade. Word of his death might never reach his father, but if it did, he hoped that dying in battle might restore his honor, and that of his ancestors.

As they moved forward, dust rose from the many stamping feet, and though it tickled their noses and coated their throats, none of the soldiers coughed.

To his relief, his troop had been moved back from the front line. Their brigade was the middle of three, and his troop was ten rows back and slightly left of center. Though relieved to learn they weren't in the front row, An-Chi knew that nine rows could vanish quickly if the enemy fought well.

They first marched at parade pace and the dust billowed up around them on this windless day. The banners on their spears barely fluttered, and even though they were at the front of the formation, the dust quickly grew so dense he could barely see further than a few rows in front of him.

A horn sounded and the pace increased to a fast walk. Then another signal and all spears lowered to point forward. His long spear, nearly twice his body length, pointed at the gap between the two soldiers in front of him. His short sword clapped dully against his heavy metal armor as sweat poured down his face, and soaked his undershirt and pants.

Two short blasts and a long one increased their pace to a jog. When a slight breeze thinned the dust, An-Chi could see glimpses of faces as the heads in front of him moved back and forth, creating brief openings for him to peer through.

Though he didn't dare turn to look, he heard the thundering hooves of the cavalry charging by on both sides, and joined the others in shouting for them to destroy the enemy.

He heard a triple horn blast, but it was far away, which meant the enemy was charging at a run.

It is too early, he thought. *It will take too much out of them.*

He waited anxiously, anticipating the same command from his own leaders, and was thankful it did not come. The roar of the oncoming enemy filled his ears as his brigade moved down a shallow slope, giving An-Chi a view of the charging army. He was awed when the sun lit up the yellow sleeves of their undercoats, and the green caps on their heads. He saw a soldier in the lead trip, falling on his face to be run over by his comrades. Two others, further back also fell, warping the formation as those behind struggled to avoid tripping on them and also being trampled to death.

He heard a sound much like a thousand bamboo sticks being snapped together and looked up to see a flurry of arrows flying toward the enemy. Soon after, an equivalent number came their way.

"Raise shields!" the sergeant shouted.

The running enemy seemed to having trouble holding their shields up and they were falling in great numbers. He also noticed their reinforcements were not moving up as fast as they should.

Their formation is falling apart, flashed in his head as gaps appeared in their line. If those in the lead did not maintain their formation, the soldiers behind could not provide support. Without proper alignment, some might even spear their own comrades when the two fronts collided.

An-Chi understood why they had been keeping a slower pace. The enemy was now running up a slope and expending precious energy lugging heavy armor and weapons uphill. His army, on the other hand, was fresher, and would have the advantage of attacking from above, the slope allowing them to gain speed with less effort.

When the enemy were within fifty paces, the hail of arrows slowed and three blasts from their own leaders started the entire brigade running. Gripping his spear, he focused on the splotches of yellow in front of him, unmindful of what his troopers were now doing. They would fight bravely, or not, but he was going to charge into the oncoming enemy and kill as many as he could.

Some say life or death is pure accident, but for a soldier, it is a matter of will.

The words of his father brought focus to his mind and strength to his arms as he aimed his spear, pumped his legs, and screamed at the top of his lungs.

The two forces collided with a thunderous clash of weapons, crunching bone, and screams of the dying. Because of their added momentum and freshness, An-Chi's brigade plowed through the first three lines of the enemy, some even breaking through gaps in the line.

Still many rows back from the action, he watched the fierce fighting ahead and waited eagerly for the chance to use his own weapon. Though the winded enemy soldiers started to fall back, it was not a rout, and the leading rows of his own brigade vanished one-by-one into the carnage. An-Chi and his troopers were soon stumbling over corpses, stabbing any enemy who still moved, and staying alert for weaknesses in their line.

A platoon of yellow cavalry hit their left flank, slashing and stabbing until a phalanx of blue horsemen flew into them with swords flashing, their voices carrying over the din of the battle. The enemy riders fought gallantly, but they found themselves wedged between the blue horsemen and their supporting troops. Spears stabbed them from behind as swords chopped at their throats.

A sudden movement ahead brought An-Chi's full attention forward as yellow uniforms forced a gap in the line. Now too close to use spears, the enemy pulled out their swords and slashed madly, forcing their opponents back.

Gripping his own spear, An-Chi screamed, "Spears forward."

Though the command might have seemed ludicrous, since their spears were already pointing at the oncoming enemy, the command really meant charge into the enemy.

As a yellow-sleeved warrior prepared to hack the soldier directly in front of An-Chi, he thrust his spear into the man's chest. The tip struck his metal armor and made him stumble. In such close quarters, the enemy soldier fell back a step, but caught himself as An-Chi pulled back his spear and thrust it again, only to have the soldier jerk to one side, and hack at the spear's shaft, splintering the wood.

Releasing the spear, An-Chi yanked out his sword as his opponent lifted his own weapon, but his upper stroke stopped when someone else's spear pierced his neck. Wide eyed with shock, he tumbled backwards and vanished from sight.

His heart pounding, An-Chi wanted to charge forward and start hacking the enemy, but there were still blue uniforms in front of him. The enemy's counter thrust had stopped the line and those in front of him were slugging it out: desperately hacking, stabbing, clubbing, kicking, and screaming.

"Keep pushing," he bellowed as a spear slammed into one of his men.

He didn't try to help. Things were happening too fast, and any hesitation would allow the enemy to hack their way past him.

When a spear tip appeared at the back of the neck of the soldier in front of him, An-Chi leaped forward, splintering the shaft before the yellow soldier could pull it back. The soldier dropped the remains and reached for his own sword, but An-Chi's blade nearly beheaded him before it was halfway out.

Terror, adrenaline, fear, and machismo mixed violently in his body as he hacked, clubbed, spun, and screamed with a fury that was beyond anything he would otherwise recognize. He lost track of what was happening outside his small deadly space. He no longer felt the impacts of his strikes, or heard the roar of the battle as he focused on his task. His opponents stopped being human, just flashes of yellow light that he cut and stabbed with a rhythm too inbred to think about for fear he would lose his place and stop. He felt no pain, heard no screams, thought no thoughts, just whirled, pushed, and hacked.

It was all so automatic, so much a part of him, he didn't stop until he found himself nearly alone, surrounded by prone, bloodied bodies dressed in both yellow and blue.

As his adrenaline rush slowly ebbed, he gasped for air, his body dripping with sweat, blood, and gore, his arms so weak his sword nearly slipped from his fingers.

"Troop Leader," someone yelled, forcing him to look up to see ten of his men clustered together a short distance away.

A sense of relief flooded over him. Only four of the newest recruits had been lost, and of those who survived -- men he hardly knew, and who barely knew him -- they were now bonded in blood.

He started to move toward them, but staggered as a sudden pain in his right side pulled him in that direction. Looking down, he saw blood on his pants and a slashing cut in his armor-covered outer jacket. Yanking up the hem of his armor coat, he looked at the shallow gash in his side and let out an involuntarily laugh while wondering if the person who did it had escaped with his retreating comrades, or lay dead somewhere at his feet.

A finger's width deeper, he thought as he walked toward his troopers, *and I would have been among the honored dead.*

Chapter 51

I dove into the microwaved dinner of Salisbury steak and mashed potatoes, partly because I was hungry, but also because I was unsure of what to say to Father Victor. He did his best to keep the conversation going, starting with normal stuff about weather, and how I was doing in school, but I just couldn't stop feeling paranoid. It was hard for me to trust anyone I didn't know, even if he was a priest.

"How are you dealing with the kidnapping?"

The question struck me as odd.

"I, uh, don't know. OK I guess."

What else was I going to say? I didn't want to talk about the past few days. Even if I did, how could I have a serious discussion about my past life with a person who didn't believe in them?

Then again, I knew enough about the Bible to realize it was full of all kinds of bizarre stories: Jonah being eaten by a whale and surviving, Noah and his boat impossibly filled with every animal on the planet, Moses waving a stick and parting the Red Sea, and Jesus walking on water and rising from the dead. If he could believe those, why would mine seem so strange?

"Gerry?"

I looked at his concerned face and realized I had completely zoned him out.

"Sorry," I responded as the weight of my troubles drained what little strength I had left. "I need to go to bed, if that's OK."

"Considering what you've been through, yes," he said while pointing at our dirty plates. "Go on ahead. I'll take care of this."

Pushing my chair back, I stood. "Thanks. Good night."

I took a hot shower, replaced the bandages covering my wounds, and crawled into bed with the hope of deep and mindless sleep. However, as much as I wanted it, I tossed and turned, feeling tense and fearful until I could stand it no more and rolled out of bed to pace the room. That didn't help either, probably because such a small, sparsely furnished room made it feel like I was on death row, waiting for the dawn.

Moving to the room's only window, I peered out, but jerked back when I saw a car parked on the opposite side of the street. There was no street light, but a yard light from the church illuminated the car, and also, unfortunately, glared off the driver side window so I couldn't see if anyone was inside.

After watching for a moment, I shook my head and crawled back into bed, not feeling any less tense, but after I closed my eyes, I found myself marching along with a large number of people. I could feel my heart pumping so hard it made my head ache, but I also felt a sense of anticipation…a really strong feeling that this was a very important event for my other self.

A horn sounded again and we broke into a jog. Someone was chanting and I, along with everyone around me, was responding. Two blasts on the horn and I lowered my spear, then three blasts and I was running, screaming, and it felt like charging onto the field at the start of a football game, but hugely more intense.

My muscles twitched, spasmmed, and jerked as the world around me filled with flashes of blue and yellow. I was screaming at the top of my lungs, my arms flailing, body twisting and turning so much I fell out of bed, but kept jerking and twisting even when firm hands grabbed my wrists. It wasn't until pain exploded in my right side that I opened my eyes to see a terrified Father Victor staring down at me.

"Gerry!" he screamed. "Wake up."

The intense "dream" left me so suddenly I went completely limp, my head thumping loudly against the hardwood floor, but I barely felt it. Gasping for breath, I looked around the room until I was sure where I was before looking up at the reverend.

"Shit," was all I could think to say.

After a moment's hesitation, he seemed to realize he still had a death grip on me, and let go. My arms dropped like wet noodles, but when my right elbow struck my side, the sharp pain made me bark a loud, "Ow!"

Grabbing my T-shirt, I lifted it to expose a slashing wound

"Lord in Heaven," the reverend cried. "How did that happen?"

I can't describe the convoluted thoughts streaming through my head at that moment, but after a brief hesitation, I shook my head.

"I can't explain it. At least...not in any way that you'd believe."

Though his eyes turned suspicious, the expression quickly faded as he started to rise.

"I'll get something to patch that up and then we need to get you to the hospital."

Grabbing his hand, I held on when he tried to rise.

"No! That's the first place they'll look."

He resisted only briefly before looking at me. "How would they know?"

The dampening effects of the adrenaline rush were rapidly fading, making the wound more and more painful.

I felt my head shaking. "Is there a doctor you could call?"

He started to shake his head, but stopped and glanced behind him.

"This might sound a bit strange, but I know someone who might be able to help."

"A doctor?"

He gave his head a sharp shake, his expression mixed. "Well. Yes, but not a people doctor."

"Huh?"

"He's a veterinarian."

Chapter 52

"Ahhh Yes, I remember you," the lean surgeon laughed as An-Chi approached. "Arrow in chest."

As the troop leader lifted the hem of his armored jacket, the surgeon snorted derisively. "Why you here with little cut like that?"

"I'm not here for this," the troop leader responded while motioning to one of his men with a more serious cut on his arm. "But maybe when you are done with him, you can stitch this up as well."

His eyes weary from hours of constant work dealing with a massive number of wounded from the battle, the surgeon still managed to bark a laugh.

"We have trainees for that sort of work. You go see Doctor Chu Ju."

"I took them there," An-Chi responded, "but the line is very long."

The surgeon scowled. "And line not get shorter if you wait here."

When the surgeon started to walk away, An-Chi moved toward him, the pain in his side now secondary to the needs of his men. However, he had only taken a couple of steps before his sergeant's voice stopped him.

"Troop Leader."

Flinching, he turned toward his superior only to find the sergeant's attention was on the surgeon.

"My apologies for my subordinate's rude behavior, Master Surgeon."

The surgeon picked up something from the table next to him and popped it into his mouth, chewing rapidly as he looked at the sergeant.

"He should know his place," he said sharply. "See that he does."

The sergeant bowed quickly. "I will, Master Surgeon."

Looking at An-Chi, he gave the troop leader a scowl before jerking his head toward the exit. Not foolish enough to argue, An-Chi waved his men out of the surgical tent, and they fell in behind him.

After they were outside, the sergeant signaled for the men to stop, and led An-Chi some distance from them before turning to him.

"What were you doing in there?"

Bowing quickly, An-Chi kept his eyes down as he answered, "Trying to get help for my men."

"From a master surgeon?"

"He did not seem to be busy."

"And what does a lowly troop leader know about the duties of a master surgeon?"

"I…" He paused, lifting his eyes to see the scowling face of his superior. Though An-Chi had once been many stations above this lowly sergeant, he was now his inferior, and more than any other lower-ranked soldier in this army, he knew why it was critical he not challenge that.

"I apologize, My Sergeant," he said while bowing his head again. "My eagerness to help my men led me to this transgression. It will not happen again."

There was an interminably long pause before the sergeant snorted.

"See that it does not, Troop Leader."

At the sound of fading footsteps, An-Chi looked up to see the sergeant marching away. Swallowing his pride, he waved his men over, watching as the wounded limped toward him.

"We will go to the infirmary," he stated when they were in earshot, and glared at them as a challenge to anyone thinking of debating his decision.

Though he did his best to stand erect as they moved on, his men weren't as concerned with dignity, some leaning against a comrade, others limping, all showing their pain openly.

The infirmary was an open space with a dozen or more medical personnel doing their best to help the lesser wounded. The line shuffled ahead slowly as one-by-one they were stitched, patched, and splintered, but the sun was nearly set by the time An-Chi and his men worked their way to Mei-Xiu's table.

"Doctor Chu Ju," An-Chi announced as Mei-Xiu made eye contact with him. "I am happy to see you again."

Her tired face brightened only briefly before she nodded.

"I see you did not obey my orders," she said flatly.

An-Chi shrugged. "Thankfully, no," he responded, the pain in his side reminding him how close he had come to making her sarcastic request come true.

"I am also grateful."

"I lost four men, and have some wounded in need of your care."

He stepped aside to wave his men forward, noticing that Mei-Xiu did little more than nod at the wounded before moving the first to a stool.

Attendants were lighting lamps by the time she finished with his men. After sending them to their sleeping area, he turned to her.

"I have a minor injury," he announced while lifting his shirt to reveal the long slice in his side.

"It is anything but minor, Troop Leader," she admonished as she moved closer to examine it. "It is very close to the liver. If it had been half-a-finger deeper, you would have bled out before you were off the battlefield. Even now, an infection has started, and if not contained, this 'minor' injury may well be fatal."

He winced as her cool fingers touched the hot wound. "Then I am lucky to be in your capable hands."

"Be quiet and let me work. Strip to the waist."

With some difficulty, he slipped off his damaged armor coat and then the thick jacket he wore under it. He was lifting a light shirt over his head when she pressed something wet against the tender wound. He sucked in a sharp breath as she wiped away blood to reveal the redness of the skin around the injury. The sight did not alarm him until he saw the flash of concern on her face.

"Is there a problem?"

She shook her head. "It is not serious, but before I stitch this up, let me see how your face is healing."

Though she wore no perfumes, when her face came close to his, the smell of her aroused him.

"This wound is already healing, which means your body is fighting infection well."

Uncertain whether to just nod, or kiss her, he remained moot, his eyes on hers until she moved back down to press a cool cloth against his new wound. After a moment, she stepped back to pick up a bronze needle and roll of thread.

"I assume you will be fighting again tomorrow?" she asked while threading the needle.

He nodded. "I am their troop leader. It is my duty to lead them."

Her head shook, but her attention was on his wound.

"I will have to stitch this, or it will tear."

His mind in turmoil, he could do nothing but shrug in response. Thankfully, she did not seem to expect one as she bent over to stab the needle in and quickly pulled it through the skin. His muscles spasmmed slightly against the pain, but he did his best to not react otherwise.

After the second stinging pass of the needle, he looked around to discover his troopers had not gone to their beds as ordered, but were standing in a tight cluster, and watching them. Now flustered not only by his feeling for Mei-Xiu, but also because he was being watched, he straightened his back and painted a stony expression on his face, losing count of the tiny shots of pain until she straightened.

"That will do," she announced. "Of course, it is pointless to advise you to rest for a week or so."

His laugh was stopped by a stinging pain in his side. "I do not think my superiors will deem this little wound a worthy reason for missing the next engagement."

Turning abruptly, she moved to the disheveled table behind her, picking up and folding a clean cloth before smearing it with ointments from several different clay bowels. Moving back to him, she pressed the smelly poultice against the wound.

"Hold this," she demanded while turning to grab a roll of cloth.

As she reached up to wrap the cloth around his belly, the top of her head came close to his nose, and the smell of her hair made him want to put his own arms around her. Knowing they were being watched, he kept his hands by his side until she pulled back and tied the ends of the cloth together.

"Can you breathe comfortably?"

"It is fine."

She nodded, her eyes searching his, making him wonder if she really did want him to take her in his arms and kiss away the...

His thought stopped when she waved him away. "Take your gear and go to bed, Troop Leader. Tomorrow you get another chance to die."

Sensing embarrassing warmth in his face, he grabbed his clothes, and nodded stiffly.

"Tomorrow is as good a day as any."

He wanted to see her reaction to his flippant remark, but she had already turned away and was waving the next soldier in. Feeling foolish, he folded his clothes under an arm, and started to walk into the darkness, but after only a few steps he turned back to see Mei-Xiu examining another wound. When his attention drifted to the line of men still waiting for help, he knew it would be a long time before she made it to bed.

"Maybe all for the better," he muttered as he continued on.

Chapter 53

Salvation.

I don't know how it works.

This isn't about the religious version where a person obsesses over some church's concept of Jesus. What I'm wondering is how I'm going to save myself from the fate of an ancient Chinese soldier. Every time he survives a near miss, I get another nasty wound, and to make matters worse, this guy is one sword slashing, arrow piercing, or spear stabbing away from the grave and I'm tied to his terrifying rollercoaster ride.

My stomach was on a bumpy ride of its own.

"Gerry," Father Victor called from outside the door to my room. "Are you decent?"

I swallowed hard and took a deep breath. "Yeah. Come in."

The room was so small, the door just missed the bed as he pushed it open. To my utter surprise, Remmy and Jasmina were standing behind him.

"Am I glad to see you," I exclaimed without rising.

Remmy moved quickly into the room, taking my hands in hers.

"I heard you were hurt again," she said anxiously.

Before I could respond a thought occurred to me.

"How did you find me?"

Looking sheepish, Remmy turned to Jasmina who smiled like the Cheshire Cat.

"We had some help," she said while turning toward the door.

My jaw dropped when Barbara Foltzman stepped cautiously into the room, looking like a fish totally out of water.

"Hi, Gerry," she nearly whispered as she tiptoed to one side of the door, appearing self-conscious as her eyes looked everywhere but at me.

"But how?"

Jasmina put a hand on Barbara's shoulder. "We thought Remmy would have a part in your past life, but it turned out to be someone else."

"Who is she? Er, I mean, who *was* she?"

Barbara gave an exaggerated shrug, releasing a quick squeal as a grin grew to dominate her thin face.

"I've always, like, wanted to be a doctor," she announced. "I was so totally excited when Jasmina figured out why."

My mouth dropped open as I jerked my attention from Barbara to Jasmina to Remmy.

"Barbara is Mei-Xiu?"

When I looked back at Barbara, she was nodding emphatically. "Totally cool! Huh?" She laughed. "I suddenly had this kind of, I don't know, connection to you, and instantly knew where you were."

"You led them here?"

She jerked a nod. "Outrageous, huh?"

My attempt to rise was stopped by a sharp pain in my side. Groaning, I fell back into the pillow supporting my back.

"Wish you were a doctor now," I whined. "This hurts like the dickens."

"Someone is coming very soon," Father Victor announced to the crowd now filling the small room.

"Good," Jasmina sighed. "Then we can get you out of here."

Feeling something like a pin poking into my wound, I lifted my shirt to see stiches miraculously sewing up the gap.

Flinching with each stab of pain, I released the shirt and shook my head. "I'm not going anywhere."

"You have to!"

Not wanting to move while I, or rather An-Chi was being stitched up, I pointed at the bandages on my cheeks then opened a hand to show that injury as well.

"I am so totally cut up, I can hardly move," I groaned. "If that crazy doctor finds me, we'll just have to deal with him here."

"And how is he going to find…"

We all turned at the sound of heavy footsteps in the hall to see the malevolently grinning Toilet Face pointing a double-barreled shotgun at us.

"Prease not to move," he demanded hoarsely, his black eyes jerking from one surprised face to another, his fat lips pulled back to reveal large, irregularly shaped white teeth. "I shoot good. You die."

Chapter 54

Nearly exhausted, An-Chi pulled on his shirt as he walked toward his tent, barely feeling its course fiber rubbing his back because of the many pains accentuating each movement. Thanks to the doctor's ointments, the pain was less than it had been, but combined with his fatigue, it was enough to make him want to stop right there and lay down.

He was passing a row of supply wagons when a misstep threw him off balance and his reaction sent a stabbing pain up his side. He stopped and bent at the waist until the pain stopped, but before he could rise, the familiar buzzing sound of an arrow in flight sent him into a squat. When the missile thunked into the side of a nearby wagon, he dropped to a knee and turned toward the sound. Even in the dim light, he could see the still-vibrating red shaft with white fletching.

Immediately aware the arrow was meant for him, he scrambled behind a wagon and peered out to look for his attacker.

"Assassin in camp," he bellowed. "On your guard."

The call for help produced movement at the edge of his vision, and he turned to see a figure vanish behind the mess tent. An-Chi lurched from his hiding place as voices around him called out in response.

"Behind the mess," he shouted, his feet pounding the ground as he tried to ignore the pain in his side.

He rounded a corner to find two startled soldiers, their spears at the ready. Suddenly realizing the men could not tell his rank because he was out of uniform, he announced,

"I am Troop Leader Ban. Did anyone pass you?"

"No, Troop Leader," one of the soldiers answered anxiously. "We just arrive. See no one."

A faint snap drew his attention back to where he had come to see a shadow vanishing between two wagons.

"This way!"

His speed limited by his injuries, he did the best he could, but was nearly breathless by the time he reached a cluster of wagons. Running recklessly among them, his sword drawn, he searched the deepening darkness, frustrated by how many places there were for his attacker to hide.

More voices shouted around him as he motioned to the two soldiers following to split up and take different sides before turning himself to set as fast a pace as he could manage while peering down each row, but with over one-hundred wagons in this group, he already knew it was hopeless.

Unwilling to give up, An-Chi continued on until he saw a flicker of movement on his right. Cutting in that direction, he ran full out with his eyes on the spot, but when he got there, movement further on pulled him down another row. His heart racing, he struggled to ignore the growing weakness in his legs.

He broke out of the cluster of wagons to find himself faced with row upon row of small tents belonging to the general's elite troops.

"Alert," he bellowed. "Assassin in camp. Stop anyone suspicious."

Soldiers rose from tents and nearby camp fires, those standing opposite An-Chi displaying their surprise at his declaration. He was at a loss of what to do when he heard a bellowing cry that stopped abruptly. Ignoring his many pains, An-Chi took off at a full run. Others were rushing into the open, heads appearing above tents, people shouting questions, and looking around. Though his lungs were burning, An-Chi did not slow until he came upon a body sprawled on the ground, the head split open by the powerful downswing of a sword.

Hurrying past the corpse, An-Chi was soon at the corner of the tent complex, appalled to see hundreds of confused faces staring at him from every row and path around him.

"Did anyone see him?" he cried.

Shocked faces, puzzled expressions, and shaking heads greeted him in response. Several soldiers appeared with upheld firebrands which cast a flickering light around them. As one moved close, An-Chi spotted a bit of white poking out from under a nearby supply tent and moved quickly to it.

"In that tent," he commanded as he motioned toward it with his sword.

Even though it was too dark to see inside, two soldiers rushed in, fumbling around in the darkness until a firebrand came close enough to illuminate their search. The lead soldier quickly reappeared with a heavy soldier's coat and a clutch of red arrows with brilliant white fletching.

Feeling light headed, An-Chi stared at the arrows for a long moment, fatigue, shock, and disappointment stopping all thoughts before he gave his head a shake and waved his sword at those around him.

"He has changed clothes," he shouted. "There is an assassin among us. Look for anyone suspicious."

While some soldiers ran off, screaming his alert as they went, most just looked around at their comrades and shook their heads. There were close to seventy-thousand soldiers in the camp, along with thirty-thousand support staff and camp followers. One inconspicuous spy would have no trouble blending in long enough to slip into the deepening shadows and escape.

Realizing he was no longer in danger, An-Chi felt his strength vanish and let his sword drop until its tip thumped the hard ground.

"What is happening?" a captain asked as he pushed through the cluster of soldiers around An-Chi.

Though hardly able to stand, he stowed his sword, and snapped to attention along with everyone else.

"We have an assassin in camp, My Captain."

"Where?"

An-Chi pointed at the soldier holding the arrows and coat. "He shed his uniform and slipped in among our troops."

Without hesitation, the captain turned to a sergeant. "Double the perimeter guard. Arrest anyone trying to leave. All soldiers return to their troops. If he hasn't already escaped, we will find him."

The sergeant jerked a quick bow and hurried off, shouting commands as he went.

The captain turned to An-Chi. "How did you discover this assassin, Troop Leader?"

An-Chi also gave a curt bow. "He tried to kill me, and missed only because I stumbled as he released his arrow."

"Show me where this happened."

"Yes, My Captain."

Setting as fast a pace as he could manage, An-Chi marched back to the wagon and pointed at the sheared-off shaft sticking from its side. After his superior examined it, An-Chi pointed at the mess tent.

"He was standing somewhere over there when he released his arrow. After calling out the alarm, I chased him to a cluster of wagons, and it might have ended there had he not killed a soldier nearby." He pointed at what remained of the arrow. "It appears he doubled back and tried to retrieve his arrow."

"Did you see his face?"

An-Chi bowed slowly. "Humble apologies, My Captain. He was never more than a shadow."

Turning toward the mess tent, the captain hesitated for a moment before calling, "Where is the cook assigned to this mess?"

A disheveled man appeared from the crowd, his clothes stained from a long association with cooking, hands showing many scars from his profession.

"I in charge of mess, My Captain," the man said hesitantly.

The captain pointed at the tent. "There has been an intrusion, and your stores may have been poisoned. Destroy them and get a fresh supply for morning."

Looking dismayed, the cook started to protest, but quickly stopped himself and bowed low.

"Yes, My Captain."

"And put two guards at each mess tent. They may try again."

"Yes, My Captain."

Turning to An-Chi, the captain asked, "And what of you, Troop Leader?"

"Sir?"

"Why were you here so late?"

Giving a quick bow, An-Chi lifted his shirt to reveal the bandage on his side, now stained red from the aggravation of his recent activity.

"I was having a cut stitched, My Captain. An injury from today's engagement."

"What division are you in?"

"White Tiger, Sir."

Nodding, the captain turned to look at the mess tent again. "They fought well today. The enemy was thoroughly routed. If I am any good at guessing their intentions, I would say they will sue for peace in the morning."

"It will be a great victory for the Emperor."

Waving a hand dismissively, the captain shouted, "Bring the mess cook back."

After a moment of distant shouting, the rotund cook reappeared.

"Yes, My Captain," he said while performing a deep bow.

"I have another idea."

"Sir?"

"I will send a dozen prisoners. Feed them the food in question and if they live until morning, you can use it for the troops. If they become ill, destroy that which they have eaten."

The cook smiled. "Yes, My Captain."

The officer turned to a nearby sergeant. "Deliver the prisoners and do the same for all of the mess tents. We do not know how long this intruder has been in camp. He may have poisoned them all."

"Yes, My Captain," the sergeant barked before running into the crowd.

Facing An-Chi again, the captain smiled. "Get some rest, Troop Leader. General Lü Bu is a determined enemy. We may still need your valiant troopers."

Chapter 55

"How did you find him?" Jasmina asked, her wide eyes on Toilet Face's double-barreled shotgun.

"You stupid woman. Easy to follow."

"Oh God," Remmy moaned. "This is my fault."

"Shut up!" Toilet Face shouted as he jerked his weapon around to point at one person then another. "I shoot everybody."

"What do you want?" Jasmina asked desperately.

Toilet Face stabbed the shotgun's barrels in my direction. "Him."

"But why?"

He smiled malevolently. "Not your business to know."

"You intend to kill him?"

Ignoring her question, the thick-bodied thug waived a hand toward the back of the room.

"All against wall. Move now!"

Though the pain was dramatically reduced, I still groaned while struggling to rise.

Pointing at me, Toilet Face gave his head a sharp shake. "Not you."

His back to the others, he did not see Father Victor lurch forward to grab the gun's barrel. The priest reflexively yanked it toward the ceiling, Toilet Face resisted, and both barrels discharged with a thunderous explosion.

Debris rained down as the pair struggled for possession of the weapon. Ignoring my many pains, I pushed off the bed, hurled myself across the space between us to stab a finger into the Chinaman's left eye.

Howling like a tortured banshee, he let go of the shotgun, and fell backwards with both hands over the injured eye. My momentum kept me on top of him as both of us fell in slow motion, his long-drawn-out scream only a dull sound to my stunned ears. Just before we hit the floor, I gave his head a hard push, slamming it so hard the screaming abruptly stopped.

I suddenly felt an overpowering need to be off this murderous oaf, but the screaming pain in my side took away all the strength in my legs, and in the narrow hallway there was no way to roll sideways. I pushed with both hands, sliding down his body until I could stand and move away from him. Only when my legs hit the bed did I take my eyes off Toilet Face and see the stunned Father Victor leaning against the wall, both hands gripping the shotgun's barrels.

"Call the cops!" I gasped, my attention jerking from the stunned priest to the unconscious murderer and back.

"The phone is in the living room," Father Victor moaned, his wide eyes still on the weapon in his hands.

With Toilet Face blocking my way, I was paralyzed, and just couldn't muster the courage to crawl over him.

"Who has a cell?"

"I do," Remmy announced as she struggled to extract it from her tight pants, but in her excited state it just wasn't happening.

"Hello," a higher-pitched voice called from the back of the room. "I'd like to report an attempted kidnapping."

We all jerked around to see Barbara Foltzman with a cell phone pressed to her ear.

"Yes," she continued more calmly than I felt. "We're at the Episcopal Church in Rockaway Beach." She hesitated a moment before nodding. "The kidnapper's knocked out right now, but he might wake up at any moment." Her expression turned confused as she listened. "You don't know their address?"

Still holding the shotgun with one hand, Father Victor held out the other, his voice shaky when he said, "I'll...I'll...Let me speak with them."

Passing the phone to him, Barbara folded her hands in front of her chest and smiled at me.

"And I always thought you were, like, this boring guy." She giggled nervously. "Who knew?"

Chapter 56

An-Chi stood at the edge of the small field and watched his new troopers march along with other recruits as they prepared for the battle they all hoped would not happen.

Leading this pathetic troop will not restore my honor, he mused while watching the newcomers struggle to keep up with his only slightly more experienced men.

It had been two seasons since his disgrace, but the need for redemption had not faded. His head shaking, he looked up to see another troop leader approaching and gave a quick bow in greeting.

"Hello, Troop Leader," the newcomer said while motioning to An-Chi's men. "I see you also have club-footed dolts."

Smiling grimly, An-Chi nodded. "Two years of war has been a hardship for our reserves."

The troop leader barked a laugh, "What reserves? All I see are farmers fresh from their fields, though if they were as clumsy with a plow as they are on the march, it is a wonder they did not starve."

The comment made An-Chi laugh. "We will be lucky if they do not run at the first sign of the enemy."

Nodding, the troop leader patted the weapon on his waist. "That is what my sword is for."

Returning his attention to his men, An-Chi suddenly felt alarmed and turned to face the threat. Though he found nothing, a word appeared in his mind, no, it was more like two words, but he had no idea what they meant.

Shot gun?

He worked to calm himself, reasoning that it was part of the strange voices and sensations plaguing him since he had been shot with the arrow.

There must have been a curse on that arrow. A witch's spell intended to drive me mad.

The pain in his side flared as he felt an overwhelming sense of fear: the fear of a young boy facing danger. He fought it down and forced himself to stay focused on his men.

"Stay together," he shouted angrily as he hurried to match their pace. "Straighten your lines."

The men were obviously trying hard, but still not marching as a unit. Swearing under his breath, he moved up beside them to shout an order, but a loud noise, like a massive thunderbolt, made him jerk back and duck, his eyes immediately searching the area for the source. To his utter dismay, no one else reacted to the sound.

"Troop Leader?" his equal called from behind him.

He turned to see confusion on the man's face.

"Did you hear that?"

The troop leader shook his head. "I heard nothing unusual."

An-Chi looked up at a cloudless sky. "It sounded like thunder."

The man shrugged. "Then the spirits are playing with you. Maybe they are saying they will strike the enemy down for you, since your men don't seem capable of doing it."

Angered by the flippant remark, he growled, "My men will be ready when the time comes. The enemy will lose ten for every one of ours."

His head shaking, the troop leader said, "Or maybe they will just laugh themselves to death."

Hurrying to catch up with his men, An-Chi took one last look around before shouting, "March together! One. Two. Three. Four. Keep up the cadence!"

He continued to count, and soon saw improvement in his stumbling troopers, but the progress gave him little comfort.

How can I defend myself against the mystical powers of a witch?

He no longer worried about his own life, but the more tragic and far reaching consequences of failure, and the further disgrace it would bring to his father, family, and ancestors.

Chapter 57

Though my heart was still racing as I watched Father Victor tie up Toilet Face, Barbara seemed to be enjoying herself.

"That was seriously cool," she gushed. "The priest totally saved the day."

"Watch yourself," I warned the reverend. "He's immortal."

Father Victor gave me a puzzled look, but it was Jasmina who spoke.

"This is one of the people chasing you?"

I nodded as the priest finished tying his knot, and again picked up the gun by the barrel, though he appeared unsure as to what to do with it.

"Did you say this guy is immortal?"

I shook my head. "I'm not sure how he does it, but he's probably a couple of thousand years old."

The reverend pointed at the unconscious form lying at his feet. "Him? He can't be a day over forty."

I didn't know how to respond until I saw a knife on Toilet Face's belt. Slipping it from the sheath, I pulled back his sleeve and made a shallow cut in his forearm.

"What are you doing?" both the priest and Jasmina cried at the same time.

Looking up at them, I held the sleeve back and pointed at the thin line of blood beading above the cut.

"Give it a minute."

All four watched in stunned silence as I counted to thirty before pulling out Toilet Face's handkerchief and daubing up the blood to show only a slight scar where the cut had been.

The priest gasped as Jasmina sighed, "This is new."

Rising, I handed the knife to Father Victor. "This guy works for a Doctor by the name of Long Gang, and he's the one who wants me dead."

He pointed at the bound figure. "And what is his name?"

Shaking my head, I pushed the handkerchief back into the Chinaman's pocket. "I only heard Doctor Long speak it once. He called him, Toilet Face."

"You're kidding."

I shrugged. "Maybe it means something different in Chinese, but that's what he said."

The silence that followed was hard to tolerate.

"What are we going to do?"

The four other people in the room looked at each other, their faces clearly showing they had no idea, until Father Victor finally spoke.

"The police are on their way, and they can deal with this guy."

"And what about the doctor? What's to stop him from hiring someone else to do his dirty work?"

"If he shows up here, they can arrest him as well."

My chest tightened as my head shook. "I'm not waiting around for that."

"But you can't leave. You are the one he tried to kill."

I felt my head shaking, my anger flaring at the impossible stupidity of this situation.

"Toilet Face wasn't here to kill me," I shouted, my frustration being too much to contain. "He was supposed to take me to his master. *He* wants to kill me."

"Why?"

I couldn't stand it. The pain in my side was now masked by a sudden flare of rage, but no matter how much I wanted to slam a fist into this priest, a lifetime of Mom's obsessive teaching stopped me.

I jerked my attention to Jasmina, her mouth open, eyes wide, then to Remmy who looked equally shocked, but it was Barbara who stopped me. Her eyes were nearly slits, mouth curved up in a questioning smile, head slightly to one side.

"Why *does* this guy want to kill you?" she asked cautiously.

"Because he's a crazy loon," I shouted. "He thinks I'm connected to some two-thousand-year-old soldier in China, and if he kills me, he kills that guy."

"He can't do it," Jasmina insisted.

Using my bandaged hand, I pointed at the two cuts on my face, and then the bleeding wound on my side.

"He damned well can."

The room went deathly silent with me the object of everyone, but Toilet Face's attention. They were so focused on me that everyone jerked as one when the big man groaned and started to move.

As he rolled onto his side, I realized the reverend was still holding the shotgun by its barrel, his attention totally on us.

"Watch out!" I cried, but Toilet Face was already kicking forward to knock the reverend's feet out from under him.

Dropping the weapon, Father Victor fell to hands and knees as Toilet Face slipped his bound hands under his unbound feet and was up so fast none of us had time to react. I was still trying to decide what to do when the Chinaman sprinted down the hall.

I finally regained my balance and charged after him, but had no clue as to how I was going to overpower a maniacal killer who outweighed me by a good thirty pounds, probably all muscle.

At the front of the house, I saw Toilet Face fumbling with the front door knob, and I charged full steam ahead with the intention of tackling him. Unfortunately, he had the door open and was sprinting through it before I could reach him.

Gasping for air, I stopped at the door, surprised at how out of breath I was after such a short run. Thankfully, the husky Chinaman was standing at the bottom of the porch's steps, his bound hands over his head, and three of Rockaway Beach's finest slowly approaching him with guns drawn.

My muscles tensed, and I suddenly felt desperate to get away from there, but when I turned, my way was blocked by the reverend and my friends.

"We have to leave."

Jasmina, Remmy, and the reverend were all shaking their heads, but Barbara's eyes were almost glowing.

"Where would we go?" she asked excitedly, as though I'd just announced the desire to go someplace exotic.

The other three jerked around to give her an exasperated look before Jasmina said,

"You can't keep running. That will only make things worse."

I pointed at my face. "Worse than this?"

Her head shook. "Much worse."

Behind her, Father Victor rose slowly to his feet, his eyes jerking from me to Jasmina and back.

"What exactly is going on?"

Not even trying to answer, I turned my attention to see Toilet Face and the officers in a standoff. His arms now lowered, he posed like a sumo wrestler, threatening to run over them as they slowly moved in, their guns at the ready, faces tense. The man who couldn't be killed didn't seem to care that any sudden move would bring lots of pain. He, like me, wanted to get away at any cost.

Another cruiser screeched to a halt in the parking lot, its flashing blue lights adding to the already surreal scene as two more officers piled out and sprinted to support their comrades. Toilet Face was screaming in Chinese. Short, terse, demanding statements erupted from him, and even though the officers didn't understand, I was sure they got the gist from the intensity of his vocalization.

"Go away! I kill! Son of Heaven need me."

A shudder ran through me, and my anger vaporized as I stared at my shaking hands. I looked again at the still-screaming Toilet Face, his swinging fists keeping the officers at bay.

My shoulders slumped on their own and wobbling legs forced me to take a quick step to the doorway and lean against the frame.

"He speaks English," I shouted to the officers, then thought, *but he doesn't think it.*

The last statement brought a clarity that surprised me. I looked at Jasmina to see her attention was on the action outside. It was now obvious that I didn't need to get away from anyone to resolve this. Jasmina would again be the key in unlocking the answer, but I would have to go somewhere I had never actually been, and didn't really want to go.

A cry from outside pulled my attention to two officers trying to muscle Toilet Face to the ground. They would have had a better chance of making a rhinoceros kneel.

I more felt than heard myself yelling something in Chinese. Toilet Face and the officers turned to look up at me, their faces expressing the confusion I felt.

"What did you say?" Jasmina asked with alarm.

I leaned my shaking head against the door frame and let out a weak laugh.

"Take me to the Son of Heaven."

Chapter 58

"White tiger division at the ready," the officer screamed. "March forward."

Wedged in with thousands of other soldiers, An-Chi was relieved to see his men keeping up as the phalanx moved toward the dust cloud rising on the opposite side of the field. Though Mei-Xiu had applied a fresh poultice to his wounds, freeing him from the distraction of pain, he had refused her offer of an elixir to numb his other aches. Once engaged in battle, he would feel none of the pains now nagging him, but could ill afford the slight edge even a small amount of opiates would take away

The pace of their march seemed almost frenetic: the drums beat faster, officers screamed as they urged the men on. For their part, the foot soldiers shouted their marching chants more emphatically, their countless feet stamping in nearly perfect unison as they headed toward oblivion. The phalanx picked up the pace sooner than last time, their commander's voices sounding shrill against the monotonous pounding of drums and synchronized stamping of so many feet.

He suspected his generals were eager to repeat their successes of the previous day by intimidating the enemy with a more aggressive attack. Just the same, An-Chi worried that with so many recruits replacing the killed and injured, the faster, more demanding pace might backfire on them.

His worries were quickly abated when they passed over a slight rise, allowing him to see the enemy was still getting organized, their soldiers not yet moving in perfect synchronization. The left of three divisions was still not aligned with the other two, their cavalry prancing impatiently behind.

The two armies were still several hundred paces apart when each side's cavalry raced past their foot soldiers, the riders screaming at the top of their lungs, their horse's hooves turning dry dirt into billowing clouds. In this open plain there was little opportunity for strategy. The two groups of horsemen simply slammed into each other, hacking, stabbing, beating their opponents in the hope that brute force would win the day.

The dust stirred up by the cavalry, and the soldiers around him, partially obscured An-Chi's view of the approaching enemy force. Thankfully, a slight breeze blew tantalizing openings in the dust, exposing a group of horsemen here, part of an approaching phalanx there. His first clue that the two cavalries had met was the rider's excited shouts mingled with the shrill cries of the wounded and dying.

An-Chi could see a noticeable hesitancy in his newest recruits. This would be their first experience with death on a massive scale. It obviously and understandably terrified them.

"Eyes forward, troopers, pace to the drums," he bellowed. "Victory for the Emperor."

To drown out the rider's death cries, the captains started a chant,

"To the fight! To the fight! To the fight!"

An-Chi shouted along with his men, but he could see their enthusiasm waning as their moment of truth approached.

He had slept little the night before, his rest being disturbed by dreams of the previous battle, and later by the glaring stare of his angry father. Finally giving up, he rose a short time before the horns woke his troopers, using the extra time to stretch sore muscles, flex stiff joints, and warm up his many wounds. It would not do for his troopers to see their leader in obvious pain.

Despite the lack of sleep, he felt alert and eager to engage the enemy. While warming up, he had been struck with the conviction that whatever happened today was going to be the resolution to all his problems. Though he wasn't sure exactly what that meant, it was a feeling he didn't want to lose.

"Rise up! Rise up!" he had yelled while nudging the soldiers sleeping beside his tent.

They rose sluggishly, but after a quick breakfast, and some time on the parade grounds, they were marching as a unit, stamping out their aches and pains, and shouting out their fear.

"To the fight! To the fight!"

Horns blared, signaling full charge. The brown cloud that represented the cavalry fight had moved to their left, and he had the feeling their horsemen were gaining the advantage. Through the hazy dust, he could see the enemy's third division was now properly aligned with the others, and they were running full out as well.

An-Chi's troop was five rows back from the front line, meaning they would encounter the enemy sooner than last time, and at the pace they were setting, the wait would not be a long one. He shouted to his men, more for himself than anything, since everyone was screaming, venting their fear and struggling to keep up to avoid being run over by those behind them.

"Shields up!" he screamed as enemy arrows began falling all around them. Three men fell in front of him, then two more. As they were trained to do, his troopers moved forward to fill the gaps. The two armies were only a hundred paces apart by the time An-Chi and his men were up to the front. His own shield holding at least a dozen arrows, he strained to hold it up as he ran. Two of his men had already fallen and the arrows were still coming. So were the enemy troopers, their angry-scared faces now clearly visible through the thinning haze of dust between them.

"Keep your line," he demanded as the rain of arrows slowed.

Fifty paces to contact, An-Chi and his men were now screaming at the top of their lungs, the sound so loud he could hear nothing else. Even so, he kept shouting at them to stay in formation.

Looking ahead, he realized the enemy front line had dissolved, each man running at his own pace, the order of the formation had degenerated into a mass of screaming men, their fear overcoming discipline.

"Hold formation," he screamed while glancing to the left to see there was still a line.

The sound of a horn pierced the noise: the command to close ranks. The men slowed, moved close, and lowered their spears, each man's shield overlapping the soldier on his left as he was protected by the shield on his right.

"Keep it tight," he bellowed as the disorganized enemy collided with their line.

The enemy's spears mostly bounced harmlessly off shields, or armor plating while An-Chi's front line speared throats, arms, and legs. As the first row fell, they marched over them to get at the next. When the fighting grew too close for spears, they left them in the dying enemy and pulled out swords to stab and hack anyone who came close. For each soldier the disciplined army lost, ten enemy troopers fell. Before the opposing commanders could even begin to regain control, their soldiers were stumbling and falling because of the mounting pile of corpses and thrashing wounded under their feet.

Another horn sounded, calling for them to move forward and push the disorganized enemy back into the spears of those behind them. Many tripped, falling on their backs to be speared or hacked where they lay. Though the enemy front line wanted to pull back, the mass of bodies pressing in from behind stopped them, turning what might have been a strategic retreat into a massacre.

"Go for their throats," An-Chi commanded.

Knowing they could not stab through the armor plating covering their chests, he urged his men to stab at the most vulnerable and exposed spot on their enemy's body. The throat might be harder to hit than the thick body, but once pierced, it almost always brought quick death.

On the enemy's side of the line, the scene was total chaos. Many of those trying to flee had dropped their weapons, and when they were unable to retreat, soldiers from An-Chi's side hacked them down.

Though it was difficult for An-Chi's men to walk over the corpses, their locked formation gave them a stability the enemy didn't have, and as they pressed into the disorganized mass, the carnage only got worse. He could tell the men around him were realizing the benefit of keeping formation, because though the closeness of their bodies limited their ability to swing their swords, the enemy were still falling in droves and slowly retreating.

An-Chi was fighting with all his might when his sword was suddenly torn from his hand.

"Sword," he screamed while reaching back to the solder behind him.

Before the trooper could hand him his weapon, a spear tip slipped past his shield and pierced his left side. He gasped, trying to turn as the spear tip twisted, but could only drop to his knees, crying in pain as he fell backwards off the spear. Collapsing to the ground, he hardly noticed the soldier behind him charging forward to fill his spot. Pain turning his vision red, he rose to hands and knees, but in this low position he was jostled and kicked as those above him fought for their lives.

Certain that if he lay down he would be trampled, he fought through excruciating pain and slowly worked his way toward the rear. Knees and thighs pushed and jostled him, feet stomped his fingers, making the pain so overwhelming he thought he would never make it, until a pair of hands lifted him up and walked him into the clear.

He was nearly delirious when the soldier carefully lowered him to the ground, muttered something, and vanished back into the mass of men. Lying on his side, he kept his eyes closed as each heartbeat brought a paralyzing explosion of agony.

Lost in the ochre glow of pain, he sucked in short, agonizing breaths that tortured his body until shock finally dulled his senses. When his brain started functioning again, his vision cleared enough to see dull, wide eyes in an upside-down head that was barely attached to its shoulders, blood running in streaks from the gap in his neck. The sight made him shudder, and brought on even more pain.

The sounds of the continuing battle finally reached his barely conscious brain, but it was the thunder of hooves that forced his eyes open again. A small cluster of cavalry were heading his way, their attention on the fighting. Fire-red pain stopped him from rising to get their attention. The best he could do was hold up a hand, waving it weakly at the pounding hooves heading his way.

He needed air-filled lungs to yell, but pain kept him gasping and helpless to do anything more than watch the galloping horses approach, their hooves kicking heads and stomping the arms of corpses in their path. He was certain the hooves growing ever larger in his vision would surely crush him under their ponderous weight as the thundering grew louder and louder, and...

A high-pitched, unintelligible scream pierced his distressed mind just before the hooves jerked to his left and passed so close they shook the ground and peppered him with dirt clods.

"Someone will come for you, Soldier," a voice shouted as the horses raced past.

He tried to relax, but even his sagging body brought pain as he looked back to see the last row of soldiers continuing to move away from him, revealing hundreds of bloody corpses in their wake. A sudden spasm in his side pulled him onto his belly, his forehead pressing into the dust as he released a desperate groan, and tried to will the agonizing pain away.

When his eyes closed, he found himself looking up at a strange face, definitely not Chinese, dressed in odd clothes. Two other burly men in dark uniforms were holding tightly to a larger Chinese man. Though the man did not look like anyone An-Chi had ever seen, he somehow knew he was the thin, threadbare simpleton who tried to kidnap him.

It is the pain, he reasoned as he sucked in short breaths.

A young woman suddenly towered over him, her face showing alarm and fear. He felt a strong attraction to her, but it was another young woman behind her with strange kinky hair, he was sure he knew.

"You..." he started to say, but was stopped by another spasm. "...can heal me."

The first girl jerked around to look at the second one before twisting back, her mouth open, eyes questioning.

"What did you say?"

Another spasm choked off his answer, and left him gasping.

"Please save me, Mei-Xiu, if only for my father's sake."

The girl knelt quickly beside him, her eyes wide, head shaking.

"Your father?"

Spots peppered the scene as their faces grew to fill his vision and then slowly faded away.

"I have disgraced him, but I must live if his honor is to be restored."

The women abruptly vanished, their faces replaced by a darkening red background populated with undefined shapes that ebbed and flowed until everything gradually sank into an oppressive darkness.

"Forgive me Father."

Chapter 59

After watching the cops muscle Toilet Face into a patrol car, I staggered back to the bedroom. When Barbara followed me, I turned to say something to her, but was stopped by an intense pain in my side. Screaming, I stumbled backwards and fell onto the bed, my contact with even that soft surface being the most painful thing I had ever experienced. Feeling a terrifying warmth against the hands covering my side, I looked down to see my own blood oozing between them.

Father Victor was suddenly over me, but his words were drowned out by Remmy's screaming. Then Barbara's face appeared, and as she pushed back her hair to stare questioningly at me, I started speaking, as though possessed.

"You...can heal me."

"I think he's speaking to me," she said, sounding shocked.

"Please save me, Mei-Xiu. If only for my father's sake."

"Your father?" Barbara asked, her face expressing the confusion I felt.

Black spots peppered my vision, and the scene was suddenly replaced with a row of soldiers moving slowly away from me.

With my eyes closed, I strained against the pain, but could still hear Remmy screaming for an ambulance, the sound of a phone dialing, and Father Victor moaning, "Lord have mercy."

*   *   *

In the dark space of a ghostly world, I found myself kneeling before a candle-covered alter and desperately praying to small figurines, asking them how I could achieve salvation.

When the figurines offered no answers, I began to realize from both the smell and the sound around me that I was in a hospital. An involuntary cough produced a gasp on my right just before my bed shook.

"Gerry!" Remmy cried as I made a fruitless attempt at swallowing before opening my eyes.

Mom and Dad must have heard Remmy cry out because they came rushing in, their faces showing the same anxious concern as my girlfriend.

"How are you feeling, Son?" Dad asked hopefully.

Responding was impossible because my tongue felt like a dry potato. When my words came out all vowels, Remmy stuck a straw into my mouth, and I sucked in cool water.

Knowing I would soon be able to speak, my first thought was to say I was OK, but how could I?

"Where's Jasmina?" I asked, knowing the answer from both Remmy and my parent's faces.

The first real surprise was my mother's conflicted expression as she looked everywhere but at me.

"I need her help, Mom," I insisted, not taking my eyes off her until she finally looked at me. I pointed at my left side. "This can't be *explained* away, and I'm sure Father Victor will agree with me."

Her eyes jerked from my girlfriend to me and back before she let out long sigh and gave a curt nod. Sucking in a breath, Remmy hurried from the room, only to reappear a moment later with both Jasmina and the reverend. Behind them, I saw a uniformed police officer peer in, and just as quickly turn away to scan the hallway.

"How are you doing?" Jasmina and the reverend asked at the same time.

I was in too much pain to find that funny.

"I'll…be OK."

"This isn't over," Jasmina warned.

Though swimming in a pool of pain-killing opiates, I was clear-headed enough to nod.

"I'm still connected to him," I said while slowly lifting a hand to point at my side. "And I think this surgery may have totally saved his life."

"Wouldn't that be hard for him to explain?" the reverend asked, his tone curious, but not without a hint of doubt. "What I mean is, where did the stitches come from? Wouldn't he be labeled a witch or something?"

Jasmina let out a derisive laugh. "Killing witches is a Christian thing. Ancient cultures thought of them as healers, among other things."

"Yes, but stitches? Isn't that a fairly modern concept?"

I felt my head shake. "The Chinese were successfully performing surgeries, like, centuries before it was 'discovered' in Western Europe."

"Really?"

Moving close, Jasmina asked, "When was your last contact?"

"I think it was just before I woke up. He was wondering who had shamed him and how he could earn his way back into his father's favor."

"Shamed him? How?"

I felt my head shake. "I dunno exactly, but it totally got him kicked out of his family. He was, like, a colonel in their army when this happened, but lost his rank and everything. I think he's trying to earn repentance by starting at the bottom and working his way up again."

"But why does this doctor want to stop him?"

My head was still shaking. "My counterpart doesn't know anything about him."

"I do," Barbara announced, making us all turn to face her.

Her kinky hair pulled back into a puffy ponytail, she wore blue jeans, black sneakers, and a yellow tank top under a black one with the words "You shouldn't be looking here." spread across her small breasts.

"You what?" Jasmina asked.

Barbara shrugged. "You said I was, like, connected to this Mei-Xiu person." When none of us responded, she shrugged again.

"Well, I had this really strange dream last night, and I think she was in it."

"What happened?"

Giving her nose a quick rub, Barbara shifted her feet and folded her arms across her chest.

"Well, she so thinks An-Chi is a dork, but she's also kinda hot for him."

I heard a click in the medical equipment next to me and turned to see flashing lights on the device with a tube that ran into my IV. As Jasmina was asking why Barbara thought An-Chi was a dork, I felt myself losing focus.

After briefly squeezing my eyes shut, I looked at Barbara and tried to concentrate on her response.

"Well, I mean, like, he's fighting in battle after battle, and she knows he's so gonna get himself killed. What girl wants to hook up with a nutter like that?"

"But you said you knew why the doctor was after me," I said anxiously.

Barbara huffed a derisive laugh. "Well, it's so not like the dude doesn't know himself."

Adrenaline now countering the effects of the pain meds, I tried and failed to sit up.

"He doesn't. I asked."

"He so totally does. He just doesn't want to admit it."

"Who is it?" Jasmina asked insistently.

"His wuss of a brother."

Faces flashed in my mind, some were children, others a bit older, but all young. Barbara nibbled on a finger and stared at me as a name finally popped into my head.

"Pi?"

"Ya," she said, dragging the word out as though implying that I, or rather An-Chi should have known all along.

"But he's only nine-years old."

"Not him, exactly," she explained. "I mean, the kid's got loads of smarts, and he actually ends up being an emperor of China. But Pi's mom isn't your mom, and she doesn't know that's gonna happen, so she's trying to eliminate the only successor standing in her son's way."

"But the doctor said something about being emperor himself."

She laughed. "That's the problem with hiring a bad dude to do your dirty work for you."

"But I don't get the impression the doctor wants to kill An-Chi, or at least not right away?"

Huffing a laugh, Barbara shook her head. "Didn't you pay any attention to what we learned about China in class?"

Letting out a sigh, I felt my own head shaking. "Could you get to the point?"

"The doctor knows the future because his present person can somehow connect with his past self, probably much like you are doing with the general's son. By the way, An-Chi's real name is Cao Ang, and his dad is a warlord named, Cao Cao, who has too much power for the doctor to take down directly. His big weakness is this Chinese obsession with family honor."

She did a quick 360-degree spin and looked at me. "You said Cao Ang had been disgraced in some way, right?"

When I nodded, she shrugged. "Then the doctor probably had something to do with it, because dishonor of the son reflects on the father."

"Which explains why someone doesn't want him to succeed in regaining his honor," Remmy shouted.

"Maybe," Barbara said, "but whatever the dishonor was, it wasn't enough to bring his dad down."

"So what happened?" I asked.

Barbara looked down at her hands for a moment before her eyes rose to meet mine. "According to the history books, Cao Ang finally restored his honor, and totally saved his dad's life by giving him his own horse after General Cao Cao's mount was too seriously wounded to carry him."

I stared at her for a long moment before saying, "That makes him a hero, not a threat."

"But if the assassin, like, kills you, the old man totally dies in that battle. Since your brother would be too young to take his father's place, there would be a huge power void in the region. With a few more strategic deaths, a person with the right connections, and a flair for the dramatic could fill it."

"But how does the woman you are connected to know this?"

Barbara sighed. "She was helping her father when a dying soldier confesses to being part of an attempt on An-Chi's life."

"He was supposed to kill An-Chi?"

Barbara nodded. "He was, but he got cut up in some kind of skirmish and died on the operating table."

"Wait a minute," Jasmina asked. "Was that guy's face painted green?"

Barbara's shaking head made my gut cramp. "Nah. He was, like, a common foot soldier."

Snapping my eyes closed, I tried to make contact with An-Chi, but got nothing.

"He's still unconscious," I moaned while looking from Jasmina to Barbara and back. "I can't see anything."

"I'm so going to send someone to help," Barbara announced.

"It won't do any good," I countered. "You're easily two or three kilometers from the battle. If the assassin is already there, no one can run or ride fast enough to save me."

"Oh God! There has to be something we can do."

"We can pray," Father Victor announced.

"Pray?" I protested. "That won't accomp…"

Jasmina gripped my arm, and I turned to see her staring at the reverend.

"That just might work."

"What?" I cried.

Looking at me, she shook her head slowly. "Prayer is a process of focusing the mind, and communal prayer is two or more people doing exactly the same thing, only with more power."

"To what end?"

"If we all focus our thoughts on one objective, and channel that energy through you, we might be able to wake An-Chi."

"Father?" my mother asked uncertainly.

"That's not exactly what I was talking about," the reverend said hesitantly. "I can't possibly condone…"

"…praying to God for Gerry's spirit to awaken and show him the light?" Jasmina interrupted.

"Well, yes. I guess we could pray for that."

Rising, Jasmina motioned for everyone in the room to crowd around me.

"The reverend will lead us, but I want each person to take the hand of the person one each side, and focus your prayer on Gerry."

As Father Victor moved up beside me, Jasmina positioned herself between him and me, taking our hands, but leaning toward the vicar.

"Keep it direct and to the point. We need to wake him quickly."

Looking hesitant, the priest stared at me for a long moment before taking a deep breath.

"I will start the invocation, and then follow with, 'We pray for Gerry's spirit to wake up.'. You will repeat the last line after me, and we will continue to repeat it until Gerry is confident his…uh…spirit is awake. Are we ready?"

When everyone nodded -- some eagerly, some hesitantly -- he took another deep breath and said,

"Heavenly Father, we invoke your help for Gerry Patterson. We pray for Gerry's spirit to wake up."

"We pray for Gerry's spirit to wake up."

"Gerry," Jasmina whispered. "Close your eyes and concentrate."

I snapped my eyes shut, staring into the mixture of black and gold floating across my vision.

"We pray for Gerry's spirit to wake up."

The voices started merging into one as I tried to make a connection that seemed surreal, and yet I knew was out there, if "out" is the correct word.

"We pray for Gerry's spirit to wake up."

Coughing involuntarily, I felt a stirring, like there was something alien moving inside me. The glow of my eyelids changed in color briefly and then I was looking at some kind of hairy red ball. It took a moment to realize it was a person's head. The sight should have shocked me, but instead I felt only confusion as my counterpart looked around.

To his left, a cloud of dust showed that the battle was still going on, but had moved far away. Slowly turning in the other direction, he saw bodies everywhere. The corpses from each side lay next to, or on top of each other, mixed together in death in a way they never could have been in life.

My heart raced when I saw a pair of boots running toward me. When they stopped about ten feet in front of me, I looked up to see the same scowling face I'd seen when this all started. His face was no longer green, and his uniform color had changed from yellow/green to red/blue, but the fish-scale-shaped armor plating made me gasp as he stepped over bodies as though they were simply trash in his way.

"We meet again, Cao Ang," he said as I looked up into his black, emotionless eyes. "For the last time, I trust."

Chapter 60

An-Chi felt numb, but as he stared at the newcomer, a strange question erupted from his lips

"Did my brother send you?"

Without responding, the other took a quick look around a field littered with bodies and equipment before lifting his sword.

As he prepared to rise, An-Chi felt something pressing into his side, and quickly wrapped his fingers around the hilt of a sword.

"What do you want of me?" he insisted.

The assassin strode forward, his sword at the ready, but not over his head, as that would attract attention. Three steps, a slight hesitation, another look around, then four quick strides until he was within striking distance.

"Your head," he said while lifting his weapon.

Grimacing, An-Chi rolled toward the attacker and thrust his sword up to pierce his left thigh. Without hesitating, he immediately rolled away, managing three revolutions before trying to rise. To his dismay An-Chi was on his knees when the attacker's sword slammed his shoulder with a loud clang.

The impact knocked him over, but as he fell, he dropped his shoulder and did a somersault. The assassin kept up with him, delivering another bruising blow to his side. Rising again to his knees, An-Chi blocked the next attempt as he tried to ignore the throbbing wound in his side. He briefly lost sight of his opponent's sword, but a flash of light on his left made him instinctively pull his sword around to deflect the slashing blow and then parry away a stabbing move.

Knowing he had little time left, An-Chi put all of his effort into rising to his feet, but managed only one step before his heel slapped a body and he nearly fell. The effort to stay upright tore at his wound, but he used the pain to maintain focus, jumping to his right to avoid another slashing blow. His movements were slow, his opponent's blade ringing as it bounced off his armor again.

Smiling wickedly, the assassin shoved his blade toward An-Chi's face, forcing him to step to his right, and the effort made him stumble and drop to one knee. Gasping as pain exploded in his side, An-Chi hardly noticed the blade slicing through his topknot until the ball of hair bounced off his shoulder.

Like a chess player, an experienced soldier knows the timing and duration of each move he and his opponent can make. Such knowledge allows him to anticipate and react to his adversary, and with muscles weakened by his recent traumas, An-Chi knew he was out of options.

With shaking hands, he held up his sword to block the next blow, but the powerful impact sent it flying and threw him onto his butt. Knowing he did not have the strength to rise, let alone outrun his opponent, An-Chi looked up to see his attacker take a labored breath, his movements unsteady as his blade rose over his head. Instead of striking, the assassin seemed to lose his balance and stumble back a step.

An-Chi did not notice the sweat beading up on the man's suddenly pale face because his attention was on the blade looming over him. Not willing to turn away, he sucked in a quick breath and prepared for the coming blow, only to see the man's eyes grow wide before they rolled back into his head. A moment later, his knees buckled, and his body thumped to the ground.

Stunned by this unexpected development, An-Chi tried to rise, but barely got to his knees before losing his balance and falling onto his back. Pain limiting him to short, choppy breaths, his body trembling as he lifted his head to stare at the inert form, unsure of what had happened until he saw blood oozing from the hole he had earlier made in the dead man's left thigh.

The threat now gone, his head flopped back, arms shaking, but he refused to let his eyes close.

"I will not die here," he swore to the many corpses around him.

Chapter 61

"Aaaggghh," I groaned through gritted teeth as the pain in my side increased.

"What is it?" a nurse's voice asked.

My eyes were closed, riveting my attention on the scene unfolding before me. An-Chi had just dropped onto his butt, and I knew with certainty, because he knew with certainty, that this was the end.

The sword rose, its glistening blade reflecting the midday sun, but I wasn't thinking about how beautiful that magnificent weapon was, just terrified that it was going to come down and split my head in two.

And then, to my utter amazement, his eyes rolled up and he collapsed.

"Oh my God! He's dead."

"Who?" Jasmina cried.

"The assassin," I announced, my eyes popping open to see the startled faces around me.

"What are you talking..."

The nurse's question was interrupted when the entire room erupted into cheers.

"What is going on here?"

Complete exhaustion overcame me, and I closed my eyes as she said,

"Your incision is bleeding. I need everyone out of the room while I take care of it."

Though I knew I was still looking through An-Chi's eyes, all I could see was his hands and dirt.

Are you OK?

At first I thought he hadn't heard me, but before I could ask again, I heard a faint,

I am alive.

However, instead of sounding like he was relieved, it was just a simple statement.

I wanted to ask more questions, but the nurse's voice pulled me back to the present.

"Mister Patterson? Are you with me?"

Opening my eyes, I saw her concerned face and tried to smile, but even that minimal action was too much for my exhausted body. I took a slow breath, and gathered enough strength to respond,

"Yeah. I'm fine now."

"What was all that about? Why were they cheering?"

I could just feel the last bits of energy escaping my body.

"It's hard…to…explain," I answered haltingly. "Maybe later."

As my eyelids drooped, she shook her head.

"I've got to change your bandage," she said as my eyes closed. "It might hurt a bit."

I felt my head shake weakly. "No it won't."

*   *   *

I was surprised to wake up in an empty room. Well, nearly empty. Mom was sleeping in a chair on my left, but true to form, she awoke with a start when I picked up the water mug from the side table.

"You're awake," she said needlessly.

Though my hands were shaking, I took a sip and nodded. "How long have I been out?"

Covering her yawning mouth with a hand, she looked around. "About an hour, I guess."

"Where is everybody?"

"The nurse said they'd all have to wait outside until the doctor had a chance to look at you." Shaking her head, she let out a nervous giggle. "Of course, no nurse on this planet could keep me out of here."

"And the doctor's not been here yet?"

Rising, she moved to the side of the bed and took my hand.

"Yes, but he said no one was to disturb your sleep."

Feeling her hand squeeze mine gave me a sense of comfort I couldn't describe. Just the same, I had to ask.

"Do you believe in what has been happening to me?"

She hesitated for a long moment, her face going through several different expressions before she smiled and looked at me.

"I believe you believe it's happening."

My anger flaring, I pointed at the cut on my cheek.

"You and Dad were watching when this happened," I growled. "And Father Victor was right in front of me when An-Chi got stabbed in the side. How can you possibly think I'm faking this?"

Tears dribbled down her cheeks, she shook her head.

"I'm not saying..." She sucked in a breath, chewing on her lower lip for a moment before continuing. "This is all so bizarre. I have no idea what's going on."

"Well I do," I said with a confidence that suddenly vanished as I said it. "Sort of."

"What do you mean, 'sort of'?"

I shook my head. "I don't know all of why I'm connected to this guy, but there's a doctor and he's immortal and...wait a minute."

"What?"

"Oh my God."

"Gerry. You're scaring me."

I felt my head shaking again as I squeezed her hand. "I need to speak with Jasmina...and Father Victor."

"Why?

"There isn't time to explain." I lifted her hand and squeezed it again. "Please, Mom. Get them for me."

She hesitated a long moment before hurrying from the room, and returning in less than a minute with the pair.

"You should be resting, Gerry," Jasmina announced as she entered.

"The doctor," I said insistently. "Didn't he say he learned how to be immortal from some old woman?"

"I think so, yes."

"And then he killed her."

"Uh huh," she answered cautiously.

"How was that possible? She was immortal too."

"Oh my," Jasmina said. "She must have given him whatever it was that made her immortal, and that means there's a way to defeat him."

"How would we find out?" the reverend asked.

I felt my head shaking. "Toilet Face would know because he's most likely the one who killed her."

Jasmina's head was shaking as well. "Well, he's not likely to tell us, is he?"

I held up my hands, but they were so unsteady it made me woozy.

"The only way to know is to ask him."

Chapter 62

A sudden jolt shook An-Chi awake. Disoriented at first, he gasped upon realizing he was on a wagon piled high with corpses. Pushing a bloated arm off his face, he looked around at the broad valley they were passing through and slowly came to realize that the wagon was moving away from the fighting. He could still hear sounds of the conflict, but when he looked in that direction, all he could see was dust floating above a small rise behind him.

So many parts of his body ached it was difficult to take a deep breath, let alone gather enough strength to yell, but he knew that whoever was driving this wagon had mistaken him for a corpse, and was taking him to a mass grave.

"Hello," he gasped, barely above a whisper.

Realizing no one would have heard him, he sucked in as much air as his aching chest would allow and tried again.

"Hello!"

As the wagon rolled to a stop, he heard a strangled cry.

"Back here," he called. "Get me down."

A pair of excited voices jabbered away as two scraggly-looking peasants appeared, their eyes wide, voices straining with such a high pitch he might have mistaken them for women.

To his utter surprise, he could not understand what they were saying as they shrieked and pointed at him.

Exhausted, he let his head thump back against the corpse under him, closed his eyes, and tried to make sense of the strange voices. Finally becoming annoyed with the gibberish, he shouted,

"What are you saying?"

The two hesitated before speaking again, and then each tried to out-shout the other. After a confusing moment, An-Chi relaxed his mind and the words started to make sense.

"What you do there?" the elder screamed. "We no carry living people."

"Watch out, Uncle," the other wailed. "It spirit of dead soldier."

"Spirit? No! That freeloader."

"Ahhh, noooo" the younger cried, his arms flapping. "It eat our testicles. It kill our children."

An-Chi wanted to laugh at these pathetic creatures, but the reality of his situation annoyed him.

"I am not yet a ghost, you cretins, but if I die on this stinking heap, my vengeful spirit will do far worse than eat your testicles." Lifting his head again, he sucked in a deep breath and bellowed, "Get me down!"

The elder slapped his hysterical nephew before climbing onto the back of the wagon and pulling on An-Chi's boots. As he slid off the pile, the old man caught him and lowered him to the ground.

Instead of pulling away, the man started pawing through An-Chi's clothes.

"You hitch ride. You pay," he demanded. "Give money."

Angered by the man's insolence, An-Chi slapped his hands away, but when he would not stop, he smacked his left ear. Caught off guard, the man fell to the ground, howling as he pressed a hand to the side of his face.

Seemingly fearful of more abuse, the man jumped up and scurried around the side of the wagon, screaming, "No freeloader. You get ride, you pay."

The effort took what little strength An-Chi had, but he managed to stay upright by leaning against the cart as he scowled at the man's stunned nephew.

"Where is the camp?"

Now mute, the young man stabbed a finger toward the east and said, "Five *li* that way."

"Five *li*? An-Chi muttered as he looked across the expanse of waving grass between him and the safety of his barracks.

"You not make it," the old man taunted. "Carrion birds peck out your eyes long before we get back."

His anger giving him a shot of adrenaline, An-Chi straightened and took a wobbly step away from the wagon.

"You not walk so far," the nephew almost whispered as he looked toward the distant camp and back to An-Chi. "You better off stay with us."

"I will be fine," An-Chi grunted as he carefully put one foot in front of the other and staggered in the direction indicated.

"Carrion for birds!" the elder shouted while walking away. "Carrion for birds."

As the world around him spun, An-Chi staggered, caught himself, and tried to set an even pace.

"One. Two. Three. Four," he chanted with each stride. "One. Two. Three. Four."

The shock of each footfall pulsed in each of his many wounds as he marched under the beating sun, and struggled to keep his focus. He barely felt the grass sweeping past his legs, and struggled to regain his balance each time a random spot of uneven ground sent him staggering.

"One. Two. Three. Four," he shouted as loud as he could and kept putting one foot in front of the other, unsure if he was heading in the right direction.

He kept his eyes on the ground ahead, afraid to look up, for fear of seeing birds circling overhead. Sweat poured down his face when a faint sound made him look up to see a break in the horizon ahead. Not a break really, but a small speck that grew and shrunk, appeared and disappeared, its shape distorted by the rising heat. It didn't really register with him as it gradually grew in size, blurring and solidifying into something grey against the green grass, floating on it like a ship on water.

Soon the grey blob split into two, then four shapes repeatedly rising above and sinking into the grass. Though he still could not focus on them, he recognized the shapes, not by their appearance, but because they moved, not like bobbing boats, but galloping horses.

The thought brought relief, but the resulting relaxation almost made him fall. He staggered, caught himself, staggered some more before resuming his pace. His attention was now on the beasts, feeling comfort in the sound of their hooves thumping the dry ground. They were only twenty or so paces away when shadows slipped off their backs and ran toward him.

"An-Chi," Mei-Xiu screamed. "An-Chi!"

He started to cry, the sobs pulsing in his chest so hard his arms shook, and the sudden, overwhelming relief made him stumble, his legs suddenly useless as he crashed hard onto the ground. He expected pain, but was too numb to feel anything, too exhausted to do more than lay with his cheek in the dirt, his chest still convulsing, drool running from the corner of his mouth, his muscle control completely gone.

He could hear Mei-Xiu calling him, feel her lifting his head, pressing a water jug to his mouth, and felt the coolness as it flowed in, choking him.

Sorry, birds, he thought as soft voices murmured above him. *No meal today.*

Chapter 63

"I've never been inside a jail before," Jasmina confessed as she followed an officer down a narrow corridor with Father Victor and Barbara close behind.

"For sure," Barbara agreed. "This place is totally creeping me out."

"It can be quite intimidating at first," the reverend responded. "In fact, now that I think about it, it is unsettling every time I come here."

Jasmina nodded. "I think that's the intent. Don't you?"

He almost whispered a laugh and nodded. "One would hope."

They stopped when the officer held up a hand and called, "Open on Hallway Two."

As the door slowly and noisily rolled aside, he turned to them.

"Sorry folks," he said. "This guy is so combative we can't let him out of his cell. You'll have to speak with him through the bars, but don't get close. He won't hesitate to grab you."

Nodding, they passed through the door, and heard the officer call, "Close on Hallway Two."

They followed the officer to the end of the hall, feeling decidedly claustrophobic after the door clanged shut behind them. As soon as the cell's only occupant saw them, he rushed forward to slam his hands against the bars, and scream in Chinese.

"What's he saying?" the reverend asked as all three pressed their backs against the opposite wall and stared wide-eyed at him.

"Wow!" Barbara barked. "He seriously wants out. He just keeps saying over and over that he, like, has to get out to help the doctor."

After a moment of railing against the bars, Toilet Face let out a sob and sank to his knees, moaning words that made Barbara shake her head.

"Man, he's totally, like, dedicated to this doctor dude. He's crying about how angry his boss will be when he finds out he failed."

They all stared at the sobbing prisoner for a long moment before Jasmina pushed away from the wall and turned to Barbara.

"Ask him why no one can kill him."

Barbara looked confused. "Really?"

Nodding, Jasmina moved halfway across the hallway and made eye contact with the sniveling Toilet Face.

"Just ask him."

Jasmina glared at him as Barbara translated her question.

To everyone's surprise, he responded in English. "I immortal. I live forever."

"Why are you immortal?"

He shook his head. "Not know why. My master make it so."

"How?"

Giving her a guarded look, he slowly rose while fumbling in his pockets until he produced a jade-green amulet about the size and shape of his pudgy little finger.

"Hey," the officer cried. "You're not supposed to have that." He moved quickly to the bars, his hand held out, palm up. "Hand it over."

Toilet Face's face was nearly blank when he held out his own hand, but still inside the bars. Looking perturbed, the officer reached in to snatch it from him, but the prisoner was faster, his other hand clamping his wrist and yanking so fast, the officer slammed hard into the bars before he could even cry out.

Slipping the amulet back into his pocket, Toilet Face reached through the bars and hammered the officer's head into the metal and he immediately went limp. It all happened so fast, the startled threesome had no time to scream before the prisoner was yanking at the keys on his victim's belt. When they would not pull free, he grabbed the officer's throat, screaming,

"Get me out or he die!"

The threesome was still too shocked to react when a siren blared and two officer rushed in, their Tasers drawn.

"You let me out!" Toilet Face screamed. "You let me out!"

While one officer rushed the three civilians down the hall, another moved in to zap the excited prisoner. When he didn't release his victim, his partner returned to fire a second device into the Chinaman, finally sending him to the floor.

As they were hurried away from the cell, Jasmina screamed, "He has an amulet in his pocket. Take it from him."

Without waiting for a response, the threesome hurried down a second hallway to the front of the police station where a police woman guided them into what appeared to be a break room.

"You folks wait right here," she ordered.

"Please," Jasmina insisted as she turned to leave. "Get that amulet in his pocket. It should stop his violence."

"Will do, Ma'am," she acknowledge before vanishing from sight.

While Jasmina paced the room, Barbara sat at the small table and played with sugar packets. Father Victor stood guard by the door, watching and listening for something to report. All three rushed out of the room when they heard an ambulance siren, but before they could get to a window, a heavyset officer blocked their way.

"Good morning, folks. I'm Captain Marshall. I need to ask you about what went on in there."

"Is the officer going to be OK?" Jasmina asked.

The captain nodded. "He'll have one heck of a headache, but otherwise, I think he should be fine. The ambulance is just a precaution."

"That's a relief."

"I understand that one of you speaks Chinese."

Barbara held up a hand. "That would be me."

"Why did this guy attack you?"

She shook her head. "He didn't attack me. It was my friend, Gerry Patterson."

"And where is he?"

"He's in the hospital, 'cause someone cut him up real bad."

"Cut him up? Why is that?"

She hunched her shoulders. "It's all, like, totally weird. I don't really know how to explain it."

Jasmina moved in to wrap an arm around Barbara's shoulders. "Excuse me for interrupting, Captain, but did you get the amulet away from the prisoner?"

Marshall stared at her for a moment before pulling a plastic bag from his pocket.

She stretched out a hand. "May I?"

The captain hesitated again before handing it to her.

"Oh my God," she exclaimed as the bag touched her palm.

She took two quick steps to the small table and sat in a chair, her eyes locked on the green lump inside the bag.

"This is so powerful."

"I beg your pardon, Ma'am?"

Her eyes closed, she pressed the amulet between her palms. "Do you know what this is?"

His expression skeptical, the captain looked at the priest. "No, Ma'am."

"Oh yesss," she hissed. "That's what this is all about."

"Ma'am?"

"Shhh! I'm travelling through time."

"I beg your pardon? Did you say you were travelling through time?"

Her eyes still closed, she nodded. "That's exactly what I'm doing, and in a few minutes I'll know why this is…"

She stopped when the captain snatched the bag from her. Her face the picture of puzzlement, her wide eyes staring at him as he held the amulet out of reach and glared at her.

"Why did you do that?" she protested. "I was almost there."

Captain Marshall shook his head. "I don't have time for such foolishness. That wild man hurt one of my men and I need answers."

Though Jasmina opened her mouth to protest, her expression quickly softened as she rose from the chair.

"We'll tell you all we know, Captain," she said solemnly, "but I need to spend some more time with that amulet."

Pushing the bag into his pocket, Marshall shook his head. "It's evidence, and we'll keep it safe until it's no longer needed."

"But my friend's life is in danger. I need to use it to find his killer."

"You're friend is dead?"

"No, he's about to be if we don't stop him."

"Stop who, Ma'am?"

Jasmina sighed, her annoyance obvious. "A two-thousand-year-old assassin."

"Two-thousand?"

Nodding adamantly, she stabbed a finger in the direction of the cells. "And that crazy man in there is his accomplice."

Chapter 64

The room swam as though he were looking at it through simmering heat. He couldn't move from the chair as his father came in, his expression dour, body tense.

"You have betrayed me," the elder man stated.

"No, Father. That is something I would never do."

"No?" his father shouted angrily. "Then tell me why my enemy already knows my plan for attacking him, a plan I confided only to you."

"But I have spoken of this to no one, not even my closest friends."

Turning quickly, the elder man held up a knife, making Cao Ang gasp when he recognized the inlaid dragon on the handle.

"And are you also going to deny killing my secretary? You were seen leaning over his dying body!"

"I was there when he died, but I did not..."

"Leave this house!"

Shocked by the declaration, Cao Ang looked quickly around the room until his eyes fell on the one thing he had not remembered seeing: the round, pink face of his younger brother, Pi.

Could it be you?

"Could what be?" a feminine voice asked.

Turning toward the sound, An-Chi opened his eyes to see Mei-Xiu's confused face staring down at him. The previous scene had seemed so real to him he had trouble believing it was really her.

"What?" was all he could think to say.

His question seemed to befuddle her, and it was a long moment before her confused expression changed to a smile.

"I am pleased to find you awake," she said modestly, though her eyes glowed with happiness.

An-Chi looked around the tent before asking, "How did I get here?"

"We found you wandering in a field. You were delirious."

He started to sit up, but she rushed over to stop him.

"Do not move! You are badly wounded."

"But I feel almost no pain. How can this be?"

She pointed at several bronze needles sticking from his skin. "I administered *Chen* to help with the pain. It has fewer side effects than the opiates. You will heal faster without the risk of addiction."

"But I must report back to my sergeant," he protested. "He will think I have deserted."

Her head shook as she turned away. "Most of your brigade will not return from this battle. The casualties are high."

"Higher for them than us, I hope."

"Will it matter? Those who survive this battle will just be fodder for the next."

"Of course it will matter," he argued angrily. "We fight for the honor of our people. General Lu Bü is a demon!"

"Not such a demon that he cannot find tens of thousands of young men willing to die for him."

Throwing his covers aside, An-Chi sat up, feeling a sudden pain in his side as he did so.

"I will not tolerate such disrespect for my general," he said while swiping the brass needles from his skin. "Bring my uniform."

Jerking around to face him, she stared blankly for a moment before waving a hand at a nearby box.

"They are in there. I had the blood washed from them."

Despite the pain, he hurried to the box, and too angry to worry about his nakedness, grabbed his pants before turning to find Mei-Xiu on her knees picking up her acupuncture needles.

"Do you feel no loyalty to your people?" he asked.

After picking up a needle, she turned to look at him, her eyes revealing a sadness that nearly made him gasp.

"I do," she said flatly. "I show it every day by helping my fellow doctors patch up your wounded and maimed so they can go back out and die."

"To not fight would be to submit to an unjust ruler."

She opened her mouth, as if to respond, but after a brief pause she simply nodded and turned back to her chore.

"You think me a fool," he blurted, not sure why her opinion meant so much to him.

She stopped, her head bowed, shoulders sagging for a moment before she rose to face him again.

"You are what you are. I can do nothing to change that."

His side aching, he clinched his teeth and pulled on his pants. Grabbing the rest of his gear, he stormed from the tent, nearly crashing into a merchant standing outside.

Grunting in pain, he quickly changed direction to avoid a collision with an overweight merchant standing just outside the tent. Without an apology, he raced off, his mind filled with confusing feelings he could not even define. Yet somewhere among all that anger, an alarm was sounding, warning him of imminent danger. As he passed the entrance to the next tent, he looked back to see the merchant still watching him, his demeanor relaxed, expression curious.

He stopped, turning to face the overweight man with white-powdered face, dangling earrings, and oversized topknot tied with a red ribbon. As though fearful of his gaze, the man quickly pulled his colorful silk coat around his body, making the flowing sleeves swing wildly as their tips nearly touched the ground. The merchant's mouth seemed to pucker, his head jerking back as though a fly had flown into his face. When An-Chi did not turn away, the merchant waved a hand dismissively and vanished into Mei-Xiu's tent.

Somewhere in the back of his mind, a voice was telling him to go back and check on this strange person, but his anger got the best of him. Turning on his bare heels, he continued on, glancing back one more time before thoughts of the tent and its occupants were lost in the confusing arguments in his head.

Chapter 65

"We have to get that amulet," Jasmina insisted as she stood next to her car with Barbara and Father Victor.

"You can't be serious," the priest protested. "It's just a pretty stone."

"It's far more than that, and you know it."

Looking offended, he straightened and crossed his arms. "I know no such thing. You're just playing off this confused person's superstitions."

"And you're just hiding behind the ancient delusion that the church has even a clue as to what the almighty wants from us."

"I beg your pardon?"

"Excuse me," Barbara called in her warbly-soprano voice.

When the verbal combatants jerked around to glare at her, she almost fell backwards while pointing back at the police station.

"I think that cop wants to, like, speak with you."

Almost as one, Jasmina and the reverend did a quick spin to face the approaching officer.

"Sorry to disturb you, folks, but..." Looking decidedly nervous, he glanced back at the stationhouse before holding up the plastic bag containing the jade stone. "The captain was looking at this and it kinda shocked him...in some way." He held the bag out to Jasmina. "He thought maybe you should have it for now, as long as you promise to bring it back when you're done with it."

"Shocked him?" the priest asked.

Shaking his head, the officer looked uncertain. "I don't really know. He pressed it between his hands like your lady-friend did and he kinda winked out for a moment. When he came to, he seemed mighty agitated. He said it was really disturbing and he didn't want it in the stationhouse anymore."

"Just like that?"

The officer nodded. "Just like that, Sir."

Jasmina snatched the bag from his hand, pressing it between her palms as she took two steps back and closed her eyes.

The other three people watched as her body twitched, head jerked from side-to-side, and her expression changed rapidly from joy to anger to anguish, and to joy again.

"I think I'm almost…oh wow!" she cried.

"What is it?" the reverend asked anxiously, his hands almost to his mouth.

Her eyes popping open, she released a nervous laugh and turned to the officer. "I need to speak with your captain again. Please take me to him."

"What did you discover?" he asked while following her back to the station.

"I now know how to catch the killer."

"You know where he is?"

Still walking, she held up the bag. "No, but this amulet will bring him to us."

"I don't understand."

Slipping the amulet from the bag, she pointed to one end. "This has been broken in two, and it stands to reason that the doctor has the other half."

"Can he use his half to find you?"

"Quite possibly, but the key point is that when the two pieces are brought together, he has the ability to physically connect to a past point in time.

"But why hasn't he done this before now?"

"He can connect, but there's more to it than that."

"More?"

She nodded enthusiastically. "If he can permanently join the two pieces, he will have something that does a lot more than make him a time traveler."

She stopped abruptly forcing her three companions to do likewise.

"It will make him a god."

Chapter 66

His stomach aching, mind reeling, An-Chi released a loud sigh and stopped. Dropping his sword and armor coat, he pulled on his undershirt before slipping into his heavy coat. Lifting his eyes to the sky, he stared at the stars and wondered why he was so shamed by Mei-Xiu's declarations.

"Why does she vex me so?" he growled while looking in the direction of Mei-Xiu's workplace.

The gnawing sense of danger further confused him until he remembered the red ribbon on the merchant's topknot.

The same as the assassin's!

Picking up his gear, he tried to run, but almost fell when his sudden movement tore at the stitches in his side. Moving as fast as his battered body would allow, he rushed past a cluster of officer's tents and located the front flap of the medical facility.

"Mei…" he started to say as he rushed inside, but checked himself. "Chu Ju!"

Groaning as he stopped in a cluttered space too small to hide a woman and an obese merchant.

"Chu Ju," he called again, uselessly looking behind her exam table before yanking open the doors of a tall cabinet, his eyes searching as his mind tried to grasp what might have happened.

He was desperately scanning the room when he spied a small bamboo scroll in the middle of the floor.

Carefully, painfully scooping it up, he unrolled the bound wooden strips, five rows of carefully drawn Chinese characters, five characters on each.

"If you won't come by force, you will now come willingly."

He struggled to make sense of it until the tent flap opened and the thin, scrubby creature who had tried to kidnap him appeared.

Pulling out his sword, An-Chi prepared to defend himself, but upon seeing his weapon, the newcomer pulled back, a look of terror on his face.

"No," the pathetic creature cried. "You not come, he kill her."

"Who is he?"

"He is my master," he answered as though the answer should be obvious. "And he not wish to kill Cao Ang. Just talk."

An-Chi looked at him suspiciously. "How do you know my real name?"

The servant shrugged. "My master know much. He very wise man."

"And he only wants to talk?"

"And trade, maybe."

"Trade what?"

"That only my master know."

"And if I choose not to come?"

The emaciated head shook slowly as his thin lips curved up into a malevolent grin. "Your doctor friend, she die."

An-Chi hesitated while searching the small space for some idea as to what was going on, and not surprised that Mei-Xiu's workplace didn't provide it.

"I must let my sergeant know I will be gone."

"No," the servant stated insistently as his head shook. "You come now. No more wait. You come now!"

Taking one more look around, he started toward the entrance, but Toilet Face lifted a hand.

"You leave sword and armor."

An-Chi gripped the sword tighter, wanting to lunge forward and behead this pathetic creature. When he realized what that might mean, he felt his shoulders sag, if only a little, but it was enough to make the servant smile as he took a step back and held the tent flap open.

"Do not go," screamed in An-Chi's head as he dropped the sword, along with the rest of his gear, and walked out of the tent.

Chapter 67

She watched the car enter the gravel parking lot, dust rising in its wake as it slowed, the driver's head moving back and forth as though searching for something. She was standing on a long and narrow dock that ran parallel to the lake's muddy bank for some thirty feet before angling out into deeper water. When the doctor finally looked her way, she gave a sweeping wave.

She could see the doctor moving slowly from the car while still looking around for any sign of a trap. She knew the move was just habit, because even if police cars raced into the parking lot, he would come to her. He needed the other half or Toilet Face would not be able to travel with him through time.

"Missus Maxell?" he shouted more loudly than was necessary.

She gave an exaggerated nod, but said nothing. Looking around one more time, he stepped onto the dock and made his way to her, initially appearing confident until she realized he was walking down the center of the dock, and glancing nervously at the water.

Immortal, maybe, she was thinking. *Inhuman, no.*

"You have the amulet?"

"You don't like the water?"

Though he did not answer, the question made him glance right then left toward the muddy bank some twenty feet away.

"You can't swim, can you?"

Scowling, he focused his attention completely on her. "I am here to recover my property."

She pulled her left hand from her pocket, the jade-colored stone nearly glowing as its end protruded from her fist.

His pace increased, and though he was ten feet from her, he stretched out a hand.

"Give it to me and I will be on my way," he said, his arm now fully extended, eyes eager, lips curved up in anticipation.

When his hand was only inches from the stone, she pulled away from him and moved quickly to the edge of the dock, her arm stretched out over the water. Having no time to think, he lunged after her, but stopped short of the edge, grabbing at her other arm as though to pull her back. As his fingers wrapped around her right arm, she opened her left hand, leaving the stone balanced precariously in her shaking palm.

Inching closer to the edge, he reached for the amulet, but she countered the move by reaching back with her right hand to grab his waist and push, a move that caused her left hand to rotate away from him, and forced him closer to the edge until he was leaning precariously over the water.

His fear of the water seemed to vanish as he made another grab at the stone, but smacked her wrist instead, sending the amulet into the air. Releasing an anguished cry, Long Gang stretched as far as he could, his toes on the very edge of the dock, body leaning as he desperately tried to capture a prize already out of reach.

Twisting her body, Jasmina put all her strength into pushing forward with her right hand, but as he started to fall forward, he grabbed her shoulder, and pulled. She barked a laugh, tilted her own body toward the water and they both tipped over like falling trees to slap the dark surface of the lake.

As she entered the icy water, Jasmina pushed off the doctor and swam away to surface several meters from him. His arms slapping the water, Long Gang gasped for air while trying desperately to reach the dock. Finally gripping the deck, he started to rise from the water, but something pulled him back under for a moment before he reappeared, to gasp, sputter, and plead for help while slapping desperately at the dock's pontoons.

Finding a handhold, Jasmina made no effort to help him as she floated in the cold water, smiling when a black head appeared next to the doctor to push him up against the dock.

Seeing the wet-suited diver, his face covered with a mask, the doctor initially screamed in terror, as though a demon from the deep was coming to devour him. His look turned incredulous when the diver lifted his mask and asked,

"Are you alright, Sir?"

Long Gang jerked his attention from the shivering Jasmina to police cars racing by on the highway, their lights flashing. He followed their progress as they turned at the northern edge of the lake, entered the parking lot, and stopped behind his car.

"You cannot kill me," he screamed at Jasmina as another black head rose from the water next to her.

"Can't we?" she asked the second diver as he lifted a mesh bag from the water.

Long Gang's eyes went wide when he recognized the two nearly identical shapes inside the bag. Letting out an anguished cry, he freed a hand and began patting his pockets.

"I think we can now," Father Victor announced while lifting his diving mask. "But I'd rather we didn't."

Releasing a shivering laugh, Jasmina nodded. "I'd rather we didn't either."

Chapter 68

"Yaaaa!" Long Gang cried as though someone had stabbed him.

Doubling over, he stumbled a few steps before catching himself and straightening.

"Something is wrong," he said more to himself than the bound and gagged Mei-Xiu.

The merchant ignored her muffled protests as he staggered to the mouth of the small cave.

"The stones. Something is wrong with the stones."

Beyond the mouth of the cave, he saw two figures: one was tall, but despite the many injuries Long Gang knew he had, he walked with a determined stride. The other was short and thin, and scurried along just behind the first. Though they were too far off to make out features, there was no doubt that his servant was bringing the troublesome soldier to his lair. He leaned against the cave's entrance and watched them approach. Though he was briefly puzzled that Toilet Face was not prodding An-Chi to hurry, Long Gang felt his heart swell upon seeing the soldier.

As they drew nearer, the merchant could clearly see An-Chi was not tied up, nor did Toilet Face have a weapon pointed at him. The sight made Long Gang chuckle.

This cave is outside the camp, he thought happily. *And so, troop leader, you are now a deserter, and the unwitting fool who will start a chain of events that will make me Son of Heaven, and very soon afterward, Emperor of the entire world.*

Though he knew a merchant's word carried little weight, he also knew others who would gladly implant the right message in the military tribunal's minds. Lacking any contradictory evidence, An-Chi would be convicted in absentia of desertion. Even better, Long

Gang would also make sure he was condemned as a liar as well. He had given a false name upon enlisting, and had not revealed his dishonor and banishment by his father, General Cao Cao. While this would surely lead to him being publicly executed, adding to his father's shame, Long Gang had an even more delicious end in mind for An-Chi. When he was done with him, the general would lose the respect of his men, and without it he could not lead.

The merchant wanted to shout for joy, but a sudden bout of nausea ended his celebration. Hand over his mouth, he looked out to see Toilet Face stumble, double over, and throw up.

"What is happening?" he groaned as An-Chi stopped only briefly to look at the retching servant before continuing on.

Toilet Face scrambled to his feet, and raced to catch up, but the effort only made him stumble and fall again.

"The stones," Long Gang grunted while fighting another cramp that threatened to double him over. "My future self has lost one of them."

Grabbing the leather pouch holding his half of the stone, he staggered back from the cave's entrance, using the darkness to hide his lack of composure as the pair approached. Though it took a great effort, he put on a confident face when the soldier entered, blinked rapidly and looked around.

Releasing the pouch, he hurried to a small table in the middle of the cave and lit a paper lantern before turning to see his disgusting servant stagger in, looking even paler than usual.

"Master. He is here."

Struggling not to react to the absurdly obvious statement, Long Gang turned his attention to An-Chi.

"You are a deserter," he said flatly. "I need not tell you what the consequences of your rash behavior will be."

An-Chi's face was stern. "I am here to rescue the doctor you have kidnapped."

Though another wave of nausea swept over him, Long Gang did his best to maintain a casual air, made harder by his whimpering servant now writhing on the floor. Fighting his cramping stomach, he suddenly had an inspiration that pleased him enough to make the nausea a minor issue.

"A pity that your superiors will not see it that way when they find your bodies."

He fought the feeling of being under water, something that had terrorized him since childhood. The sensation made him blink and struggle to maintain his train of thought.

"It will look to them like a violent rape by a disgraced soldier." He shook his head. "What will the great general think of that, do you suppose?"

An-Chi jerked a no. "I am already disgraced in his eyes."

The nausea now almost completely gone, Long Gang took a step away from the table and waved a hand dismissively. "But that was a private matter, known only to a very few people. However, this disgrace will not be so easily contained." He chuckled. "In fact, he will not be able to contain it at all."

"My father is much stronger than you think," An-Chi said defiantly.

Laughing again, the merchant shook his head. "I do not think you understand. Before you are even dead this evening, word of your disgrace will be spreading. Your father will probably be the last to hear of it, but by then the damage will be so widespread he will have no choice but to take his own life."

"He would never do that," An-Chi protested.

"It matters little because there will be a note explaining it all."

"An assassin? He will never get past his guards!"

Smiling malevolently, Long Gang nodded. "In fact, it will be one of his precious guards who will help start his journey to the place of his ancestors."

"No!"

The merchant nodded again, this time more emphatically. "I am afraid, my dull friend, that all has been prepared for me to replace your father, and with even more clever intrigues, to also take over the other general's armies, one-by-one until I am declared the Son of Heaven for all of China."

"You? A lowly merchant?"

Long Gang suddenly felt like he was under water again, which made his stomach cramp. Despite the turmoil, he managed to bark a laugh.

"Such sweet irony, don't you think?"

Thankfully for Long Gang, An-Chi had turned to survey the cave and did not see his discomfort.

"Not if I kill you first," An-Chi cried as he abruptly charged toward the obese merchant.

Because of the injury to his side, the troop leader's pace was unsteady and lacked much speed. When An-Chi stumbled to his left, Long Gang quickly shifted his bulk in the opposite direction, drawing the soldier toward the cave's center. An-Chi had only covered half the distance between them when Long Gang yanked on a thin string, and a large net rose from the dusty floor to lift the soldier into the air.

His nausea fading, the merchant picked up a walking stick and prodded the struggling soldier, forcing him to look at him.

"Such brutish behavior will not help you, Cao Ang," he sneered. "In fact, it has led you into my little trap."

"You will not get away with this!"

"I already have. Your arrival in this cave has altered the future, and started a chain of events that will soon make the entire world bow down to me." As the trapped soldier struggled, Long Gang continued, "In fact, my first act as emperor will be to order your doctor friend here," He motioned to Mei-Xiu at the back of the cave, "to make you the first of my many eunuchs." He laughed. "But do not be concerned, my brutish friend, you will not hold that role for long. You are worth far more to me dead than alive."

An-Chi's head jerked around, his change in expression making it clear he saw the bound girl for the first time.

"She would never do that!"

Shaking his head, Long Gang waved a hand at Toilet Face, and pointed toward a narrow opening in the back of the cave. The sniveling servant rose unsteadily and vanished through it.

Laughing again, the merchant turned to look up at his captive. "As a matter of fact, she will."

Mei-Xiu whined when Toilet Face appeared with a stumbling captive, the short man's hands tied behind his back, eyes covered, mouth gagged.

"Either she does what I ask, or she can watch as I perform surgery on her unfortunate father. I can assure you it will be a slow and painful procedure which he will not survive."

"Why are you doing this?"

Long Gang stared at him for a moment before barking a laugh. "Because I am a god, you simpering fool, and I can do what I wish."

Turning away from An-Chi, he waved a hand at a small depression in the cave wall.

"Put her father in there, and bring the woman to me."

Toilet Face pushed his sluggish captive into the alcove, tripping him when he had gone far enough. The doctor crashed to the hard floor, groaning as he rolled onto his back. His head shook slowly while Toilet Face tied a cord around his ankles.

An-Chi watched Toilet Face move to Mei-Xiu and lift her up. She tried to strike him with her bound hands, but the effort was weak, and even against the emaciated servant, ineffective.

Long Gang laughed as An-Chi thrashed against his bonds, but after a moment, the merchant sighed, and moved to the room's only table. Picking up a large needle, he used a red ribbon to attach it to the end of his walking stick and then dipped the tip into a small container.

Looking up, he saw the soldier had produced a knife that must have been hidden in his clothing and was cutting at the netting.

"A valiant effort, but it will do you little good," he muttered as he moved under the struggling captive.

He could see that An-Chi was so focused on cutting himself free, he would not see him lift the stick to stab him. However, he took great pleasure in hearing the soldier cry out when the needle struck home.

"Do not think I underestimate your fighting prowess, Cao Ang," he sneered. "Even injured as you are, I am sure you are a formidable foe, but this little prick will take care of that. It will make your muscles too weak to resist us as we prepare you for castration.

However, I take great satisfaction in knowing it will do nothing to dampen the pain."

Saying nothing, An-Chi continued to work at the ropes until he finally cut a large enough hole to free himself. Long Gang smiled when he saw the drug was already taking effect, and his captive's clumsy effort sent him crashing to the stone floor.

Mei-Xiu gave out a loud, but muffled cry of alarm as An-Chi rose unsteadily to his feet, staggered, and fell, his knife clattering across the cave floor.

"Well, well, well," Long Gang said condescendingly. "That witch's potion is rather fast acting, is it not?"

An-Chi tried again to rise, but Toilet Face rushed in to push him back down. As they struggled, the soldier slammed a fist into the servant's forehead, sending him onto his rump, looking dazed. However, even with his attacker out of the way, An-Chi could not rise from the floor.

Seeing that the drug was taking effect, Long Gang moved hesitantly toward him, his walking stick up and ready to stab him again. He was almost to An-Chi when the soldier did a quick roll toward the merchant, grabbed his knife and stabbed its blade into his opponent's left calf.

"Ooooeeee!" Long Gang screamed, his walking stick clattering to the floor as he grabbed at the knife, but it was gone by the time his hands reached the wound.

Afraid his captive would make another attempt, he jumped back, stumbled and dropped to one knee. He quickly looked up to see An-Chi tossing his knife in Mei-Xiu's direction before his eyes rolled up and he went limp.

Growling against the pain, Long Gang tried to rise, but could only manage to get halfway up before he dropped back to his knees.

"Toilet Face!" he screamed, but instead of responding, his servant remained on his back, his hands over his face.

Seeing that An-Chi was barely moving, the merchant gritted his teeth against the pain and willed himself to his feet, but when he looked around, the woman had the knife and was sawing through the bindings on her ankles. He started to move toward her, but was stopped when An-Chi grabbed his foot with one hand and pressed the fist of his other into the wound. The effort was feeble, but excruciating, amplifying the pain enough to send the screaming Long Gang back to the floor. Continuing to howl, he kicked free of the soldier's weak grip and struggled to his feet, but before he could recover enough to make another attempt at rising, Mei-Xiu had freed her hands and was on her feet.

Rather than attack him, she moved quickly to the soldier.

"An-Chi!"

Focused on An-Chi, she did not see Toilet Face until he was on her back. While they struggled, Long Gang pushed himself up and took two hops toward them on his good leg. He was preparing to take a third hop when he bumped into a chair and fell. His teeth grinding from the pain, he rolled his corpulent body until he reached the wall, only then looking back to see his featherweight servant was still keeping the flailing woman occupied. Growling angrily, he clawed his way up the stone wall until he was on his feet again.

"You cannot kill us," he shouted.

As though in response, Mei-Xiu stabbed over her shoulder with her knife, speared Toilet Face's cheek, and threw her screaming attacker off. The howling servant pressed both hands to his face and crashed to the ground, his feet kicking air as blood oozed through his fingers.

"But I can cause you a lot of pain," she panted, her attention jerking from the wailing servant to his master.

When she started to move toward her father, Toilet Face jumped up with one hand still covering his face and moved between them.

Despite the pain, Long Gang pushed away from the wall, doing his best to look steady as he smiled at the terrified woman.

"I am already healing from Cao Ang's attack," he said as boldly as he could. "He will be of little use to you, and my servant will keep you from your father." He watched her attention shift from the soldier on the floor to her father, obviously unsure who to sacrifice in order to save the other.

"Do as I ask and you and your father will go free."

"Huh?" Toilet Face asked, his lust for vengeance obvious.

"Do not be concerned," Long Gang said soothingly to Mei-Xiu. "He wants to cut your heart out, but will do as I say."

"Let my father go now."

Long Gang shook his head. "I am afraid that will not be possible until you do as I ask."

"How do I know you will not kill us anyway?"

The merchant shrugged. "Because, in the overall scheme of things, you do not matter. Once this soldier's emasculated body has been discovered, the future will be mine to control and I will have no need to harm you."

Long Gang watched her expression carefully, knowing she wanted to believe the lie because it was a chance to save her father. He had to stifle a smile as her gaze switched between the two men, but he knew she would make the right choice, a choice that would leave them all dead.

He imagined the scene: the brutalized woman's body next to Cao Ang's castrated form, his throat slit, arms slashed, apparently by the angered father who discovered the soldier had raped and killed his daughter. It would only be natural for the father to commit suicide after dispatching Cao Ang.

Toilet Face would spread the alarm, which would bring military guards. He had already made sure the news of this disgrace would spread faster than a wind-driven grass fire.

I have already won.

Chapter 69

I awoke with a start…a decidedly sluggish start: barely able to open my eyes, hands shaking, head as heavy as a cannon ball. At first I fought against the unknown force holding me down. Struggling to see what was happening to me, I forced my eyes open and scanned what I could see of the room, but saw nothing out of the ordinary. Trying to call out was fruitless as my tongue was numb and unresponsive.

When it finally occurred to me to use the call button, my arms were already too heavy to lift, my body sinking into the mattress, head lolling back. I struggled against closing eye lids, no longer sure why I was resisting, but somehow knew I had to.

The effort was wasted, and when my eyes finally closed, I expected total darkness, or at least the reddish glow of light filtering through my eyelids. Instead, I was looking at the back of a woman.

"How do I know you will not kill us anyway?" she was asking.

A man answered, but I couldn't make out the words because my other self seemed to be struggling with the same sluggishness I was experiencing. Despite our combined condition, I felt a powerful need to protect the woman.

You have to get up, I was thinking. *She needs your help.*

I could sense his struggle to position himself to rise as his attention shifted between two men, but like me, his arms and legs weren't cooperating.

He looked up again and I could see a really fat man favoring his left leg and a thinner one holding a blood soaked hand over his cheek.

The doctor? Toilet Face?

You must help me! An-Chi demanded. *I need your strength to overpower them.*

While watching the scene unfold, I could feel my body growing weaker and weaker, as though I were slipping into a drug-induced sleep. An-Chi looked at the blood-smeared pinprick on his arm.

You've been drugged?

The slow up-and-down motion of my vision made it clear he was nodding, and then I could understand what the other man was saying.

"Once his emasculated body has been discovered, the future will be mine to control and I will have no need to harm you."

Emasculated?

Panic popped my eyes open and I was once again in the hospital room, my mother asleep in the chair beside my bed, and the only person in sight.

"Mmmooooommmm!" I groaned weakly, but it was enough to shock her awake.

"What? Huh?" she asked groggily before pushing herself out of the chair. "Honey? What is it?"

Shaking my head, I tried to speak, but each word took all my strength. "No...drugs...danger...don't let...kill me."

Mom was suddenly over me, her eyes wide, mouth open. "What is it, Honey? Talk to me!"

"Someone drugged...me. Muscles...weak. Can't move."

"Help," she cried as she grabbed the nurse's call button and I heard the click-click-click of repeated pressings. "Somebody help!"

I've no idea how long it was before a nurse came, because I was at the very edge of consciousness by the time she arrived. Mom took it from there, creating an exaggeration of my statement that included an unknown man slipping in to put something in my IV.

The nurse kept her cool, and soon more people were piling into the room, anxious voices filling my groggy brain with noise, shadows moving across my vision until someone bent down beside my bed and cried, "Look at this!"

Peering through half-opened eyes, I saw Father Victor holding a small bottle, but though he spoke with urgency, I couldn't understand the words. It didn't seem to matter, as gravity overpowered my eyelids and their closing shot me back to the cave where the woman was still standing between me and the two men.

Someone bumped my bed, jerking me back to the present. I looked up to see a nurse sticking a needle into my IV tube. When done, she looked at me, her face strained, eyes probing, lips pursed.

I felt the effects almost immediately.

"Doctor, he's coming around," the nurse was saying. "That was a close one."

The word "doctor" sent a wave of panic through me as I jerked my head around to the physician and breathed a sigh of relief when his pleasant, Hispanic face smiled down at me.

"How are you feeling, Mister Patterson?" he asked in perfect English.

I licked numb lips, but had no trouble keeping my eyes open.

"Better. What happened?"

"It appears someone snuck in here and injected a drug into you. If we had not caught it when we did, you might have died."

I looked up at him, feeling puzzled. "But how? There's a cop at my door."

The doctor shook his head. "He left half-an-hour ago. It seems the police have captured the man trying to kill you."

"And his accomplice?"

The doctor shook his head. "I guess they thought they had him as well, but maybe there was more than one. It appears we'll have to keep a closer eye on you."

"How?"

"We're moving you to intensive care until another officer can get here."

"That won't be necessary," my dad announced, his stocky body a commanding presence as he barged through the open door. "I'll make sure nobody bothers my son."

"Thank God you're here," Mom cried as she crashed into him, her arms squeezing his body so tightly, even my muscular Dad grunted as she buried her face in his chest.

Wrapping his arms around Mom, he turned to the doctor. "The cops called and said they were taking the guard off his door. I dropped everything and came right over, but it seems I wasn't fast enough."

The doctor shook his head. "Fortunately, we were able to administer an antidote quickly."

"Well, he won't get a second chance," Dad said emphatically.

I looked up at all the adults standing around my bed, their conversation so intense they hardly noticed I was still in the room. Closing my eyes, I found An-Chi still on the floor of the cave. I no longer heard the conversation around me as I watched what he was seeing, my heart pounding when I realized that though the two men trying to kill him looked very different from the ones after me, they were actually the same people.

As strange as that was, I was suddenly distracted by a faint buzzing at the edge of my consciousness, like a distant mosquito heading toward me. The cave scene was surreal: blurred movement, hollow voices that echoed so much I couldn't make out what they were saying.

I wanted to swipe at the mosquito, but An-Chi resisted. It was only then I realized the two men were focused on the woman and ignoring him.

They think you're unconscious!
Yes.
What are you going to do?
Quiet! They must not hear you.
Only you can hear me.
Then I must be mad.
That makes two of us, Buck-o!
Buck-o? What is that?
Well, it kinda means friend, or something like…
Shhh! They are coming our way.

The buzzing grew more intense as the one An-Chi referred to as the merchant limped toward the woman, but instead of defending herself with the knife in her hand, she tossed the weapon toward me. I could feel An-Chi's muscles tensing as the merchant reached for the woman, but even more importantly, the cave was taking on a greenish glow as he planted the foot of his good leg next to the woman's and gripped her arm.

Die now, An-Chi was thinking as he grabbed the knife, did a quick roll, and stabbed it into the merchant's good leg.

The fat one's scream mixed with the buzzing as he toppled to the floor, but An-Chi was already rolling to one side, thankful that the drugs I had been given also gave him more strength.

Only quick reflexes saved him from being beheaded by Toilet Face as his sword passed inches from An-Chi's head. Rolling again, the soldier rose quickly to his feet, and froze as the thin man raced toward him, sword held high, his face a mixture of rage and fear.

Waiting until Toilet Face was starting his down-stroke, An-Chi faked a move to the left then lurched right and forward to slip past his unprepared attacker's weapon, and bring his knife around to stab him in the side. While that sort of strike -- painfully slicing someone's liver -- would cause a normal person to slowly bleed to death, the howling servant barely hesitated as he did a quick spin, and struggled to manage the heavy sword in preparation for another assault.

He started moving toward An-Chi when the cave filled with a green light and everyone froze.

What is happening? An-Chi asked, though whether he thought it or spoke out loud, I wasn't sure.

At that very moment, I wasn't sure, but hoped it had something to do with Jasmina.

I think it has something to do with...

My mind went blank as a face materialized in front of me, a face with distinctive Chinese features.

Father!

Chapter 70

Standing on the dock, a shivering Jasmina stared at the pieces of stone in each of her open palms, mesmerized by the power emanating from them.

"Oh my God," she exclaimed.

While Captain Marshall's officers pulled the shivering Long Gang from the lake, he turned to Jasmina.

"The stones are moving," he stated anxiously. "What are you doing?"

Her head shaking, she kept her eyes on the slowly rotating stones. "Nothing. They're moving on their own. It's some kind of magic."

"There's no such thing as magic," the reverend announced as he lowered his air tank to the deck. "It must just be a power source we don't yet understand."

"The p...power of a g...god," Long Gang stuttered through chattering teeth.

The priest shook his head. "It may seem so, but I doubt anything in our existence is that powerful."

Her eyes on the stones, Jasmina was also shaking her head. "I think what he means is..."

She stopped when the two pieces clicked together, and a green glow instantly enveloped her.

"No," Long Gang screamed. "I must use blood from human liver to join them."

"Lord in Heaven!" the reverend cried.

Captain Marshall started to move toward Jasmina, but stopped when her hair flared out around her head.

"Oh my!" she cried as the green glow intensified and little arcs of energy flashed in her hair. "Stay back everyone."

The priest and the police chief stumbled back along with the startled officers standing next to Long Gang. That left the doctor alone to stare at Jasmina.

"You cannot do this!" he protested. "The crystals are *mine*. It is *my* destiny to rule the world."

Though Jasmina was shaking her head, she remained silent as a glowing green sphere expanded and darkened until more figures began to appear: two men in fighting postures, and a woman watching a corpulent man lying on the floor in obvious pain.

"What the hell?" the captain cried as the two standing figures jerked around to look at him.

"It wasn't a human liver you needed, Doctor," she shouted over a growing buzzing that seemed to come from everywhere. "It was two people who had a connection that even they weren't aware of. You picked the right two people to connect your timelines, but you were the wrong catalyst."

"But there must be pain," Long Gang screamed. "Their agonizing sacrifices are needed to make the connection powerful enough. How you do it?"

"An-Chi," Jasmina screamed. "Watch out!"

Jerking to one side, An-Chi barely avoided Toilet Face's attempt to slash his throat. Doing a quick spin, he jammed his knife into the servant's right arm, and the sword clattered to the floor.

Toilet Face howled as he jumped back, his free hand gripping the new wound. It was only when he stopped backpedaling that An-Chi seemed to notice the small leather pouch hanging from a thin strap around his neck. It might not have caught his attention even then had it not started rising in the air as though it wanted to float over to Long Gang, but was restrained by the strap.

"Toilet Face," the merchant moaned as he stretched out a hand. "Give me the stone."

Obviously confused, the servant looked down at the pouch as though he had never seen it before.

"Quickly," Long Gang demanded. "I must have it now."

The servant grabbed the pouch, but instead of undoing the strap, he clutched the bag tightly with both hands.

"You say, if I lose stone, I die."

"No," the merchant cried. "That will not happen."

"Yes it will," Jasmina countered. "That is exactly what will happen."

All four of the cave's occupants turned to look at Jasmina's glowing figure.

"Who is this?" the merchant cried as he glared at An-Chi. "You brought a witch?"

An-Chi shook his head. "She is a gift from heaven."

"She say I die if I give you stone," Toilet Face protested.

"No! She lies."

Stamping her foot, Jasmina moved a step closer to the servant. "He has been treating you like dirt all these years. Why would you assume this will be any different?"

"Do not listen to her," Doctor Long Gang cried as he moved to the edge of the sphere growing around Jasmina. "She is a demon and only wants to destroy us all. Give stone to me and you live forever."

Though Toilet Face could see the screaming doctor, he could not hear his words.

"What he say?"

Jasmina shook her head. "He is outside your world, my friend. Do not be concerned with him."

His face contorted by his anguish, Toilet Face looked from Jasmina to the screaming doctor, and finally to the merchant before shaking his head.

"I must obey my master," he said, but kept a firm grip on the pouch.

Still stunned by what they were seeing, An-Chi and Mei-Xiu gawked at Jasmina.

"Who..." Mei-Xiu started to say, but her voice faded when the reverend also moved close to the sphere.

"We are spirits from another realm," Jasmina answered for him. "We are here to stop an injustice."

"You are here to rob me of my destiny!" the merchant cried.

Stepping back from the sphere, Father Victor pointed at the ghostly figures inside. "Captain, you must arrest that merchant."

Still looking shocked, Captain Marshall shook his head. "I'm not sure I can even get to where they are." He pointed at the sphere's surface. "What is that?"

Taking a quick step forward, the reverend held out a hand, as though to push through it.

"It's perfectly harmless," he said as his hand neared the glowing surface.

"Stop!" Jasmina shouted. "I don't know what will happen."

"But I do," the priest said calmly before pressing his hand against the sphere.

Chapter 71

General Cao Cao's face vanished and I felt a sudden shock, as though someone had plugged me into a low-voltage circuit.

"Where did he go?"

Mom leaned over to push a lock of hair from my forehead. "Where did who go, Sweetie?"

Her steel-blue eyes and blond hair seemed completely out of place. On the other hand, compared to Mei-Xiu, Remmy's curly red hair and green eyes looked exquisitely exotic. The strangeness of the situation made me hesitate.

"I was in a dark cave trying to fight off this really fat guy who wanted to…"

I stopped when Mom gently patted my cheek. "You were just dreaming, Dear. Your father and I have been watching you the whole time. There have been no strangers in here."

Mom's denial that anything strange was going on, made me so mad I wanted to jump out of bed and run away, but a slight movement brought sharp pain and made it clear I was going nowhere.

"A Chinese doctor is trying to kill me. I didn't dream about that!"

My shout almost turned into a scream when Mom shook her head. "And by now the police will have him in custody. He can't hurt you anymore."

"You don't understand," I moaned. "The one they are arresting isn't…"

A flash of green stopped me, and before I could remember what I was saying, the scene slowly changed until I found myself on a dock staring at Jasmina.

On my left, An-Chi was slowly rising to stand next to Mei-Xiu. Leaning on her, he turned toward a fat man struggling to get to his feet.

"Get up," Barbara demanded, and I twisted around to see her standing beside my bed, but my parents were nowhere around.

"No way! I can't…How did you…" I suddenly realized all my aches and pains were gone. "This is seriously bizarre."

Shaking her head, Barbara pointed at the moaning fat man, and I felt my jaw drop.

"Whoa. Can they see us?"

Barbara shook her head. "I don't think so. At least, not yet, but we have to stop them."

"How?"

Acting as though I wasn't even there, the ancient Long Gang finally reached his feet, groaning as he hobbled to one side of the cave, and slowly bent over to pick up a spear.

"I have already started to heal," he growled as he straightened and took an unsteady step toward An-Chi. "Now you die."

"I'm afraid not," Jasmina countered, her voice surprisingly calm considering the situation.

I couldn't even speak I was so flabbergasted, and even more so when the whole room flashed from yellow to green and back several times.

Realizing that Jasmina was looking behind me, I turned to see Father Victor wearing a wet suit as he passed through the sphere wall, and before I could absorb what had happened, the room strobed yellow/green again as Doctor Long Gang burst into the space.

"Didn't someone handcuff him?" Captain Marshall yelled, but the doctor seemed not to hear as he rushed toward his ancient self, nearly falling when he crashed into the part of the sphere wall facing the merchant.

Waving his arms at his counterpart, he shouted, "She has the stone!"

"You can't go in there," Jasmina announced, though to me it sounded more like a question.

Ignoring her, the doctor pounded fists against the glowing surface.

"You must hurry. Her power is growing," he cried while pointing to his neck, as though he had a pouch there as well.

"He can't hear you," Jasmina said. "He probably can't even see..."

A cry of alarm from the merchant stopped her, and we all turned to see his shocked face as he stared at us for a long moment.

"I guess he had to expect something like this was going to happen," I said. "After all, he sent himself into the future."

Dropping his spear, the merchant grabbed his own pouch and briefly closed his eyes as he muttered something I could not hear. An-Chi, Mei-Xiu, and Toilet Face were gawking at us until the merchant barked a laugh, jerking their attention to him as he balled one hand into a fist and did a credible imitation of a windmill before under-handing something in Jasmina's direction. A ball of green light flew across the cave, hitting the sphere and bouncing into the ceiling. The explosive impact sent rock flying, knocking the merchant down, and forcing An-Chi and Mei-Xiu to duck for cover.

"What was that?" I cried.

"The power of the crystal," Jasmina explained.

"What are we going to do about it?"

She shrugged. "Nothing. My whole crystal is more powerful than his half. He can't hurt us in here."

Pointing at An-Chi and Mei-Xiu, I asked, "But how do we protect them?"

Jasmina shook her head. "I don't think he cares about them anymore. I'm guessing his plans have changed."

I looked at the merchant to see the pouch around his neck stretching out toward his servant, whose own pouch continued to point at his master.

Seeming to realize what it meant, the ancient Long Gang stabbed a finger at his servant.

"Give me your stone!"

Looking totally confused, Toilet Face clutched his pouch and looked from Jasmina to his master and back.

"Quickly, fool. We must stop her."

His body tilting toward his master, the servant started choking as the thin leather strap, wrapped twice around his neck, cinched tighter and tighter.

"Cut it loose," the doctor screamed as he moved along the inner edge of the bubble his fists repeatedly bouncing off the surface in a vain effort to push through.

The choking servant pulled out his knife, but as it came up, his eyes rolled up and he collapsed.

"We have to do something," I cried while also hurrying to the edge of the sphere to gape at the scene before me.

Though obviously in considerable pain, An-Chi rushed to the fallen servant, grabbed the knife and cut the pouch free. Despite his best effort to hang onto it, his was too weak and the pouch quickly slipped through his fingers.

The ancient Long Gang was taking a step forward to catch it when a body passed between him and his prize, snatching it from the air. Mei-Xiu did a complete flip in the air to land on her back, both hands gripping the pouch, her arms stretched out toward the howling merchant who lost his balance and fell onto his corpulent belly.

"We have to go now!" the reverend shouted as he reached through the sphere's wall and pulled me inside. While I was still recovering from shock of what happened, he was pushing me toward the wall facing the cave.

"But we can't..."

When I was close to the wall, I looked down to see a wide gap between the platform Jasmina was standing on and the cave floor. Before I had a chance to wonder if I could cross it, the reverend bellowed, "Jump!" and shoved me into the wall.

Pushing off as hard as I could, I went airborne and crashed into a surface that seemed to shudder as I passed through it and bathed me in a strobing yellow-green light. Rather than pass through it quickly, I seemed to almost stop in midair, suspended over what appeared to be a bottomless gap. Looking back on it, I should have realized that we were travelling back two-thousand-years in time. I shouldn't have expected it to happen in an instant. While I was suspended over oblivion, and my only thought was,

How the hell am I going to survive this?

The reverend seemed to catch up with me, and upon reaching the other side, we exploded out to land hard on the cave floor. I nearly went into shock because it felt like I'd been blasted with a high-pressure, electrified water hose. Jumping up, I gasped, stumbled, and might have fallen again if the reverend hadn't been holding my arm. When I looked at him, it was obvious he wasn't all that steady himself.

Everyone outside the sphere, except Mei-Xiu stopped to watch us, their faces making it clear they were as shocked to see us as we were to be there.

"...go through this..." I stopped when I realized I'd started that sentence nearly two-thousand-years in the future.

Shaking his head, Father Victor pushed me towards Mei-Xiu, shouting, "Help her!"

Still unsteady, I took two off-balanced steps and nearly fell on Mei-Xiu. As soon as my hands and knees touched hard rock, I crawled to her and grabbed the pouch just before it slipped from her grip.

"No!" the ancient Long Gang cried as he rose up, lurched toward us, seemed to trip over his own feet, and fell back to the floor.

When he tried to push himself up again, Father Victor landed on top of him, smashing one of his corpulent cheeks against the floor as the struggling merchant screamed in frustration.

So totally caught up in her struggle to keep the pouch, Mei-Xiu barely glanced at me before turning her attention to the struggling pair. Though Doctor Long Gang was stuck behind the sphere's wall, I could see he was also shouting, but stopped at the sound of metal scraping across rock.

Mei-Xiu and I turned as one to see a gasping Toilet Face rising from the floor, both hands gripping the hilt of An-Chi's sword as he slowly staggered in our direction. I wanted to defend myself, but was afraid to release the stone. Of course, what could I do? I had no weapon of my own, and rolling away left Mei-Xiu exposed.

"Kill them," the merchant howled.

Mei-Xiu let out a squeak which I probably mimicked as Toilet Face took a deep breath, and groaned through gritted teeth at the effort of lifting the sword. I ducked my head in anticipation of the blow, but instead heard a loud gasp.

When the sword clattered to the stone floor, I looked up to see the wide-eyed Toilet Face sink to his knees and tilt forward, revealing a pale-faced An-Chi behind him, one hand holding a bloody knife, the other covering his bleeding side.

"An-Chi," Mei-Xiu cried when he slowly sank to the floor, his white teeth clinched against the pain.

She started to rise, but stopped when the stone moved in her hands. I tightened my own grip, somehow certain that even though my hands were wrapped around hers, our hold on the pouch was tenuous at best, and if either of us let go, it would break free and make straight for its other half.

"I must help him," Mei-Xiu cried, her wide eyes expressing a terror I was also feeling.

I jerked my attention from An-Chi to Jasmina to the reverend still on top of the merchant, but gasped when I saw a smoky stream of light flowing between our hands and the merchant's crystal. As the light grew brighter, the pull on the stone grew stronger.

"We can't hold it much longer," I cried.

"Jasmina," Father Victor pleaded. "You have to do something."

"What?" she asked anxiously. "I'm just acting as a catalyst. This thing has a mind of its own."

"Ask it for help!"

"How?"

"*Pray* to it."

From her expression, I guessed it was all Jasmina could do to keep from laughing at the absurd irony of a priest telling her to pray to a stone. I gasped when my body started sliding over the rough floor.

"Do it!" I exclaimed. "We can't hold it much longer."

Jasmina hesitated only briefly before closing her eyes, and bowing her head until it nearly touched her closed fists. Though she began mumbling words, they were drowned out by the merchant's protests.

Feeling an overwhelming sense of alarm, I looked around to see the doctor had turned his attention to the praying Jasmina, and as I watched helplessly, he charged at her, grabbing her hands and trying to yank them down.

The effect was nearly comical. Jasmina didn't budge and the doctor's thin frame was pulled into the air by his own effort. When he was head and chest above her, his hands slipped free, dropping him with such force that his face slammed into Jasmina's fists and sent him sprawling onto the floor.

Before any of us could react, Jasmina's stone rose above her hands and a beam of green light shot from it to our stone. Mei-Xiu and I both fell away as the leather pouch vaporized and a second beam went from that crystal to the one hanging from the merchant's neck. When he reached up to grab the now-glowing crystal, a third beam shot from it to Jasmina's stone to close the triangle.

The merchant howled as he yanked back smoking fingers, but an instant later, he and the ancient Toilet Face vanished. Their more modern equivalents were shaking their heads as they slowly rose to their feet, but both were now wearing different Chinese clothing. Toilet Face's physique was halfway between his emaciated ancient self and the husky modern version. The doctor appeared gaunt, and confused, and as he looked around, he didn't seem to see the rest of us.

"We're travelling forward through time," Jasmina announced, her eyes closed, voice low and gruff, as though she were in some kind of trance. "It's about one-thousand A.D, and the Song Dynasty is at its peak. This merchant is learning about the future so he can alter it to suit his plans."

She hesitated when a ball of light pulsed around the circuit several more times, the Chinese pair changing each time until the doctor was dressed in modern clothes and his servant's body had thickened and stretched into the thug who had tried to kidnap me.

"Time has shifted again," the otherworldly Jasmina announced. "We are in the present.

The doctor and Toilet Face looked at each other, their expressions confused and uncertain.

"It's over, Doctor," Jasmina continued. "Without the stones you will soon be gone."

Toilet Face started to move toward the edge of the sphere, but his master waved him back.

"I need those stones!"

Her eyes still closed, Jasmina shook her head. "It is too late for that, Doctor. Even I can't touch them now. They will soon go back to where they came from."

"How can you know this?"

"We have met spirits like this before," she said calmly while nodding toward me. "Haven't we, Gerry?"

"We have?" I asked uncomprehendingly.

"They are like the ones I exorcised from you and Remmy last year, but these were trapped inside the crystal."

"How?"

"We have long known crystals can hold various types of healing and destructive energy. A spirit is just another form of energy and they were somehow trapped inside this one."

"They?"

She nodded. "At least a thousand of them. That is why the crystal is so powerful it can traverse time itself."

"But how will they get out?"

"Passing through the portal will free them."

"And if it doesn't?"

She shrugged. "They believe it will, and that is enough for us."

Before Jasmina could say more, the doctor jumped up to grab the glowing crystal.

"I will not be denied!"

The whole cave lit up, its walls flashing alternately yellow and green, the pace of change increasing gradually as Long Gang screamed, his body glowing, his wailing eventually drowned out by a growing buzz as the bright triangle of crystals slowly rotated and moved around the perimeter of the cave carrying the howling doctor along with them.

Crying out, Toilet Face jumped up to wrap his arms around his master's neck, and the glow enveloped him as well, pulling them both along with the crystal. After completing several circuits of the cave, the crystals moved to the center and continued to spin slowly.

On each rotation, we alternately found ourselves in ancient China, seeing Mei-Xiu, An-Chi, the corpulent merchant and Toilet Face's emaciated corpse, and back in the present. The cycle repeated at an ever-increasing rate until the crystals were moving so fast they appeared as one continuous circle of light. At that instant, I suddenly realized that though I could still see the ancient people, they were ghostly figures who stared at us while we gawked at them.

Moving next to Jasmina, I yelled, "We have to warn An-Chi about the ambush."

Her head shaking, Jasmina turned toward me held out her hands, palms up.

I grabbed them and held on tight as the cave began to spin around us, the effect making me dizzy. The lights were a solid ring now, with no sign of the attached men as an opening appeared in the darkness on my right. Still gripping Jasmina's hands, I felt myself being pulled toward the black hole, felt its bone-numbing cold and an emptiness that brought tears to my eyes. When Jasmina started to lean as well, the ring streaked toward it. The instant the lights were inside, the opening snapped shut, cutting off all sound and light. In the sudden blackness, I realized there was no floor under us and we were falling.

"What...is...happening...to...?"

I lost my hold on Jasmina when I slammed into the hospital bed, bouncing out to sprawl onto the floor. She landed on the floor next to me, both of us gasping for air as screams and shouts of joy and concern erupted around us.

Before I could react, hands were pulling me up, arms hugging my neck, people shouting. I looked up to see my mother's face, distorted with a mixture of shock and joy.

"What in Heaven's name happened?" she cried. "Where did you go?"

My mind so full of confusing thoughts, I struggled to come up with an answer until the words just popped into my head.

"Ancient China."

I'm not sure she was listening as she pulled me into a bear hug, not remembering that only a short time ago I had a life-threatening hole in my right side.

Chapter 72

"You want to explain what's been going on," Captain Marshall asked as he stood in my hospital room and watched me pull on socks. "What happened to those Chinese characters?"

Shrugging, I looked at Jasmina, which drew the captain's attention to her as well.

"You're not likely to believe us," she said. "Even if you did, we have no proof of any of it."

Shaking his head, he looked at her for a moment before turning to me. "And what is it exactly you don't have any proof of?"

"Doctor Long Gang, and his assistant, which he called Toilet Face, never existed in this time."

"Don't bullshit me, lady. I saw them."

"What you saw was a sort of an ethereal representation of them projected into the future, but they weren't really here."

The captain continued to shake his head. "Sorry to disappoint you, Ma'am, but this Toilet Face character is currently taking up space in one of my cells. Even if he escapes, I've got photos, fingerprints, and computer records."

"I don't think you do," Jasmina insisted.

"What are you talking about? It was one of my men who took that green stone from him." He was looking from Jasmina to me and back. "What the heck was with those stones, anyway?"

Jasmina opened her right hand, revealing two pieces of green crystal, each about the size of a finger. "When held together end-to-end, they allowed us to travel through time."

Barking a laugh, the captain shook his head again. "Yeah right. I'm betting the things I saw on that dock were made by some kind of digital projection. Is that it?"

"No, Captain. What you saw wasn't really anything at all."

"Come again?"

"Call your office and ask them about Toilet Face."

"I don't need to do that to know what happened."

After pulling on my T-shirt, I faced him. "She's telling the truth and one call will totally prove it."

"And how will it do that?"

"The dude's gone and there's, like, no record he ever existed."

Captain Marshall opened his mouth to respond, but hesitated for a moment, his expression mistrusting, as though waiting for someone to deliver the punch line. When neither of us spoke, he pulled out his phone and dialed.

"Johnson. Captain Marshall here. What have you learned about that Chinese guy we arrested last night?" I couldn't hear the response, but it was short. "No, I mean that big husky oriental who calls himself Toilet Face. He's in the back cell." This time the response was slower and indecisive. "What do you mean there's no Chinaman in cell six. I helped put him there myself." Another pause, but this time his face shifted from angry, to confused, to shocked. "Yeah. Right," he announced before breaking the connection and turning to Jasmina.

"What's this all about?"

Without flinching, she locked eyes with him and answered, "I'm still not exactly sure how it worked, but the doctor had what he believed was a magical amulet. Unfortunately for him, and lucky for us, it was broken, and he didn't have the ability to join the two pieces, which only gave him enough power to send himself and his assistant, Toilet Face into the future.

"I, on the other hand, am blessed with a gift that allowed me to join the pieces and connect their combined energies. That is what pulled us back two-thousand years in time and let us to take the gems from him."

"Meaning?"

"He never got the chance to use the full power of the crystals, and when he lost them, the things he did in our time never happened."

"Just like that."

Looking at me, she shook her head. "No, it wasn't quite that simple, but we're here now, so obviously we succeeded."

"You killed him?"

She held up a hand and waggled it. "Technically, no. Of course, even if we had, that was nearly two-thousand years ago. How would you go about prosecuting us, especially when you have no proof they were ever here?"

The captain stared at her for a long moment before shaking his head again. "What about the priest? Does he remember any of this?"

I looked at Jasmina, and did not find her confused expression assuring.

"I don't know," she finally answered. "We just got back. I assumed he returned to his parish."

Lifting his phone, the captain dialed again.

"I'd like to speak with the Father Victor, please," he announced, pausing only a moment before shouting, "Are you shi...are you kidding me? Who's in charge? Well, let me talk to him then."

Giving us an angry glare, the captain hurried from the room to continue his conversation.

"Oh my God!" Jasmina exclaimed as she turned to me, her eyes wide with amazement. "Do you know who he was?"

"Who are you talking about?"

"The Reverend Victor," she laughed. "He was Beauregard."

"The dog that, like, protected me last time?"

"No, not the dog, but the entity who occupied the dog's body. He was here all along and we just didn't know it."

"Was he the one who dropped the bottle on my hospital bed so the doctors would know what Long Gang used to immobilizewsed An-Chi?"

"I think so."

"Whoa!" I exclaimed. "That's totally freaky. How did he know?"

She shook her head. "I'd guess he's watching you all the time, and only appears when you need him."

"Like a guardian angel?"

She laughed. "Yeah. Something like that."

I looked around the room, feeling suddenly frustrated that someone could see me and I couldn't see them.

"That's kind of…uh…weird. Don't ya think?"

"I think you are a very lucky young man," she said while nodding. "Twice now, he's saved your life. Not many people have an eternal protector watching over them."

"Yeah," I said slowly, drawing it out as I tried to adjust to the idea of never again having a private moment. "I guess so."

"Son of a…" Captain Marshall was saying as he marched back into the room, cell phone in hand, voice trailing off when he saw me looking at him. "They never heard of a Reverend Victor, and there's no damage to the rectory ceiling." He looked at me. "No one remembers you staying there. This is crazy!"

I felt myself nod slowly, my exhaustion, and Jasmina's recent revelation keeping me from caring all that much about the captain's dilemma.

"It never happened," Jasmina insisted. "No one was hurt, and no laws were broken." She pointed at my face. "See? Gerry was never injured."

"So how is it I know about these wounds you say he never had?"

She shrugged. "Call it a group hallucination. We all got caught up in something that wasn't really happening."

"I'm not sure I can settle for that."

"What choice do you have? You're the only one who is going to make a fuss, and everyone else involved will have no idea what you are talking about."

His eyes flicked from Jasmina to me and back. "You two do."

Jasmina's laugh sounded silly, but I think, for that reason alone, it felt good to hear it. Captain Marshall seemed to be affected in the same way, because he laughed too.

"Right. The three of us had some kind of communal dream, is that what you're saying?"

"What dream would that be, Captain?"

"About these Chinese guys and their…" He stopped when she smiled at him. "No Chinese guys?"

"No Chinese guys."

"No attempt to take over the world?"

Sighing, Jasmina shook her head. "No one person can do such a thing. It's been tried."

Slipping the phone into his pocket, the captain let his hands drop to his side.

"I won't forget this happened," he insisted.

"Nor will we, but there's no way we can tell anyone about it."

"Yeah, right. I guess you have a point, so I'd better be getting back to the office and see what's really happening around here."

Jasmina nodded. "And we'll be returning to the Valley. I doubt we'll trouble you again."

Shaking his head, he started for the door, but stopped after two steps and turned back. "I'd appreciate that very much."

After watching the captain leave, I asked, "What are we going to do?"

She shrugged. "There's not much to do, except go home and wait for the next adventure."

I lifted my hands to see no scars or cuts, but the memory of that pain was still there as I groaned, "*Another* adventure?"

"Most definitely."

"How do you know?"

"Beauregard is still here. He won't leave until he knows you're safe."

Feeling my chest tighten, I looked around the room again, hoping to see some kind of distortion in the air that might reveal his presence, but then it occurred to me that he was a spirit and they are just energy.

Trying to relax, I took a deep breath. A flash of light on my right made me jerk around, but there was nothing there.

Was it a reflection or a spirit?

"Can we speak with him?" I asked anxiously. "Ask him what he knows?"

Her shoulders sagging, Jasmina nodded. "Maybe after we've had a chance to recover from this. I'm too tired to try right now."

Though I followed when she turned to leave, I couldn't help looking back over my shoulder. Guardian angel or not, the idea of someone always watching me was totally creeping me out.

I stopped at the door and looked back into the room one last time.

"Just don't watch me in the bathroom. OK?"

Epilogue

"Are you sure you want to do this?" Jasmina asked.

I held up a medallion, its polished surface engraved with beautiful Chinese characters 伟力 that translated literally into *wěilì*, which I was pretty sure meant "mighty force".

"I want to give him this," I said while pointing at the two green crystals in Jasmina's hand. "You think there's still enough energy left to make it happen?"

She nodded. "The spirits who once occupied these crystals are gone, but I think there's enough for one more trip."

"I so totally don't like this," Remmy protested. "I should be going too."

"Sorry, Remmy," she said, "There's only enough for one person." She nodded to me. "I'll send you back to when his division is preparing for the final battle, but you'll only have a few minutes." She turned to Barbara and Remmy. "Though we'll be able to see the people on the other side, they'll be ghostly images and we'll only be able to hear what Gerry is saying."

Both girls hesitated for a moment before nodding as one. Turning back to me, Jasmina held both halves of the crystal and slowly moved them together. A green glow appeared around her, growing larger and larger until it also encompassed me. Within seconds, the room faded to a transparent haze and I found myself standing in the open entrance of a tent.

When I sucked in a breath, a surprised Cao Ang jerked around to face me. He looked much like a terracotta soldier, except for his brilliant red and blue uniform, his glimmering armor, and the healthy color of his skin.

"Hi, An-Ch...er...Cao Ang," I greeted. When he didn't respond, I added stupidly. "You're preparing for battle?"

He hesitated for a long moment before nodding. "Will you be accompanying me?"

"No," I said while fiddling with the medallion in my hand. "I just wanted to give you something."

Leaning over, he picked up his shining sword, slipped it from its scabbard, and held it up, not as a threat, but just to admire it. I'm not sure why, but I felt my chest swell with pride, and understood what this upcoming battle meant to him.

"I will fight once more at my father's side," he said matter-of-factly before lowering the weapon. "I need nothing more."

I felt an urgent tapping on my shoulder, and turned to see the ghostly outline of Barbara, her finger stabbing me.

"What will happen to Mei-Xiu?" she asked.

"Mei-Xiu?"

A surprisingly, lusty feeling filled me as Cao Ang's eyes moved to a small painted portrait on a nearby table.

"She has returned to her family's home, and I sent a go-between to approach her father. We will be married after our forces have destroyed Zhang Xiu's army and killed him."

"Why not now?"

Cao Ang shook his head. "Do you not have proper procedures that must precede a wedding?"

I shrugged. "If I really wanted to marry a girl, I suppose we'd just run off and do it."

Frowning Cao Ang shook his head. "That would be shameful. Her family would never forgive her, nor would mine accept her as my wife. I could not bring such disgrace to someone I love."

"Yeah," I sighed. "I can totally respect that."

"Will you be betrothed to the one you called Barbara?"

The shock of his statement froze my tongue, and a good thing too. Barbara was standing right next to me, and though I was certain she couldn't hear Cao Ang's question, my response would have given her a clue as to what he was asking.

"I'm not ready for anything like that yet."

"Do not wait long, my friend. Life can take unexpected turns."

Though his statement took my breath away, more insistent tapping on my shoulder made me jerk around to look at Barbara.

"He can't go into this battle. He'll totally be killed."

"Is that spirit speaking to you?" Cao Ang asked as he looked at Barbara.

"Can you see her?"

He nodded. "Yes, but I cannot hear her words."

I shook my head. "It's nothing. She's against war."

Slipping his sword into its scabbard with a snap, Cao Ang picked up his shield, felt its heft and smiled.

"Maybe someday you will come to China and meet my descendants. I will tell them of our great adventure together, and they will welcome you with much happiness."

"Yeah," I responded, trying not to show the sadness I was feeling. "I'll do that."

The space around me flashed yellow, and I briefly turned to see Jasmina shaking her head.

"I've gotta go now," I said.

Cao Ang was holding up a hand, as though he wanted to say more, but before words came out he vanished in a flash of green light. I turned to Jasmina, seeing tears in her eyes as her ghostly figure turned solid again.

"Why didn't you tell him?" Barbara cried angrily. "You could have saved him."

Looking at her, I shook my head.

"It totally wouldn't have mattered," I said calmly. "He'd have gone anyway."

Tears flowed down her cheeks as she sobbed, "Why?"

Her question stopped me for a moment, because I totally understood why. This was about deeply held traditions that defined his love for Mei-Xiu, the respect of his father and his ancestors, the fate of his country, and his place in the cosmos. China needed him to be at that exact spot, on that exact day with the horse his father, General Cao Cao needed to escape the ambush. The general had to continue the fight that ended the Han dynasty, and that could only happen if Cao Ang made the ultimate sacrifice for his leader.

Feeling the weight of the undelivered medallion in my hand, I turned to Barbara, and wanted to explain all of that to her, but only managed,

"Because that was the way he wanted it."

THE AUTHOR

Growing up on the Oregon coast, Cliff has enjoyed telling the stories rattling around in his head. His books are an opportunity to share his out-of-this-world adventures with a wider audience.

A fifth-generation Oregonian, Cliff has been a farmer, logger, and business owner. He now lives in the Jefferson, Oregon, working as a computer support consultant for small businesses up and down Oregon's beautiful Willamette Valley.

For more information about Cliff's books, and more, please visit:

www.scovellbooks.com

Photo by Andre Lindauer